FAT HOPE!

The Bet That Changed a Life

This edition first published in paperback by
Michael Terence Publishing in 2025
www.mtp.agency

ISBN 9781800949959

Cover design (AI)
2025 Michael Terence Publishing

Michael Terence
Publishing

This book is dedicated to…
My lovely daughter, Rana,
my dear Granddaughter, Isabella,
& the long-suffering Hubby, John.

SATURDAY 13th NOVEMBER

George awoke at the crack of noon. Then he clutched his temples as the usual alcohol-induced Saturday morning pains ricocheted round his skull when he moved his head. Oh God, a fun Friday night to start the weekend enjoyment was such hard work!

Suddenly something stirred in the bed beside him and he tensed uneasily, unable to look sideways. Oh please let it be one of his own chat-ups and not an Ugly Bird Bet! Why had he, Edward, Rodney and Stefan started the stupid game? It wasn't as though any of them needed the money! And it had been going on for far too long now. It was really time they stopped doing it.

Stefan had started it. They'd all been casually eyeing up a group of girls who had just come into the Duck and Grouse, their local pub.

Edward had muttered, 'I quite fancy that blonde one.'

'Oh, I had my eye on her!' Rodney had added.

'I'll toss you for her,' George had suggested, producing a £2 coin.

And Stefan had said, 'Listen to you all. You're completely brainwashed by the Media.'

'What do you mean?' 'What are you on about?' 'No we're not,' his friends had all protested.

Stefan had sighed. 'You Brits are all the same. You care more about someone's visual appearance than their personality. That blonde's mates could be witty and interesting, and she could be thick and boring. But do you chat up the witty ones? Oh no! You think you score points if you pull the prettiest one. And a lot of them aren't so pretty when they wipe off all the layers of muck plastered over their faces. You'll put up with her loud shrieky voice wittering on about herself, saying Like this and Like that and how she broke a nail today until you can't stand it any more. Then you'll dump her and go after another look-alike, often with big, rubbery injected lips and surgery-enhanced boobs, just so everyone can see you with a beautiful girl – even though most of her is artificial.'

George had tried to look hurt. 'Ooh, that's not true – well, not always. I quite enjoy a bit of conversation sometimes. Girls expect it. They like a chat. I'm a good listener – well, for a while. I look on it as foreplay!'

They all laughed.

'OK,' said Stefan, 'Go on then, I bet you can't chat up the one on the right.'

'Oh no, that's taking things a bit too far! She's…'

'Ugly,' agreed Edward, 'Right, I bet you £20 that you can't chat her up, be really charming to her, and-'

'Spend the night with her,' continued Rodney, 'And I bet you £20 too.'

'And me,' added Stefan, 'After all, appearance isn't everything, is it? And actually, she's got nice eyes if you look closely.'

George shuddered. 'I don't want to look closely.'

Digby the Duck and Grouse landlord joined in, leaning his large stomach against the bar. 'Yeah, I'll have twenty on that. Even our George can't turn on the charm or get it up if his heart's not in it!'

'Thanks a lot, Digby. You doubt my capabilities. Anyway, why don't one of you do it?' wailed George.

'Because we put you forward first. Now off you go,' said Stefan, patting George on the shoulder and pushing him gently across the room.

And that's how it had started. And George won the bet, by the way.

Ugly birds could be great in bed if you were drunk. They were always desperately grateful- and gratefully desperate, and usually fun too!

He tried to raise his head and look over his shoulder, but couldn't manage it. There had been a biological change in the night. All his body weight had moved upwards. He was solid lead above the neck and liquid jelly below it.

Slowly and painfully he turned his head on the pillow. No luck there. The room was swaying like a heat haze. He focused for a few seconds and looked beside him again. But she'd pulled the cover right over herself so he couldn't see who she was. All he could see was the top of her head.

Trying to recall any of the last night's events was hopeless. It was just a fast-moving blur. Total lager-induced amnesia. Was there something wrong with him, or was his brain doing him a favour?

Who the hell was she?

Best to be on the safe side and get out. George gently turned back the duvet, placed one foot on the ground and started to slide his weak, feeble body out of the bed.

And an arm snaked across his waist, pulling him firmly down on the mattress. He thought his head was going to split in half as it crashed down on the pillow, which had turned to concrete.

Horrified, George looked up and nearly screamed. She must be a descendent of Cyrano de Bergerac, he thought as her face loomed over him. She was a human version of Concord. He was sure the tip of her nose would stick in his ear as she kissed him. And her teeth; they were like the plastic ones you get in Christmas crackers.

He nearly screamed again when she clamped her hand between his legs, but he couldn't as he was fighting for air and blood circulation, and his vocal chords were blocked.

His voice came out in a faint croak.

'Morning George,' she chuckled, looming closer. George turned his face away and shut his eyes.

Obediently his manhood (manhood? What a strange expression! He didn't feel very manly at the moment) instinctively obeyed instructions and pointed upwards, despite George trying to stop it. The last thing he wanted was sex. He just wanted to go back to sleep, preferably on his own.

She was on top of him, riding him like a Grand National steeplechaser, shouting, 'Yeah! Come on!' while staring at the wall above the bed. He was half-expecting her to produce a riding-crop as they jumped over Beecher's Brook and galloped past the winning post. And it was a photo finish!

'Oh George, you were WONDERFUL!' she gasped predictably, rolling onto her back.

'Oh, um, so were you,' George forced himself to say, then equally predictably before he could stop himself, 'Er, what's your name again?'

***

George soaked his aching body in a deep bath. 'I can't go on like this,' he said to Oswald, his plastic duck, 'I'm giving up betting. It gets me into too much trouble. And I'm giving up women too. I'm just going to have quiet sessions in the pub, drinking with my mates.'

He groaned, laid his flannel over his face and completely sank into the soothing warm water. Then he re-emerged. 'And I might cut down on my drinking as well. It's too much hard work the next day.'

Oswald bobbed up and down and said nothing.

***

'How did you get that black eye, George?'

'Maybe he got a nose stuck in it, Rodney.'

'Oh very droll, Stefan. Actually she punched me.'

'Punched you?' they all said in unison. 'Why? What did you say?'

George shook his head, then wished he hadn't. 'Why do you all assume I said anything?'

'Because you always do, George,' Edward said, and they all nodded in agreement.

'Is this some new kinky form of foreplay?' laughed Digby, pointing to his blackening eye, and everyone else laughed except George.

'Oh, just cough up my winnings, you lot,' he snapped. 'And this is the last time. All Ugly Bird Bets are off from now on.' He held his hand out while everyone obediently felt for their wallets.

Edward counted out four fives. 'Here you are George,' he said, 'You certainly deserve it.'

'Too right,' Stefan nodded, dropping two tens into George's open hand, 'I never thought you'd go through with it. She was the ugliest bird yet!'

'Oh I don't know,' George bluffed, 'She was pretty good at, um…' His voice tailed off and he shuddered, resting his hands on top of the bar.

'Lucky you were so drunk, George. Cash or credit?'

'Credit, Digby. And I'll have four lagers and a breakfast, please.'

Almost every day without fail the four friends met at the Duck and Grouse and planned their social life; the Honourable Rodney Ponsonby-Ffinch, aristocratic layabout, Edward Marchbury-Haines, upper-middle-class layabout, and George Slater, layabout. The three of them had been friends since their school days.

Stefan Romanovitch was the only one who worked. He ran Stefan's Sweat Shop, the most exclusive fitness club around, where the rich went to get rid of their pounds. And Stefan was happy to take them!

Rumour had it that he was an illegal immigrant, a rumour that he neither admitted nor denied. He definitely had a hint of an accent, and he played at being a Man of Mystery.

One day a regular in the Duck and Grouse had loudly declared that Stefan from Russia or Rumania was probably

Steve from Romford. But the laughter had died on his lips when Stefan had straightened his huge muscular frame and the man had seen the expression on his face. He'd picked up his drink off the bar and disappeared fast into the back of the pub.

Rodney, Edward and George didn't ask Stefan any questions about his background. Rodney and Edward were too polite, and George couldn't be bothered, and didn't really care. Stefan had appeared about 10 years ago, and had naturally fitted in with the others.

Wherever he really originated from, the mystery helped to make Stefan appear even more attractive to his female clients, who were willingly treated to a lot more than just a massage, as he regularly hinted. Their age was unimportant. Their bank account was VERY important.

Stefan was almost always dressed in designer leisurewear and the latest style of trainers, most of them samples given to him by sales reps.

Old Gubbins sat in his usual place on the bar stool in the corner, with a pint of Bitter in front of him which would last for hours. He puffed on an empty pipe. He'd never adjusted to the smoking ban. 'It's taken 10 years off my life,' he'd announce to anyone who asked about the empty pipe.

'How do you know it's taken 10 years off your life if you're still alive, Gubbins?'

'Because I feel 10 years older, that's how! I can't see as how a bit of baccy can hurt other people.'

Now he stared at the men as the money changed hands. 'I can't see why every woman has to try to look like a fashion model nowadays,' he said, 'My late wife, bless her heart, had what you'd call a homely face and body. She was never a beauty. And she didn't waste our money on expensive clothes neither! When I met her, she could already lift a bale of hay on her own with no effort, and milk the cows twice a day without fail. Those cows loved her, they did. They'd all come running when she called them. And she could cook the best fried breakfast that you ever had! I loved that woman for over 30 years, and I never criticised her appearance, not ever! She had a heart of gold, she did. God, I miss that woman!' He took his pipe out of his mouth and banged the bowl on his hand, then he put it back in his mouth, sucking furiously.

Rodney nodded in sympathy. 'Yes, there's more to love than just visual appearances.'

'But it helps,' said George, 'It really does!' He shuddered again as memories of his night began to flood back.

Digby poured the drinks. 'Off to the races lads?' They all nodded. He put the lagers down on the bar in front of them without spilling a drop. 'Well don't lose too much money will you? I don't like it when my customers are in lousy moods. It's bad for business.'

Edward took a large swig of his lager. 'Aah, a hair of the dog. That's better. I don't intend to lose today. I've had a red-hot tip and I'm feeling lucky!' He was the shortest member of the group, but he was very good-looking in an obviously well-off way. He was always expensively but classically dressed, with his straight dark hair neatly styled and carefully flopping over his forehead.

Stefan smiled, or as near to a smile as Stefan allowed. He even scowled when he smiled! People blamed it on Botox, but they never said it directly to him. 'Where have I heard that before? The trouble with you guys is you don't know when to give up. I just go for a good day out. I don't ever think that I'm going to win, so I have a little flutter and leave it at that. I have a financial limit. And I'm pleasantly surprised when my horse comes first.'

'Agreed,' Rodney nodded, 'Except I have a large-ish flutter. It's expected of me - runs in the family. But I never exceed my pre- arranged limit either, and I try to spend quite a lot of time studying the form. My father would think I had a gambling addiction if I lost too much, and he'd cut my allowance. And I do win fairly often - well, often enough to be allowed to get away with it so it just seems like a pleasant pastime.'

Rodney was tall, but not as tall as Stefan. He had striking pale blue eyes and fine wavy blonde hair that reached just over his collar and constantly needed combing, and thin, pointy features with a permanent expression as though he was about to burst out laughing. He dressed casually in expensive country clothes that had seen better days.

George just sighed.

He had the ability to just throw on his clothes (as he often did) but still look good, even when they were slightly crumpled. He was taller than Edward but shorter than Rodney, with broad shoulders that looked as though he worked out regularly. But he was far too lazy to do that.

Usually he did his clothes shopping in batches and favoured modern, fashionable but casual outfits.

Female assistants in clothes stores rushed to help him choose. And he was happy to listen to their advice.

He often arranged to meet one of them later, to try on his new outfits.

***

'Daph, we've got to do something about George.'

'Oh Fred!'

'-And it's no good 'oh Fredding' me. You've got to face it Daph, that son of yours is a useless layabout.'

'He's your son too, Fred-'

'Oh, don't rub it in!'

'-And he's only young.'

'Young? He's 28 years old! I'd made my first million at his age. He's halfway to spending it.!'

'Well he's not useless. He's got a degree in economics.'

'Economics, ha!' Fred waved his cigar in the air, holding it neatly between two fingers and being careful not to drop any ash on the expensive carpet. 'He doesn't know the meaning of the word! I bet he can't even spell it! It's like passing an exam in theory for learning to swim, then diving in and drowning. And unfortunately it's my money he's drowning in!'

'But he studied hard for that, Fred!'

'Studied hard? The only thing he studied at University was the girls! Pity he didn't take a degree in sex. He'd have got 100%! They've probably got one nowadays. They have stupid degrees for everything!'

'Fred!'

'Sorry luv.'

'You always swore that our kids wouldn't have to work really hard like you and your family did.' Daph stood up, smoothed her skirt down and checked her hair in the huge ornate mirror over the fireplace.

Fred stubbed his cigar out in the onyx ash-tray and walked up behind her, putting his arms round her waist and kissing the back of her neck. 'I've never asked them to work like I did, have I Daph luv? I've always given them everything they've wanted. But I wouldn't be doing my duty as a father if I just stood by and watched them waste their lives.'

'Suzie doesn't waste her life, Fred.'

'I know she doesn't, luv.'

'She and Charles are happily engaged-'

'With no sign of a wedding being planned.'

'They'll plan it when they're ready, Fred. Our daughter's enjoying her youth, and working hard at the same time. She looks after those horses all on her own. And she's training really seriously to get into the British Showjumping team.'

'Yes Daph, and she can still find time to drive one of my lorries when I'm short-staffed, even though she's so small that she can hardly reach the pedals, and she has to sit on a cushion to see clearly out of the window. And of course she drives her horse-boxes too. She was really determined to pass her HGV Licence. All the blokes think the world of her. She's a lovely girl. I'm really proud of her.'

'But what about George? Aren't you proud of him?'

'Proud of him? Why, what's he done? Something that I don't know about? George's only talents are drinking, losing money on stupid bets - MY money of course - and screwing every attractive female - and some unattractive ones - that he sets his eyes on! He and his mates spent over an hour in the Duck and Grouse the other evening, betting on who would walk through the door next - male or female, young or old. The trouble is, they're useless at it. I won five hundred quid off them in the end! Well it was six, but George borrowed his hundred back again.'

'He's a very nice-looking lad Fred, and extremely intelligent, just like his Father.' Daph stared at her husband with her eyes openly full of love and admiration. 'And he doesn't chase girls, they chase him. So you can't blame him at his age if he goes with a few of them, can you?'

'A few of them? You're joking! He's working his way through the English race – and a few other races as well! In fact, he's working his way round the world!'

'Well at least George hasn't got any young, innocent sixteen-year-olds in the family way,' Daph said coyly.

'Are you getting at me, Daph Slater?' Fred asked, linking his arms round her slim waist and squeezing her tight.

'As if I would!' she replied, twisting round and kissing him on the cheek.

Fred let her go. 'We've got to sort him out, Daph,' he said, walking across and taking another expensive hand-rolled cigar out of a large oak humidifier in the corner of the room. He held it up to his ear and rolled it around, then he picked up a box of matches and slowly lit it, puffing happily and breathing in the Cuban tobacco aroma as the smoke curled out of the end, 'He can't spend the rest of his life just bumming around. I'm not asking him to come into any of the family businesses if he doesn't want to. I'm just asking him to earn his own living somehow. The choice is his. I'm not a snob and never have been. You know that. He can wash dishes in a restaurant if he does it well, and if he can't, or won't think of anything more ambitious or better-paid. But I'm not supporting him any longer. He can learn what it's like to budget and pay all his own bills.'

'Oh Fred!'

'Don't argue Daph. He won't have to struggle like we did. And he won't have to live in a caravan like my grandparents did. He's got his own house, and that flashy car of his. He and his mates never go far or do much. If they do, they usually get drunk and spend the next day trying to remember where they left their car. So if he stops wasting money and economises he doesn't need much to survive on. The experience'll do him good. He's not banned from here, is he? In fact, if he has to pay for his own meals we'll probably see more of him instead of just seeing him in the pub or hearing about him and what he gets up to!'

Daph sighed. 'I suppose you're right, luv.'

'I always am, aren't I?' Fred smirked, winking at her. 'I'll have a word with him this afternoon at the races.' He sat down and crossed his long legs, then picked up the daily paper from the small coffee table beside his armchair.

He looks so much like an older version of George in many ways, Daphne thought, watching him mark the names of a few interesting racehorses in the paper, but how different were Father and Son!

Fred was obviously a Romany, and proud of it, but George looked more Italian or Spanish, with longer curly hair.

George was a couple of inches shorter than Fred, and more laid back. Fred was tougher and gave off an aura of confidence.

As Fred was only 17 when George was born, they were often taken for brothers when they were together, by people who didn't know them.

They made an attractive pair.

***

'A couple of bottles of your finest Champagne and four glasses, Digby, old chap!'

'Coming right up, Rodders! Had a good day at the races then, for a change?'

Rodney nodded. 'Yes, we've had a great time, and a very financially rewarding day, haven't we Edward?'

'We certainly have. Well, most of us have.'

Digby nodded at the silent serious member of the foursome. 'George lost again has he?'

Tall, blonde Stefan slapped a huge meaty hand on George's shoulder. 'If George had the same luck with horses as he has with women he'd be a multi-millionaire like his father, wouldn't you George?'

'Yeah,' sighed George, 'But I'm shattered. I couldn't concentrate properly. I had a very rough night, I'll have you know, thanks to you lot!'

They all cheered - except George - as Rodney popped the Champagne corks, one after the other. He held a bottle out to Old Gubbins, who was sat in his usual place in the corner. 'Fancy a glass of Champoo, Gubbins?'

The old man shook his head and removed his pipe from his mouth. 'No, none of that fizzy stuff for me, thanks, Rodney. It would play havoc with my liver. I'll stick to my pint. I'm too old to change my ways.'

He sipped a minute drop of his Bitter, put his glass down on the bar and replaced his pipe between his teeth.

Edward held his glass up and waved the other arm in the air. 'Here's to the horses. Long may they run!'

'Especially the fillies,' Rodney said, squeezing sideways to let two girls get to the bar, 'And a good evening to you two lovely ladies. I haven't seen you in here before – and I'm sure I'd remember if I had! Welcome to our friendly little community.'

A tall blonde and a shorter dark-haired girl looked at him. The blonde stared at him coldly and tutted, then spoke to Digby. 'An orange juice and a Perrier water please. No ice.' She turned to her friend and said, 'Go and grab that table over there. I'll bring the drinks.'

'No, she's got enough ice,' Edward whispered.

Rodney winked at the dark-haired girl who smiled at him hopefully, then she obediently trotted over to the vacant table and pulled out two chairs. Her friend followed her, carrying the drinks. Three of the men stared at the back of them as they crossed the room.

'Are you seeing what I'm seeing?' Edward whispered.

'Yeah, I think so,' Stefan nodded, 'That girl's a natural blonde!'

George stared at the ground. He sighed dramatically. Rodney refilled George's glass. 'Come on George, cheer up. It's not the end of the world. It's only money - our parents' money at that - and we had an enjoyable day.'

'I know,' George sighed again, 'It's just that my old man won a small fortune and he doesn't even need it! And he kept making sarky remarks after each race like, Lost my money again? Good job I'm winning it back!'

'Okay George, here's a chance for you to win some of your money back.' Edward nodded his head at the two girls. 'I bet you, um, let's see, twenty pounds that you can't spend the night with that girl there.'

'Which one?' George asked, curious.

'The snooty blonde. The iceberg.'

'Oh, not her plain friend then? That makes a change!'

The friend kept glancing towards the four men, her glass held up to her face.

'No, she'd be easy. The blonde one isn't interested. She's obviously completely off men for some reason.'

'They could be a couple?' Edward suggested.

'Not the way the dark one's looking at us!' grinned Rodney.

'She's probably sulking after a break-up. I think you should cheer her up and restore her faith in us decent males, George. Let's make it more interesting,' Stefan whispered, 'I bet you a hundred that you can't pull her in ten minutes.'

Rodney nodded. 'I'm in.'

'Me too,' added Edward, 'But you have to make a night of it.'

'Yes, the whole night,' Stefan said.

'Good thinking, Stefan!' Rodney agreed.

Digby leaned his huge frame on the bar. 'Yeah, I'll have a ton on that. Go on George, I bet even you can't pull Little Miss Ice Maiden. She's right off men. It's obvious!'

'Look on it as therapy, George,' Edward urged, 'It'll be your good deed for the day, or rather, the night, cheering her up and making her happy. And it'll help you to recover from last night.'

George shuddered.

'-And you'll restore her faith in Mankind,' said Stefan.

'-And you'll make some money for a change,' Rodney urged.

'Okay, you're on. I can't refuse a bet like that, can I?' George placed the palm of his hand on his forehead, 'Let me think, let me think. Right, I'm ready.'

'Let's time him,' said Digby.

Stefan reached in his jacket pocket and produced an old stop-watch.

'Blimey, that's an antique!' Digby remarked.

'It's what I use at the gym. It always looks effective. And it's accurate too. Okay, are you ready George, three-two-one-go!'

They all stared as George strolled casually over to the two girls, bent down and spoke to them, resting his hands on the table and leaning forwards. The dark girl nodded enthusiastically. The blonde hesitated then she nodded too.

'He's offered to buy them a drink,' Rodney whispered, 'It's the only reason they'd both nod like that.'

Digby turned and sauntered along to the end of the bar and began talking to another customer as George walked towards him.

'Digby!' called George. Digby ignored him. 'Digby!' he shouted louder, 'Get your ass over here, pronto!' Digby had turned deaf. 'Okay, I want five minutes extra for injury time!' George hissed at him.

'What injury?' asked Digby, recovering his hearing.

'The injury I'm going to give you If you don't get back here quick!'

'Yes come on Digby, no cheating!' Rodney called.

Digby sauntered slowly back. 'Yes? What can I get you?' he asked.

'A rum and Coke and a brandy and lemonade.'

They all creased up. 'The orange juice and water soon went out of favour now that someone else is paying the bill,' Edward laughed.

George picked up the drinks. 'It'll be worth every penny, mate, you watch.'

Four pairs of eyes bored into his back as he walked over to the two girls and put the drinks down. Then he patted all his pockets, a worried frown on his face. He spoke to the blonde who sighed and began to reach into her bag. George shook his head and brushed her hand away, but the girl insisted and took out a wallet and brought a £20 note out, which she handed to George. He came back to the bar and paid Digby, pocketing the change.

'What are you playing at, George?' Rodney demanded, 'You haven't lost your wallet. I saw you with it just now.'

George winked at him. 'All part of the plan Rodders, all part of the plan.'

Stefan held his watch up. 'Four minutes seven seconds left.'

'As much as that?' said George, 'Oh goody. Plenty of time.'

He walked back and spoke to the blonde. She shook her head. Then he grasped her elbow, gently lifting her to her feet and led her towards the door.

Four faces stared open-mouthed as George held the door open for her with a slight bow. Then he turned to his friends and gave them the thumbs-up sign before following her out into the street.

'Of all the crafty-' gasped Edward, 'He's taken her home to pay her back the money!'

'Yeah, and the rest. Didn't put up much of a fight did she?' Digby grumbled.

Rodney shrugged. 'It's worth paying a hundred pounds to watch the maestro at work. Meanwhile, her poor friend's sitting there all alone. Open another bottle of Champers and pass me two glasses please, Digby old chap. And pour yourself a glass. You look as though you need it!'

***

George's house was in an exclusive little terrace. His car was parked outside. 'Well here we are at my humble abode,' he said, squeezing past his car. He opened the front door and, placing a hand round the girl's waist, led her inside and closed the door. He walked into the lounge and gestured to the sofa. 'You sit yourself down there and make yourself comfortable while I go upstairs and find my wallet, then I'll pour us a drink. I expect I left it in my jacket when I got changed earlier. Stupid of me!'

Halfway up the stairs he realised the girl was following him. 'It's alright,' she said as he walked in the bedroom, 'I know you've really got it. I saw you with it earlier. It was just an excuse to get me back here, wasn't it? Men are always doing that to me! I know you fancy me.'

'No I – oof!' She had his trousers down to his knees before his body hit the bed.

SUNDAY 14th NOVEMBER

'Oh, just once more, George!'

'I really don't think I could manage it.'

'Oh please, George! Pleeeeeeeasssssssse!'

'No, get off, I've got to go out.'

'Oh George, you haven't really got to, have you? It's Sunday. Can't we stay in bed all day? I could make us some breakfast. I'm good at breakfasts, and then-' She flopped on top of him and pressed her lips onto his mouth, making Mmmmmm sounds. She sounded like a dying wasp and she tasted of stale rum and coke. He tried to turn his head to the side to inhale some fresh air, but she grabbed his head with both hands and held him in a tight grip.

George tried to push her upwards to unglue her body but she seemed to have doubled in weight. 'Look dear, I've got to get ready. I'm going to my parents for lunch.'

'Ooh, can I come? Can I? I'd love to meet your parents. I bet they're great fun!' She chortled as though Fred and Daph had said something funny outside the bedroom door, 'And I'm free all day!'

'You've come quite enough, love,' George muttered with his teeth clamped together to prevent her sticking her tongue in his mouth. He tried to free himself from her vice-like grip and reach for his clothes at the same time, but she kept pushing him back.

Giving her a sudden quick shove, he sent her flopping backwards, and he rolled out of bed, bundled up a handful of clothes, dashed for the bathroom and just managed to slam and lock the door before she untangled herself from the duvet, leaped out of bed and hurled her body against it.

'George!' Her fists hammered on the door. 'Let me come in, George!'

'No way! Go on, go home now, love.'

Where did she get her energy from? He started to run his bath and automatically dropped Oswald the duck in, still clutching his clothes in front of him like a protective shield, staring at the bathroom door as though afraid that she'd burst through it.

Looking down, he realised that he'd still got one of his socks on. Oh the shame! It wasn't allowed in the Unwritten Sex Rule (or Socks Rule) Book to leave your socks on, but he hadn't had any time to take them off. She'd been attacking him until she finally fell asleep, snoring with her mouth open. She didn't look so attractive any more; in fact, she didn't look attractive at all with her hair all over the place, mascara under both eyes and red lipstick smeared all over her large injected lips and her face.

'Please George! I'll sit behind you and wash your back if you like. It's really nice. I saw it in a film once. It looked dead sexy. Come on, let me in. Pleeeeeeasssssse!'

He shuddered and leaned his forehead against the door. 'Look, be a good girl and go away now, will you?' He looked longingly at the bath. Oh boy were his aching muscles looking forward to a long leisurely soaking!

'Aaaaow, George!' She thumped on the door with both fists.

George turned round and checked that the lock was holding up against the attack, wincing at every thump. He was still clutching his bundle of clothes. The door was worryingly bulging inwards in a couple of places, he was sure. Or was he imagining it? He made a mental note to call a carpenter to reinforce it. 'Come on, be sensible will you, please? We both had a good time. Now get dressed and go home. I've got a busy day and I'm absolutely knackered before I start!' He turned the taps off and lifted a foot to step into the welcoming water. Then he lowered it again and peeled off his sock.

She started snuffling. He took no notice and she sniffed louder. ‘You just used me, didn’t you?’ she whined, ‘Men are always doing that to me. You’re all the same. You just used my body for your lustful pleasure!’

‘Me? More like the other way round, dear,’ George muttered, putting his foot down again and dropping his pile of clothes on the floor, then turning to examine his scratches and bruises on his back in the full-length mirror. He touched one long scratch and sucked his teeth in with the pain.

‘What? What was that? I can’t hear you. You’re muttering! Men are always doing that to me! You all mutter after you’ve had sex. You just used me for your own needs.’

‘No I didn’t!’

‘You did! You did, George. And now you’re kicking me out into the street like an unwanted dog!’

‘Or a bitch,’ George muttered.

‘What? What did you say?’

‘I said, Ooh, I’ve got an itch.’

‘Oh. -And I’ll never see you again, will I?’

‘Yes you will!’ Unless I see you first, he thought to himself, clenching his hands at his sides and gazing at the ceiling.

‘I won’t!’

‘You will.’

‘No I won’t. I know I won’t!’

‘Alright then, you won’t!’ George shrugged and tipped some relaxing bath gel into the bath.

Everything went quiet and George hoped that she’d gone. Then…

‘George?’

‘Oh, WHAT?’ he groaned.

‘I need the loo.’

‘Well there’s one downstairs by the front door.’

‘Okay. Um, George.’

‘Oh, what now? Please leave me alone to get ready!’

'I will see you again. I really will, won't I?' she pleaded. 'It might sound daft but, I think – I think I'm in love with you, George.'

Yes it did sound daft.

George sighed and slapped the wall with the palm of his hand. 'Look, get dressed and then, beside the phone in the hall you'll see a notepad and pen. Write down your phone number and - and your name.' What WAS her name? She hadn't given him a chance to ask her. He hopefully lifted his leg again, about to step into the bath.

'Alright then. And do you PROMISE you'll call me?'

'Yes, I promise.' George crossed his fingers.

'I bet you won't. You'll forget me. Men are always doing that to me!'

'Well I promise you that I'll never forget you!'

'Really? Oh George, that's a lovely thing to say!'

'Well, believe me it's true! Now if you'd kindly stop yelling at me through my bathroom door, I'm going to have my bath and get dressed to go out!' He realised that he'd been standing on one leg for a while, and he stepped into the bath, kicking aside the one sock he'd been wearing.

'Alright then. And George?'

'Oh, WHAT?'

She giggled. 'I promise I'll never forget you either.'

'Oh. Right. Glad to hear it.'

Ten minutes later, while George was soaking his aching body, she called through the door, 'Right, I'm going now. Goodbye George. Love you!' She made kissing noises through the closed door. 'Um, George.'

'What now?'

'You are really special to me, you know. I don't just leap into bed with every guy I meet.'

'Oh good. Bye, er? Goodbye. Um, yeah, love you too!' What WAS her name?

'Right that's it,' he told Oswald the duck, 'I'm definitely through with betting. No more stupid bets for me, and no more women or I'll never reach thirty! Maybe I'll go in a Monastery.'

No, that was a bit drastic. And at the moment he doubted if he could get down on his knees to pray for forgiveness and then manage to stand up again.

***

The Duck and Grouse was already busy, but conversations died away as George swaggered across to his usual place at the bar and everyone stared at him. He nodded to everyone as he walked past their tables, saying, 'Morning. Morning. Nice day.'

Silently, Rodney, Edward and Stefan put down their lagers, pulled out their wallets and each of them handed £100 to George.

'Thank you, thank you and thank you,' he smirked, 'And Stefan-'

'What?'

'You were right, she IS a natural blonde. Digby! Four lagers please!'

Digby walked over and glared at George while he poured out the beers. 'Cash or credit?' he snapped.

'Um, credit I think.' George nodded at the menu, chalked on a blackboard on the wall. 'At your prices it won't take me long to munch my way through what you owe me.'

Digby slapped the last lager down and started to walk away. Then he turned and came back. 'Here, hold on,' he added, 'How do we know you're not cheating? How can we be sure she didn't just take the money you owed her and leave last night?'

'How can you be sure? Just take a look at my back. It's like Clapham Junction!'

Rodney peered down the back of George's shirt and sucked in through his teeth. 'God, I hate scratchy women!' he said.

'Oh yes, me too!' agreed Edward in an I wouldn't know, but I'd love to find out voice.

'You didn't really doubt our George's talents did you Digby?' asked Stefan, slapping George on the back, making him choke on his lager and bringing tears to his eyes with the pain. Everyone laughed unsympathetically.

Edward called, 'Four more of your delicious lagers please, Digby, served with your usual charm and wit! Right, where shall we go today, chaps? The Golf Club, the Yacht Club, the Country Club or THE Club?'

George drained his lager and gestured to Digby, 'No more for me thanks.'

Digby paused theatrically, empty glass in hand and mouth hanging open. 'You what?'

'No more?' gasped Rodney, equally theatrically, 'Did my ears deceive me, or did I hear my old pal George of many years say, 'No more'?'

'You did, Rodney. I've got to go and have lunch with my parents. Dad invited me yesterday - well, it was more like a summons than an invitation. Never mind, I want to ask him for some money to buy a new car. Mine's nearly two years old now, and I've seen a nice black Merc down the road that will do me nicely. It's time he increased my allowance.'

'Right,' said Rodney, 'We'll see you later then. Give my love to that gorgeous little sister of yours, and ask her when she's going to make an honest man out of my brother.'

'I doubt if she's made a dishonest man out of Charles yet,' George said, I'm pretty sure their horses are more sexually active than they are! See you guys this evening.'

'Yes, 'bye George,' Edward called as George walked out, 'Hey Digby, remember us? We're all dying of dehydration over here!'

***

George stopped his car outside the tall wooden gates and pressed his horn, which loudly played Dixie, like the Dukes of Hazzard. He leaned out of the window and waved at the security camera above the gatepost. The gates opened and George drove through, then they closed silently behind him. His car purred along the gravel drive which was lined with rhododendron bushes, and drew up in front of the huge modern house.

Bert, the butler and Jack of all trades stood in front of the open door, his thumbs jammed in his braces. George stepped out of his car and smiled at him. 'Hello Bert, are they in?'

Bert glared at him, 'They're expecting you, ain't they?'

'Yes, they certainly are. I've been summonsed.'

'Well they're in then, ain't they?' Bert turned and led the way, shuffling along the hall and muttering under his breath.

'Pleased to see me are you, Bert?' George joked, following the old man across the spacious marble-tiled entrance hall.

'It's me back. It's really giving me jip,' Bert groaned, placing his fist on his spine. He paused outside the open lounge door, knocked and peered round the door.

He jerked his thumb at George behind him, announced, 'He's 'ere,' and shuffled off to the kitchen.

Bert had worked for Fred since Fred had started his haulage business at the age of 17. He was stocky but tough. When three thieves had broken into the yard one night while Fred and Bert were locking up the office he hadn't thought twice about tackling them. He had grabbed a lump of wood and fought the gang, sending the thieves running, or rather, limping off empty-handed, but he was seriously injured with cuts and broken bones. He was in hospital for several months, and he was unable to work for a long time.

Fred had kept him on full pay and Bert had insisted on returning to work again before he was completely recovered. He'd said he was dying of boredom. So Fred had given him light work to do to keep him mentally occupied, as general handyman, cook, and as Nanny Extraordinary when the children were young. He'd been like another Grandad, and George and Suzie had adored him. He'd always had a new game to play with them, and he could produce pennies from behind their ears.

When Fred's new dream house was completed, Bert had moved in to a small apartment on the ground floor at the back, designed specially for him. He was completely devoted to Fred and the family, and would do anything for them. His grumpy exterior hid a heart of gold, and sometimes a lot of pain.

Daph looked up from the small mirror she was holding. She had been checking her make-up, which was perfect, but slightly overdone. 'George, luv!' she cried, 'Come and give us a kiss!'

'Sherry, George? -As if I needed to ask,' said Fred, gripping his cigar in his teeth while he poured it.

'Oh, yes please, thanks Dad,' George replied, kissing Daph on the cheek and sitting down next to her on the huge expensive chintzy-covered settee.

The massive lounge was like Daph's make-up; perfect but overdone. The expensive carpet didn't quite match the expensive curtains, but it nearly did and the expensive wallpaper didn't quite match the expensive suite, but it nearly did. There was too much expensive furniture and too many expensive ornaments in the room. And the blending of antique and modern didn't quite work, but it nearly did. But what did work was the creation of a comfortable, welcoming, homely atmosphere. There were objects scattered on tables and the floor; newspapers, magazines, a tissue box, Fred's spectacles, a pair of shoes, an empty glass, a dirty ashtray, a half-empty chocolate box, an open book. It was a family room to relax in.

Outside, the patio, the pool, the gardens, the tennis court, the lake and the fields beyond the fence, viewed through the glass wall of patio doors, were a delight to look at. Fred, Bert, and a team of professional gardeners had transformed the scrubland into a landscape that would have made Capability Brown green with envy. With Fred's wealth they had been able to cheat and have full-sized trees and shrubs planted, so they hadn't had to wait for years to achieve the final effect that they wanted.

Although they employed two full-time gardeners, both long-term semi-retired workers of Fred, Daph loved to spend hours out there, snipping at plants, down on her knees with her trowel in her hand.

None of Fred's employers ever wanted to stop working as Fred was such a good boss, (and George didn't want to start) so he either let them keep their old jobs, or found them something to do part-time if they weren't as fit as they used to be.

Fred sat in a chair opposite George, crossed his long thin legs and sipped his sherry.

George examined his father. He was in good shape for his age. What was he now? He must be forty-five. A young Dad. With his dark, curly hair and weathered, tanned skin his gypsy blood was obvious. And Fred was proud of his origins. He had never denied his background. Despite all his money he was exactly the same as he'd always been - straight, honest, hard-working and down-to-earth. He never put on airs and graces, or spoke in a phoney posh voice. He had a firm handshake, looking people straight in the eyes, and he spoke loud and clearly. And people liked and respected him for it. They knew they could always rely on him. He'd never been refused a membership of a club or turned down for an invitation because of his roots. And money talks, of course.

George looked more like his mother expression-wise, although he'd inherited the Slaters' dark, curly hair and big brown eyes with long lashes.

Daph always looked innocent, and she always was. George always looked innocent, but whether he was or not is debatable.

'Well son,' Fred began, 'Lost at the races again did you?'

George nodded, shrugged and smiled. 'Never mind, better luck next time, eh?'

'Serves you right,' Fred continued, 'I told you not to bet on that filly. Dead loss she was. You always have a lot of trouble with the fillies, don't you?'

'Fred!' Daph defended her son.

'Sorry luv.'

'Well,' George bragged defensively, 'I won four hundred quid at the pub last night, so I was only a few hundred down.'

'Only a few hundred down, eh? ONLY a few hundred. Well, whoopy-doo!' Fred sighed emphatically and shook his head. 'ONLY a few hundred,' he repeated, 'Unbelievable.' He stood up and walked over to his cigar humidifier and selected one of the longer ones. He rolled it next to his ear, nodded approvingly and lit it with a match. No lighters for Fred's cigars. That was strictly taboo.

The onyx phone rang. Daph answered it. 'Hello, Daph Slater speaking. Oh, hello Grace.' She inspected her professionally manicured nails while she listened. 'Yeah? Yeah, 'course you can! Hang on, I'll just check with Fred,' She placed her hand over the receiver. 'It's Grace next door. They want to use our upper field for the summer fete and the lower field for the showjumping.'

'Yeah, sure! Tell them they're welcome to hold it here.' Fred waved his cigar in the air and walked across the room to refill the glasses. 'Not for you, George. You're driving,' he said.

'Fred said yeah, sure,' Daph repeated into the phone, 'Yeah, okay, I'll remind him.' She placed her hand over the receiver and spoke to Fred again. 'Don't forget you're playing golf with Ponsy this afternoon.'

'I won't!' Fred called, 'I'll pick him up at two.'

Daph spoke into the phone again. 'Fred said he won't and he'll be there at two. What? When, tomorrow? Yeah, that's fine. I'll see you then, Grace. Bye.' She hung up. 'I'm having coffee with Grace and the ladies tomorrow. She's holding a meeting to discuss the summer fete. Oh, and Suzie's on her way back from the stables. Oh, they ARE nice people.' Daph flicked a speck of non-existent dust from her silk designer dress. 'They'll make lovely in-laws for our Suzie.'

'Huh,' grunted Fred, 'By the time Suzie and Charles get organised and arrange their wedding, I don't reckon any of us will be around to see it!'

'Well I hope I'm still around. I'm looking forward to being a Grandma.' Daph smiled hopefully at George.

Fred shook his head, carefully lowering himself into his chair with a glass in one hand and his cigar in the other. He nodded at George. 'It's no use looking at him, although I'm surprised that he hasn't got a whole load of offspring to support, the way he spreads himself around!'

George wriggled with embarrassment. 'I don't spread myself around. And I'm just careful.'

'Fred!'

'Sorry luv.' Fred didn't look sorry at all.

Daphne patted George's knee. 'I'm glad to hear it, luv.'

'Careful? Oh, very funny. Since when? Or perhaps he can't have kids. Maybe he's firing blanks.'

'Fred, stop it!'

This time Fred didn't even pretend to be sorry.

'Blanks?' George had never considered that before. He'd always assumed that all females were on the Pill. He made a mental note to get himself checked out at the doctor's.

'Fred! Don't be so coarse!'

'Sorry luv.'

Daph glared at her husband, her eyes full of love, paused and then continued.

'Suzie and Charles know what they're doing. They're just making sure first.'

'Making sure of what? They've been together since they were kids! Perhaps we ought to get George to give them some sex education lessons.'

'Fred! You stop that talk!'

'Sorry luv. That would be a bit drastic, wouldn't it?'

'Anyway, they've seen their horses doing it often enough.'

'George! Don't you start!'

'Sorry, Mum. Oh look, here comes Grandad.' He sighed with relief at the chance to change the subject, and walked over to help the old man to his usual seat. He didn't take hold of Fred Senior as his Grandad was much too independent for that, but he was there if he was needed.

Fred Senior came in through the patio doors, his usual flat cap on his head. George couldn't ever remember seeing him without his cap on.

'Hi Dad,' Fred greeted him, 'Where have you been?'

'I've just finished varnishing the seats down in the field.'

'Oh Dad, you didn't need to bother. One of the lads could have done that!' Fred stood up and took a bottle of beer out of a small fridge under the drinks cabinet, opened the top and handed it to his father.

Fred Senior lived in a little old cottage on the edge of the estate that had been there for several centuries when Fred bought the land. He had a garden shed that was bigger than the cottage, filled with tools, tins of paint, an old car that he never drove any more, but kept polished and started up regularly, wood and materials left over after the main house was built, and goodness knows what else. 'Well you never know when it will come in handy,' was Fred Senior's motto on life. He spent a lot of his spare time tinkering around in the shed and kept it spotless, moving things from place to place, oiling and sharpening his tools with his old radio on in the background. He knew everything that was in there, and he knew at once where everything was. He could repair anything, and would rather do the work himself than have his son 'Waste good, hard-earned money, paying someone else to do it when I'm perfectly capable'.

'Oh cheers Son.' Fred Senior took the bottle and lowered himself slowly down into an armchair, grunting with the effort, and he leaned back with his legs apart. He slapped his hand down on his thigh and rubbed it up and down, sighed happily, took a long swig out of the bottle and wiped his mouth on his sleeve. 'You know me; I like to keep busy. It's good for me. It keeps the body from getting old and seizing up. And you know what idle hands do.'

'Um, nothing?' said George.

'No, come on, help me out here.' Fred Senior raised his cap slightly with one finger and scratched his forehead under his cap. 'There's a saying, isn't there? Idle hands-' He made a circle in the air with the forefinger of his free hand, encouraging everyone to finish the saying.

'Ask George. He's an expert on idle hands,' Fred said, picking up his phone from the small table next to his chair.

'Eeeugh, I'm not!' George gurgled, 'I'm always doing something.'

'Yes, well we all know what you get up to with your hands, don't we?' Fred laughed.

'Fred, you stop it!' Daphne warned him.

'Sorry Luv.' Fred tapped the details into his phone. 'Oh here we are. Idle hands make fretful minds. And here's another one; The Devil finds work for idle hands.'

Fred Senior grinned. 'There, see, told you.' He turned to George. 'So how are you getting on, Son?'

'Talk of the Devil,' Fred said to no-one in particular.

'Not so bad, Grandad. I keep plodding along.'

Fred Senior tutted and raised his eyes. 'Glad to hear it. No idle hands then? Keeping the Devil at bay are you?'

'So all these women do have their uses after all! We thought George was a ladies' man and all the time he's been fighting the Devil! We should address him as Saint George!'

'Fred Slater, I'm getting really cross with you now! George does NOT have idle hands!'

'Sorry Luv. No, it's his brain that's idle,' Fred said loudly.

'Oh Fred!'

'Sorry luv.'

'Anyway, my brain's not idle,' George replied defensively, 'I'm always out and about and doing something. I don't just lie around at home, do I?'

'No, and nor do I, and I never have, although I could do if I wanted to.' Fred's businesses were all run by efficient, loyal staff. But Fred firmly controlled them all and made sure that he was seen regularly. He renewed his Heavy Goods Licence every year so he could still drive his lorries, he inspected his properties several times a year to see if any maintenance was necessary instead of relying on the Agents, and did the same with his residential parks, always accessible to the people living there and making sure they were happy with everything. 'But I'm working and earning a living, I'm not just playing with my pals! he said.'

Bert shuffled in and jerked his head towards the hall. 'Suzie's just arrived and dinner's ready in five minutes.'

'Don't you mean lunch?' George teased, winding him up. It was an old joke.

Bert sniffed. 'No I don't! In my day you had breakfast, dinner and tea, and that was it. None of them posy, stuck-up new-fangled titles!'

'That's right Bert,' Fred Senior agreed. 'My old Mum, bless her heart, said you shouldn't go to bed with a full stomach. You mustn't eat a big meal late at night. You should give it time to settle down or you'll have indigestion and nightmares.'

'What's for lu- I mean, dinner today, Bert?' George asked, changing the subject.

'Roast beef and Yorkshire pud, followed by syrup pud and custard.'

'Puddings a la Bert. Lovely!' said George enthusiastically.

While Bert was laid up and unable to move, he had discovered a new interest in watching cookery programmes. He'd starting practising, and he turned out to be a very good cook, but he preferred basic and traditional recipes. But any restaurant would be proud to employ him and serve his cooking as everything was perfect. His Yorkshire puddings were excellent, risen high, and the roast beef would be just right, brown on the outside and pink inside.

'Don't you be so sarky, young George,' snapped Bert, 'You don't get none of that foreign muck in this house!' And he shuffled back to the kitchen, pulling the door slightly closed as he passed, and scowling with pleasure at George's praise.

The door flew wide open again and Suzie burst into the room. 'Hello, Mummy. Hello, Daddy. Oh, hello, Grandad! GEORGIE! YOU'RE HERE ALREADY!' She ran round the room kissing everyone. Suzie had only seen her brother the day before, when she was at the races with Charles. But she did everything with a breathless enthusiasm, making people feel important, which charmed everyone.

'Hello Little Sister.' George stood up to greet his sister. Suzie hugged him.

'Dinner!' shouted Bert from outside, 'Urry up before me puddings sink!' Everyone obediently rushed to the dining-room.

'I mustn't take long,' Suzie gushed, loading roast potatoes onto her plate, 'One of Daddy's drivers has gone sick so I'm driving his lorry to Essex this afternoon. The delivery's needed for the morning. Then I'm meeting Charles again this evening.'

'Well you be careful, dear,' Daphne cautioned her, 'Don't you go giving anyone any lifts.'

Suzie giggled. 'Oh Mummy, of COURSE I won't. We're not insured for giving lifts. I'll be alright!'

'Yeah,' said George, 'How is that guy who tried to mug you in that M25 service station car park?'

Suzie's huge brown eyes opened wide. 'Oh he's MUCH better! I phoned the hospital the other day to check. They've taken all the stitches out now, where he slid across his knife. And his plaster cast comes off soon. He's still wearing the neck-brace though. Poor man. When I threw him over my shoulder, I didn't know there was a car just driving in behind me. And then he bounced off it and hit that tree!'

'Poor man? He attacked YOU, Suzie, he tried to mug what he thought was a little defenceless female, all alone in the car park at night!'

'Yes Georgie, but he wasn't to know about my black belt in judo, was he? He could have been KILLED!'

'He should have been killed,' declared George, reaching out for a second helping of roast beef, pouring gravy over it and jabbing his fork in it angrily, 'He had a criminal record longer than his broken arm!'

'Yeah, people like that should be put down. That would lower the crime rate,' Fred said, 'Bloody criminals and scroungers. They think they can just take whatever they want. They think people like us owe them a favour! I worked hard for everything I've got and I never borrowed or took anything from anyone! And that reminds me, George.'

'Yeah?' George wondered if it was a good time to ask about the new car.

'Your mother and I have been talking about you.'

Daph pulled a You've been talking and I've been made to listen face, staring down at her plate.

Oh oh! Thought George, balancing peas on his fork.

'We've decided to stop supporting you,' Fred continued.

George dropped his peas. His mouth fell open, displaying a piece of Yorkshire pudding. He swallowed and reached for his wine glass to take a large gulp without even tasting the expensive red wine. 'Sto-stopped supporting me? Bu-but how will I survive? Where will 1 get my money from?'

'You'll work, son. W-O-R-K. That other four-letter word ending in -K that burns up a lot of energy, that you haven't got round to trying yet!' He moved aside as Bert cleared the plates.

'Fred!'

'Sorry luv.'

'Work?' squeaked George, 'Doing what?'

'Doing whatever you like, son. It's not that I begrudge you anything I've got, you know that. And half of it will be yours when we're dead, and half for Suzie. But it took me years of hard graft to get where I am today, and I'd hate to think of you losing everything I've worked for, just because you've no idea of the value of money.' He poured a thick helping of custard over his syrup pudding and chewed thoughtfully, looking at George. He swallowed his food and sipped his wine, examining the liquid contents appreciatively, then he continued; 'I'm not asking you to work for me, although you're welcome to if you'd like to.' George's face made it clear that he wouldn't like to. 'The choice is yours, son. Do anything you like. Start at the bottom if you want to. I'll support you and give you any help and advice you want if you decide to start your own business. It won't do you any harm. But the fun's over. The charity's stopped. You're nearly 30 and it's time to stop mucking about. As from now you're entirely self-supporting, and you'll pay your own bills.

So you'll either have to get a well-paid job, or cut down on your extravagant way of life.'

All the colour had drained out of George's face. It didn't seem like the right time to ask for a new car after all.

He had a sudden thought. 'But what about poor Mrs Blenkins? She's cleaned for me for years. I won't be able to afford to keep her on.'

'Oh what a shame! Your Mother cleans this big house on her own-'

'I prefer to do my own cleaning,' Daph added, 'Then I know it's done properly.'

'-And you can't manage to clean a little two-bedroom terraced house?'

'But I don't know how to do it! I've never done it before in my life!' George wailed.

'Aah Diddums. Oh dear, poor you. My heart's breaking for you!' was Fred's reply, scraping his plate clean, 'You're just going to have to learn, aren't you?'

'You could always go in the army. They'd teach you to clean; and they'd pay you,' Fred Senior suggested.

George shuddered at the thought. 'No thanks Grandad. I don't fancy that at all!' He wondered if he could still draw some money out on his bank-cards if he hurried, or had his father already cancelled them?

Work? Doing what, for goodness' sake? Well he wasn't going to beg and crawl. He stuck his chin out bravely.

'Right, fine, if that's the way you want it,' he sighed dramatically, like a prisoner in front of the firing-squad.

'It is,' Fred replied, spoiling the effect.

'I know I'll find it hard-'

'You can say that again!' Fred interrupted.

George carried on, 'But I don't need your charity!'

'Good, I'm glad to hear it, because you're not getting it any more!'

'I'll live on bread and water if I have to, but I'll survive – somehow!' He exhaled loudly again, poured himself a large brandy out of the cut-glass carafe in the middle of the table and cut a slice of Stilton cheese.

'Course you will, son. You'll have to won't you?' Fred lit a cigar, blew out a cloud of smoke and stood up. 'And look on the bright side; you'll be keeping the Devil at bay! Right, I'm off now. Come on, Bert!' he called, 'I'm playing golf with Ponsy!'

'Ponsonby-Ffinch,' Bert muttered happily, 'Stupid bloody name! It's like calling you Ffred! And stupid boring golf! Don't know what you see in it.'

'Come off it Bert, you're a brilliant caddy, and you love the game. Bye Luv, see you later.' Fred bent down to kiss Daph, then he draped an arm over Bert's shoulder and led him out.

'I'd better be going as well,' Suzie told her mother, pushing back her chair, 'I've got to get the lorry loaded. Bye, Grandad.'

'Goodbye Suzie. And you be careful!' Daph said, standing up and clearing the table. She paused to kiss her daughter.

'Goodbye my little angel,' Fred Senior called after her.

'I'll walk you to your car,' George said, sticking his hands in his pockets and putting on his sad face.

Suzie took hold of his arm. 'Oh Georgie, why don't you get a driving job with Daddy? It's SUPER fun! And when I stop anywhere the men are EVER so friendly, and EVER so pleased to see me!'

'I bet they are!' replied George, looking at his sister's petite figure and blonde curly hair. She was dressed in a pair of jodhpurs and a loose white shirt as usual, with her sunglasses on top of her head, but she still managed to look like a model. 'You just take care, won't you?'

'I will,' she promised.

They reached Suzie's sports car and he opened the door for her, then shut it after she'd climbed in. 'Goodbye Georgie,' she gushed, 'And DO think of something, won't you? Oh, I HOPE you'll be alright! Here,' She handed him a £50 note.

'Oh Suzie, I can't take that!'

'Of COURSE you can, Georgie! After all, they haven't cut off MY allowance, have they? And I hardly touch it. I've got LOADS in the bank! I don't need it with my wages as well; well, not yet anyway, although I probably will do when Charles and I get married! We're planning to have ABSOLUTELY LOADS of children! But PROMISE not to tell Mummy and Daddy! – I mean about the money, not the children!'

'I promise faithfully!' George shouted, jumping out of the way as she roared off, spraying him with a cloud of gravel.

Sticking his hands in his pockets again he strolled back indoors, wondering how he was going to survive. Could he talk his mother round to reversing Fred's decision? No, nobody could do that when Fred had made up his mind. And Daph never argued with Fred when he made a decision. What on earth was he going to do?

He went into the dining-room where Fred Senior was still eating his roast beef. He was a very slow eater, so everyone left him to eat at his own pace. George sat down opposite his Grandad with a dramatic sigh and poured himself a glass of cold water out of a jug on the table.

Fred Senior stuck his fork in a carrot ring, then in a roast potato, cutting a small piece off, then in a slice of roast beef. He pushed some peas on top, patted them down with his knife, dipped the little pile in the gravy and neatly popped the lot into his mouth, chewing slowly, looking at George out of the corner of his eye. George sighed again for effect, sipping his water and staring across the room, holding his glass between his cupped hands.

Grandad Slater swallowed, and drank a large swig of his beer. He didn't like wine. He thought it was too fancy. He enjoyed a traditional dark beer made in a small craft brewery. Then he leaned back in his chair, patted his stomach and burped expertly and contentedly, hooking out a piece of meat from a tooth with his little finger.

'Well, Son,' he said at last, 'So you've lost your allowance have you?' George nodded sadly and silently. 'So what are you going to do?' Fred Senior continued. 'You've got to do something, because your Dad won't change his mind once he's made a decision.'

George shrugged. 'I haven't got the faintest idea. I haven't recovered from the shock yet.'

Fred Senior took a toothpick out of a little porcelain pot on the table and picked at his teeth thoughtfully for a while. Then he said, 'Well whatever it is that you decide to do, just make sure that you do it well.'

George banged down the glass dramatically and clenched his fists and held them up in the air. 'Oh it's so unfair, Grandad! Dad's sprung this on me, out of the blue. He could at least have given me a few weeks' notice to sort something out!'

'Well you've had 28 years, son. You should have guessed that your Dad wouldn't keep forking out money forever more.'

Fred leaned forward, his arms flat on the table. 'I remember when you were born like it was yesterday,' he said with the toothpick in the corner of his mouth, 'Your Mum was sixteen and your Dad was seventeen. Everyone was horrified. Nobody thought their marriage would last, bless their hearts. But your Dad swore to Rocky, your other Grandad, who had him by the throat at the time, that he'd work hard and make us all proud of him, and not to underestimate him because he was so young. And my God, did he work!'

George had heard it all before, but he listened politely.

His Grandad paused and adjusted his cap. 'Of course, he'd been working for me for his pocket money since he could stand! But he really threw himself into the work full-time. First he worked in my scrap yard all day, and he got it really tidied up and expanded. Of course, I always kept it tidyish and I knew where everything was, but he made it easier to reach things so's he could sell more stuff. And he was leaving there and washing up in a pub at night. Then as soon as he'd saved up enough money and passed his driving test, there was no stopping him. He cleared jumble sales, sorting out paper, scrap and material into piles and selling them, and putting aside the decent books. And your Mum would wash and iron all the decent gear which they sold at car boot sales and markets. And that led on to the antiques business. He and your mother taught themselves all about it and opened a shop.' He slowly counted on his fingers. 'Then there was the haulage business and the removals. And the property business. They had their own flat before they were nineteen, and they paid cash for it, so nobody could turn them down because of their age.' He smiled at the memory.

'Then they moved and bought the terraced house, then the semi, and the detached house, plus the other properties that your Dad bought and rented out. He put every penny back into the business. If he wasn't driving lorries he was stripping wallpaper or building a new kitchen.' He gazed over George's head with a reminiscent smile on his face. He seemed to have forgotten George for a while and he was talking to himself.

'Little Suzie was born when they were eighteen and nineteen. They were so proud of you kids. Your Dad vowed that you'd both have the best education that he could afford. Then Rocky had a heart attack and your dad ran his fuel business. And when he died, Daph, your mum, inherited it. And then your Dad collapsed. Do you remember it?'

George nodded. They'd thought that Fred was going to die. They'd assumed that it was his heart. But it wasn't. It was just chronic exhaustion.

'Your Mum made him sell all his businesses. But he insisted on keeping the haulage business and the properties. He said the land would be worth a fortune one day. And now he's learnt to enjoy himself at last. He loves golf. And they visit their yacht regularly -. of course he bought it cheap off a bloke who was desperate to sell - plus trips abroad to their Spanish villa and their French farmhouse. Oh, I still can't keep up with him, even after all this time!'

'No, nor can I!'

'But you're going to have to do it the other way round, son. You've had your leisure time, now you're going to have to work for a living.' George pulled a face. 'Luckily for you, you know there's a light at the end of the tunnel. You know you'll be rich one day. So if you take my advice, you'll get your head down and graft; show your Dad that you can be independent. Make him proud of you. I know you can do it son. You're a Slater.'

He reached into his back pocket and pulled out a thick wad of notes, held together with an elastic band. He licked his thumb, peeled off two twenties and a ten pound note and handed them to George.

'Here,' he said, 'Take this. You're going to need it. If you got a job tomorrow, it'd be at least a week before you got paid, and probably more like a month. This'll tide you over if you spend it wisely - no more stupid bets. And go easy on the booze!'

George politely but eagerly reached out his hand and took the notes, then he took hold of Fred Senior's rough, varnish-stained hand and squeezed it.

'OK Grandad, thanks. Don't worry, I'm through with betting. And I'm off alcohol too,' he added, drinking the last drop of his brandy, 'And thanks again.'

Embarrassed, Grandad Slater gently pulled his hand away and stood up. 'Well I'm off for my forty winks now, as usual. And remember what I said, son. Make your Mum and Dad, and all of us, including yourself, proud of you.'

George nodded. 'I will, Grandad. And I'll make YOU extra proud of me too. Just like my Dad did.'

Fred Senior glanced back at his grandson, grunted and gave a doubtful shake of the head, raised his cap and ran his hand over his grey but still thick hair, jammed his cap back on his head and shuffled off through the back door and along the garden path to his bed in his cottage.

Daph was thumbing through a magazine in the lounge, sitting on a sofa with her shoes kicked off and her long slim legs neatly tucked to the side on the sofa. George tried out his dramatic sigh again and collapsed into a chair.

'Look at the length of these skirts!' said Daph, 'They show everything they've got. Honestly, they may just as well wear a belt! And you can see right through them!'

'Where? Let's have a look,' said George, instinctively interested. Then he remembered his new situation. He tapped his fingers on the arm of the chair a few times, and he stood up. 'Oh well, I'd better be going. I probably need to sort out some of my things, to sell them. To raise some money for food and things. To help me survive, until I get A JOB.' He paused for affect.

'Mm,' muttered Daph, not looking up.

'Maybe I'll do a car boot sale, to get some money, to live on.'

'Okay luv,' said Daph, reading her magazine, 'Give your Mum a kiss.' She made kissing noises and turned her cheek towards him.

George bent down and kissed her. 'Bye then, Mum,' he said in his most heartbreaking voice, sighing tragically, 'I don't know when I'll see you again. I'll have to save my petrol from now on. Maybe I could thumb a lift here sometimes.' He gave her a little hug and a pat on the shoulder.

'Bye, dear,' said Daph.

George was opening the front door when his mum called, 'Oh, George!'

'Yes Mum?' This sounded hopeful, he thought as he went back into the lounge.

She was standing up and bending down, trying to get her shoes on while rummaging in her Christian Dior handbag. 'Here, take this,' she said in a stage-whisper, glancing at the doorway over her shoulder as though expecting Fred to materialise behind her.

Closing her bag, she handed George a £50 note. 'It's all the change I've got. It'll tide you over for a while if you're careful; buy you petrol for interviews and things. But do try and make it last. And promise not to tell your father!'

George took the £50 note and tucked it in his inside jacket pocket with the rest of the money he'd been given, then he placed his hand on his heart. 'You have my word as a gentleman.'

Daph looked doubtful. 'I'd rather you promised.'

***

'Work?' shrieked Rodney in a falsetto voice, staggering dramatically and grabbing hold of the edge of the bar, 'Oh my God, that's terrible! And our fathers are playing golf together this afternoon. I hope your father didn't put any funny ideas about me in his head! I honestly don't think I could survive if I had to work for my living! What on earth are you going to do, George?'

George shrugged and held out his hands hopelessly. 'I haven't got the faintest idea. Not the faintest. But I've got to do something quick or I'll be completely flat broke. I stopped at my bank's cashpoint on the way here, and I made several attempts to draw out some money, and then it ate all my cards. I'm sure I heard munching noises and a burp from inside the machine. They probably have a Troll sitting in the inner workings.'

'I expect it's the Bank Manager. He looks a bit Troll-like,' said Edward.

'My Dad really means business. He's dead serious about this. And once he makes his mind up about something, there's no budging him. As far as he's concerned, he's always right. There are two sides to every argument with him; his and his.'

'I'm not sure what I'd do if I had to work,' said Edward thoughtfully, 'But I don't think that I'd mind very much. I've thought about it a few times. I've often fancied running a sort of art gallery, where local artists could display their paintings, or their sculptures, or pottery perhaps. We could have lots of launch parties, with wine and canapes. I'd take a commission on anything that was sold. I wouldn't run it myself of course. I'd get a manager, or an attractive manageress to do it for me, and I could pop in sometimes for the launch parties and to collect the money and check that everything was okay.'

'How about a boutique?' Rodney suggested, 'That would be rather fun. You'd enjoy that. We'd come in to buy our clothes at a discount, and to admire the scenery. Loud music and lovely girls.'

'Yeah, you could have a two-way mirror in the changing rooms,' Edward suggested keenly.

George shook his head. 'I haven't got any funds to start anything like that. And I don't know anything about fashion; only about what goes on inside it. I don't really take any notice of what girls are wearing. After all, it's hopefully all going to come off eventually. I just check out their bodies, and where all the zips and buttons are.'

'Do you? Wow, I've never thought of that!' said Edward admiringly.

Rodney grinned. 'I don't bother. I just get hold and pull, and they usually join in and help, to avoid wear and tear – and to hurry things up, of course.'

'I could always do with some help at the Sweat Shop if you're really stuck, George,' Stefan told him, 'There's lots to do out the back all the time.'

'Thanks Stefan, that's really decent of you, mate.' George knew perfectly well that Stefan didn't need any extra help at all. All his staff were physically fit, well-trained and qualified experts at what they did. And they all loved their jobs. George wouldn't be a very good visual example of what training could do, and he'd never train, of course. He couldn't be bothered.

'Hey, I could do with a washer-upper behind the bar. Then you could talk to your chums and chat up the girls as you usually do,' Digby grinned.

'You're really enjoying this, aren't you, Digby?' George snapped.

Digby looked hurt. 'Only trying to help, George, only trying to help.'

'You can help by doing what you're best at and pouring four more pints, Digby,' Rodney told him.

George drained his lager. 'No, not for me. I'm off. I'm really not good company at the moment. I'm not in a socialising mood. I'd rather be on my own. I'm going back home to have a quiet panic – I mean, think.'

'Don't forget to buy the papers tomorrow. There may be a suitable job for you.'

'Yeah, sure. A suitable job. Whoopee! Cheers, Edward. I'll pick them up in the morning.' George sounded doubtful as he slowly walked away.

'Cheerio, George. Chin up, old chap!' called Rodney as George left, then he shuddered. 'Poor old George! Work, how terrible! Hurry up with those lagers please, Digby, and a brandy for me as well. I've had rather a nasty shock. In fact, I'm feeling quite faint!'

'So what on earth is Juicy George going to do to earn a living?' Digby asked, putting down the drinks. 'It's even hard for qualified people to find a decent job around here. The restaurants and shops are family run. Everyone either commutes, or they move away to the cities. The railway station's shut, there aren't any buses, and the traffic's at a standstill in the mornings, and again in the evenings. I mean, what's he got to offer a potential employer?'

Edward shrugged. 'No idea. It's not a subject that I'm familiar with. We're all going to have a look in the papers tomorrow. It's a pity he can't earn a living out of females somehow. That's where his talents lie. He can make a female do anything.'

'What, you mean, be a pimp?' Rodney looked shocked. 'I know Fred said he'd be happy with whatever George did to earn a living, but I think he'd draw the line at pimping!'

'No, I didn't mean that,' Edward said, 'Although I don't think we should rule anything out at this stage. I don't really know what I meant. I was just thinking aloud.'

'Coo-ee, Stefan!' called a woman who was easily in her seventies, tottering towards Stefan and waving her hand, its long red painted nails looking lethal. She had a face-lift so tight that her pumped-up lips could hardly move, and an outfit on that would have looked ridiculous on someone half her age. The dress was low-cut, showing a vast area of her wrinkled bust, and the skirt was halfway up her thighs. She could hardly balance on the high-heeled red shoes.

'Oh hello, Agnes. Oh wow, don't you look GORGEOUS this evening? You look younger every time I see you. And my my, you've lost more weight, haven't you?' Stefan placed a hand on each of her hips and squeezed them several times.

'Oh, you flatterer, you!' cooed Agnes, slapping him on the arm and wiggling her backside, 'And my transformation's all thanks to you! You helped me to start my weight-loss and kept me going when I felt like giving up.'

She turned and noticed Rodney and Edward, and looked them both up and down, approvingly. Then she smiled, 'You'd never believe that I was a size 20 a few years ago. I was really down and depressed. But this lovely man gave me back my self-confidence, and made me what I am today! I'll see you on Thursday, darling, for my massage.' She said Massage in a very suggestive voice.

'Yes, I'm looking forward to it – as always,' Stefan said, winking at her. Agnes tottered away giggling.

Edward and Rodney stared at him. 'You haven't?' said Rodney.

'You couldn't?' gasped Edward.

Stefan just smiled mysteriously and tapped the side of his nose.

'Excuse me,' said a voice.

'Sorry,' replied Stefan, moving aside to let a young couple get to the bar.

'What would you like to drink, Dee-dee?' asked the boy.

'Orange juice.' She giggled. 'I'm on a strict diet. I want to look nice for you. Oh, and a packet of salt and vinegar crisps please.'

Stefan watched them thoughtfully as they wove their way through the Sunday night crowd and found a table where they sat holding hands.

'I know something that George couldn't make a woman do,' he said quietly, or as quietly as he could speak over the noise in the bar.

'What's that?' Edward and Rodney asked simultaneously. (Well, almost simultaneously.)

'He couldn't make a woman lose weight.'

'What do you mean?' Rodney asked.

'Well, many of my clients visit my Sweat Shop regularly, once a week or more. They spend several hours using the equipment, working out, listening to advice from my staff, having a sauna, a swim, a massage, or one of the other treatments. Then they spend the rest of the week entertaining or being entertained, eating and drinking themselves silly, and vowing to cut down before their next visit. They never lose any weight, but they're happy to pay me a lot of money to stop them putting any more weight on! And it's a well-known fact that most women are permanently on a diet - well, verbally, anyway!'

'But what about all the slimming magazines on sale? There are loads of them! Surely they must do some good?' Edward asked.

Stefan raised his eyes to the ceiling. 'Only for the people who publish them! Women buy them, take them home and read them while demolishing a coffee and a cream cake - their final, farewell cream cake, of course, and naturally, the coffee has sweetener in it instead of sugar! - and they decide which diet they're going to start tomorrow.'

'Yeah, that's right,' Digby butted in, 'They've got no idea. They come in here, announce that they're on a diet, then order a gin and slimline tonic and a meat pie. They think that one counter-balances the other. Honestly, you ought to try being in the catering business in this day and age! Whatever I have on the menu, someone will complain. There's the Veggies, the Vegans, the Dairy-frees, the Gluten-frees and the Calorie Counters. No wonder pubs and restaurants are closing down every day! Bring back the old days when people were happy with normal, proper food that I could just stick in the microwave and serve out of the packet within 10 minutes!'

'Well it's worth chewing over,' Rodney said and then he laughed. 'Ha ha, that's funny. Chewing over!'

'I bet George could make them do it,' Edward said loyally, 'I bet he could transform an overweight female.'

'Fat hope!' shouted Digby, 'Ha, get it? Fat hope! How could he? He wouldn't know a calorie if it walked in here, said Hello George, I'm a Calorie, and then kicked him up the backside!'

'What's that all about then, Digby?' a customer asked.

'It's our George. Edward here reckons he could charm a female into losing weight.'

The man flapped his hand in the air. 'No way! My missus has been on a diet for twenty years, and she's five stone heavier than when she started it!'

'I heard that, Frank!' screeched a large woman in the corner, 'Anyway, you like my curves! You said you don't like skinny women.'

'Well there are limits in both directions,' Frank said quietly, so his wife couldn't hear.

'There you are,' Digby said to Edward, 'Get George to have a go at Frank's missus.'

'He's not getting near my missus. I know what he's like!' Frank shouted.

'I think George will be relieved to know that,' Rodney muttered,

'I reckon our George could do it!' another customer called out.

'Yeah!' 'No way!' 'Sure he could!' 'Impossible!'

Digby banged his fist on the bar to attract attention. 'Right, let's do this properly! Where's Booky Bill from down the hill? Bill! Come round here!'

An elegantly dressed man in a striped suit, with lots of gold at his wrists; cufflinks, watch and bracelet, and a gold tooth, stood up. 'No chance,' he said.

Digby's face fell. 'You mean you won't take the bets, Bill? That's not like you!'

'I didn't say that did I? I meant that George had no chance of winning. Sure, I'll take the bets. I've never turned a bet down yet. It'll be like taking candy from a baby. But you've got to work out exactly what you're betting on. And you've overlooked one small point.'

'What's that?' asked someone unimportant to this story. The whole pub gradually went quiet. Everyone was listening. They all enjoyed a bet, especially at the Races, but this was a new angle. And they all knew George's reputation.

'You haven't got a female for George to work on.'

Conversations broke out again. 'Easy!' 'Loads of fat women around!' 'And they'll stay fat!' 'Nah, they all want to lose weight!' 'Sure, they WANT to!' 'Impossible!' 'No it isn't!' 'I bet our George can sort her out!' 'I bet he can't!' 'Yes, but who is she?!'

Bill clapped his hands slowly three times. 'Right,' he said, 'I'll work out some rules and let you know tomorrow. This needs some thinking about. Meanwhile you guys, don't you think it would be a good idea to discuss this with George?'

Rodney, Edward and Stefan looked at each other. 'Um, yes, I suppose we ought to,' said Edward, 'You can tell him tomorrow, Rodney.'

'Oh no, YOU can tell him tomorrow, Edward. After all, it was your idea.'

Stefan smiled. 'Don't worry, guys. He'll do it. He'll leap at the chance after he's waded his way through all the available jobs in the papers and found nothing he fancies. He'll be getting desperate then. We'll all tell him tomorrow – well, soon, anyway!'

MONDAY 15th NOVEMBER

Candy lumbered along the pavement. Her swollen feet erupted out over her misshapen shoes. The fine rain flattened her thin, mousy hair (the only thing about her that was thin) and smeared the outside of her glasses, while her tears smeared the inside. She wore black leggings that were stretched to their limit, and a long, baggy patterned top. A gust of wind threatened to blow her top up and she quickly screwed it up into a bunch and angrily pulled her coat closed.

Unaware of where she was, and unable to see, she held both hands out in front of her and blindly pushed open the door of the Duck and Grouse.

'Road sweeper wanted, four days a week, all equipment and uniform provided,' Edward read out from the paper. George shook his head mechanically, gazing down, imagining an invisible gutter full of half-finished meals and tin cans.

'Person to look after Gents' toilets. Wages negotiable, annual holidays at mutual convenience. No? Dustman wanted, training given. Oh look, George, Assistant Bar Steward urgently required for Golf Club. No experience necessary. There you are, you'd only have to do it until your father saw you. He'd be so embarrassed at being served by his son-'

'-Especially if you served him really badly and then spilt drinks over his mates,' Rodney added.

'-That he'd let you off the hook and you'd have your allowance back in no time!'

'Oh come on, you all know my Dad! He'd think it was a great joke. He'd probably order different complicated drinks for everyone so that I had more work to do. Then he's stand there and make sarky comments and laugh at me! No, the truth is, I don't want anyone I know to see me working. It would put me off. Imagine if Penny, for instance, came back from Switzerland and caught me emptying her parents' dustbin, or if Jessica saw me sweeping the road. I think it might just put them off me a bit, don't you?'

'I don't know, some females find a bit of rough a turn-on,' Stefan said encouragingly.

'Bit of rough? Oh, thank you very much!' said George, hurt. 'And you may not have noticed, but I manage OK without having to be a bit of rough to turn them on!'

'Here you are then, George,' Edward continued, 'Nightwatchman urgently required for warehouse. Immediate start.'

'Must be strong and active. Why's that, I wonder?' George asked, reading it over Edward's shoulder.

'Probably so you can run away fast when thugs break in!'

'Oh thanks a lot Stefan!'

'I wonder what happened to the last night watchman?' Edward asked, 'At least nobody would see you, not even us. You'd be asleep all day, wouldn't you? How about Assistant baker wanted. Early start. Must be adept at handling dough. Well, you were till yesterday, weren't you?'

'Yeah, very funny, Edward. You're making them up, aren't you? Oh this is dreadful!' wailed George, 'It's not that I don't want to work - well, okay, I don't - it's just that there's nothing I fancy! I can't picture myself doing any of those jobs day after day – or night after night.'

Rodney looked over Edward's shoulder at the paper. 'There must be something that'll do for now, George. How about Warm, friendly person required to work as Traffic Warden. Sense of humour required?'

George shuddered and made a cross with his forefingers.

'Aah! How about this? A job with a future! Assistant Curate wanted for Museum. That should be easy, surely?'

'I don't want to spend my time with a load of old relics,' George sighed.

'Speaking of old relics,' said Rodney, turning the page, 'Are there any rich widows looking for young male companions in the Personal column? Then you wouldn't have to work at all, George – well, not much. You'd just need to dish out plenty of charm and flattery.'

George spat out the lager he'd just swigged. 'Oh don't. That's conjuring up horrible images in my brain! Ooh, that's an awful idea!'

'Why?' asked Stefan, 'You just have to train yourself to float away and think of nice things while you're gazing into her eyes, acting all charming and interested in what she's saying, or what you're doing. Mentally count all your money, for instance.'

'I can't. I just can't.' George did an exaggerated shudder. 'It's like if you say to me, Whatever you do, don't think of a blue elephant. And what do I do?'

'You immediately think of a blue elephant, like I am now,' Rodney agreed.

'So am I,' said Edward.

'Well there you are then. Just lie back and think of blue elephants,' suggested Stefan.

Old Gubbins removed his pipe, a sign that he was about to speak, and they all looked at him, waiting to hear what he had to say. They had a great deal of respect for the old man.

'You could run my farm for me if you want, Young George. It's all getting a bit too much for me and I could do with some help.'

'Wow, thanks, Gubbins. That's really kind of you, but I don't know anything about farming.'

'Well it's easy enough to learn. It's time that's the problem. It's a never-ending, thankless job. I've known you all your life, and I know that I could trust you.'

'That really is a great offer, Gubbins. Can I think about it?'

'Course you can!' Old Gubbins replied, examining the inside of his empty pipe, 'And if you want to come up for a look round, you just let me know. You ain't lived till you watch a young lamb being born. It's up on its feet in a few minutes. And we intelligent humans take around a year to even stand up!'

'Well whatever I do, I've got to do something quick,' George said, 'It's only been a day and my money's dwindling away fast, just on bare necessities, like a round of lagers. And I'm not even thinking about the bills yet!'

'Look at this. She sounds interesting.' Rodney pointed to an ad in the paper.

'Ooh, let me see,' said Stefan, interested, 'I'm always open to offers.' He moved aside to let someone get to the bar, without looking up from the paper.

'Um, a pint of, er, that beer please. And a packet of cheese and onion crisps - no, make that two - oh, and some pork scratchings, please, and one of those steak pies as well. I'm really hungry!'

For once Digby was speechless. His eyes and his mouth were opened wide as he served the girl. He kept jerking his head at Rodney, Edward and Stefan to attract their attention.

'Well you could-' Rodney began. He glanced over his shoulder at the customer, looked away, and did a double-take that Bart Simpson would have been proud of. He nudged Edward in the back as he was about to drink his lager, spilling it down his shirt.

'I say Rodney, you nearly-'

'Look!'

'What?'

'Behind me!' Rodney hissed, waggling his head.

'My God, she's beautiful!' whispered Edward, staring openly.

'Perfect,' Stefan agreed, smiling. 'Yup, she'll do nicely!'

'What? What's going on?' George asked, a feeling of unease creeping up in his stomach as he watched his friends' odd behaviour.

They all stared at Candy as she wobbled towards a table, clutching her drink, crisps and pie. She sat down, put her drink and food on the table and fought her way out of her voluminous coat, letting it drop onto the seat behind her, then she removed and polished her rain-smeared glasses. She examined them and put them on again and had a large sip of her beer, pulled a face at the taste and ripped open a packet of crisps. A drop of rain dripped down from her hair into the crisp packet and she took out the soggy crisp, examined it, then shrugged and ate it, crunching loudly and then, rattling inside the bag and grabbing a large handful, she stuffed them into her mouth.

'Hey, have you seen…? Over there?' Digby jerked his head at the girl. As she opened her mouth to bite into the pie and everyone noticed her, a gradual hush spread through the Duck and Grouse.

With her mouth still hanging open, Candy glanced up. She dropped the pie onto the plate. She had an uneasy feeling that the whole bar was watching her, but every time she looked around, everyone was staring in a different direction. It reminded her of a horror film she'd seen once. Was she in danger? Were they all vampires or werewolves? Was this The Village of the Damned? No, she was imagining it. They were just being casually curious as she was a stranger. She just wasn't used to pubs. Then she shrugged, picked up the pie and sank her teeth into the pastry. It was hot so she flapped her hand in front of her mouth and made puffing noises while she chewed it. But she didn't stop eating it.

'Look at those HUGE thighs,' Rodney whispered.

'And that ENORMOUS stomach,' Edward added.

Eighteen stone at least,' Stefan guessed.

'Yuck,' said George.

'You haven't told him yet, have you?' Digby said.

'Told me what? What's going on?' George asked. That uneasy feeling was getting stronger by the minute. 'Oh no, no no no no! As from right now, all Ugly Bird Bets are finished from now on. Finished, Finito. No way Jose for any amount of money! They've run their course. It's over. I flatly refuse. And that's final. I'm not that desperate for money. I'd rather starve.'

Rodney, Edward and Stefan looked at each other. Stefan clamped a hand on George's shoulder. 'See that girl over there?'

'Er, yes. Funny enough I can. It's a job to miss her! So what? George said, shaking his head emphatically and trying to move away from Stefan's hand.

'Well,' Stefan continued, tightening his grip, 'There lies the answer to all your financial worries, in one neat little package, George.'

'Little?' George stared from Rodney to Edward, to Stefan, to Digby, to Candy and back to Rodney again. Then he shook his head and repeated. 'Oh no, no no no no!'

'No what?' Stefan asked, 'And it's Oh yes, yes yes yes yes! Where's your gratitude? We've all been very worried about you, and we've been thinking hard about how to solve your problem. We all CARE about you, George.'

George stepped away from Stefan's hand. 'I am not, I repeat, not, sleeping with HER! No way, not for any money. Because, A) I'm stone, cold sober; well, almost, and, B) I'd rather starve to death! I don't care if she's a millionaire. The answer is No!'

'No George, you've misunderstood us!' Rodney reassured him, 'We don't want you to sleep with her-'

'In fact, we forbid it!' Edward said.

'For now, anyway,' Stefan added as an afterthought.

George studied their faces, which left him none the wiser. 'So what exactly is my connection in this? Do please tell me,

I'm just dying to know – I think! After all, I'm obviously deeply involved in your plans in some terrible, devious way.'

Rodney, Edward and Stefan bent towards George and told him about the bet.

With the remains of the pie still held up to her mouth, Candy's eyes searched the room. It wasn't her imagination. Everyone was staring at her when they thought she couldn't see them! She could feel their eyes boring into her. She chewed rapidly, forced herself to gulp down some more beer, looked down and bit into her pie again, then she looked up quickly. Yes, their eyes were averted when she peeped in their direction. She began to fidget uneasily. Why were they all watching her? Was she really that hideous to look at? Was she a freak?

'I'm going to bet fifteen hundred on George,' Stefan announced.

'Stefan! I thought you said it couldn't be done!' Rodney said, surprised.

'I think it can be, if we do it properly, if we all watch her every day, and if you make sure you look after her properly, George.'

'Me? Why me? I just don't get it.'

'Yes, you. And it's because I'll give you half my winnings when we win, in a year's time. That's why. And we will win, won't we? You wouldn't want me to lose my money, would you, George?' Stefan grinned, displaying his perfect teeth, and he flexed his muscles. All of them.

George swallowed and tugged at the top of his polo-neck sweater. The situation had suddenly leaped up and taken him over. What had he let himself in for? Or rather, what had his friends let him in for? But what was the alternative? Work. Washing-up? Lavatory attendant? Farmer? Gigolo? No thanks. He couldn't decide which one was the worst! But in twelve months' time he could collect a lot of money - in twelve months' time?

'Hey, what am I going to live off for twelve months?'

They all thought for a moment. 'Sell your car,' Rodney suggested.

'Sell my car?'

'Well you don't use it much, do you? You're usually too drunk to drive it anywhere. It's parked outside here most of the time – that's when you can remember where you've left it.'

'Oh cheers, Digby!'

'Go on then, off you go.' Rodney gave him an encouraging push.

'Hang on a minute, there's one small point.'

'What's that, George?' Edward asked.

'While you're arguing about whether I can or can't do it, you probably haven't noticed, but I haven't actually said that I would do it. I'm still considering all the pros and cons. And I can't think of any pros.'

'That was another idea that we had,' Edward said.

'What do you mean?' George asked. Then he realised what that meant.

A hand was clamped over his mouth and his head was wrenched backwards. 'Shut up George,' whispered Rodney in his ear, 'We can all make a lot of money out of this.'

'And it could be your alternative to working,' Edward whispered in his other ear, 'Or would you rather sweep the streets?'

'Well the streets are pretty clean around here, so it wouldn't be so bad after all.' Sweeping the streets was beginning to seem quite an acceptable occupation.

'He's chicken!' said Digby, 'He knows he'll lose!' He flapped his arms up and down and trotted along behind the bar, making chicken noises.

It was raining quite hard now and sweeping the streets had lost its attraction.

'Alright,' George said lamely, 'I'll give it a try. That's the best I can do, isn't it?'

Candy was beginning to feel scared. Why was the man behind the bar acting like a chicken and glancing in her direction ? Was it the start of some primitive sacrificial ceremony? Or was he mocking her as she ate her chicken flavoured crisps?

She searched behind her for an armhole of her coat, struggling to find it and looking around her nervously while she did. How many steps was it to the door? Could she safely escape in time before they all grabbed her? She filled her mouth with crisps with one hand while she tried to get into her coat which was still wet from the rain.

'We'll talk about finances later,' Stefan hissed, 'Quick George, she's getting ready to leave! Go and do your stuff before she escapes and you miss your chance!'

'Yes, before we all miss our chance,' Rodney muttered, taking a swig of his lager.

With one huge hand, Stefan shoved George halfway across the room. Murmured conversations broke out again as George staggered sideways towards the girl, trying to keep his balance. He managed to stop, resting a hand on the table, and he stared at the huge mound of flesh in front of him. Suddenly that night watchman's job didn't seem so bad after all! Surely, he just needed to walk around the building now and then, and watch TV or take power naps the rest of the time. He'd keep all the doors locked. And he could have takeaways delivered when he wanted them. He wondered if they supplied a dog to protect him. And how hard was it to learn to milk a cow? Maybe he'd visit Gubbins' farm and have a go.

No, to hell with it. There were easier ways of making a living! He turned and started walking back to his friends with a pleading expression on his face. It nearly always worked on females, but the men were totally unmoved and unsympathetic. They all flapped their hands at him frantically, mouthing, 'Go on! Go back! And quick! Go!'

Straightening up, George forced a sort of smile on his face, which was the best he could manage. It was what is sometimes called the Tombstone Smile. Then he turned and coughed to get the girl's attention as she shoved a final handful of crisps in her mouth, and placed her hand on the table to help her to stand up, with one arm in her coat. She stared at him, wondering what he wanted.

He also had the attention of everyone in the room. They were all now openly staring at the odd couple.

Normally he would have been a gentleman and helped a female to put her coat on. But his muscles refused to respond.

'Hello,' he smiled grimly when she looked up at him, then he paused, lost for words for once. He looked back at his friends but they didn't seem to be so friendly any more. Edward leaned against the bar holding his lager, Rodney actually held up his wallet and Stefan stood frowning with his arms folded.

Candy collapsed back onto the seat. She peered behind her at the wall to see if George was talking to anyone else, then she pointed to herself with a question mark on her face. 'Me?'

George nodded. Then he coughed to clear his vocal chords; 'Do you mind if I sit down?' he asked.

Could he be the Chief of the Vampires? He didn't look like Robert Pattinson or Daniel Gillies- not that Robert Pattinson and Daniel Gillies were real vampires, of course! She shook her head. 'Wo,' she said, spraying George with little bits of chewed-up crisps.

'Let me get you another drink first,' George grimaced nobly, brushing himself down, 'Bitter is it?'

'Is it?' she replied. She didn't know one beer from another. She'd just pointed to the first pump in the row. 'Yes please. Oh, and another one of those steak pies please.

They're really nice. And a packet of crisps. I don't mind which flavour. Here, I'll pay.' She reached into her bag.

'No no, it's alright. My treat.' George's smile disappeared instantly when he turned his back on her and walked to the bar.

'A pint of bitter, Digby. And a double whisky for me. Neat. And a steak pie. Take it off my credit.'

'Don't feed her any more, George,' Stefan cautioned him, 'You're supposed to be helping her to lose weight, not fattening her up!'

'And don't you go getting drunk,' Rodney added, 'We want you in control.'

'I know, Stefan, but I've got to talk her into agreeing first. And I'm desperately in need of some Dutch courage, thank you very much, Rodney!'

'That's right George, you get in there, old chap. We're all rooting for you.'

'Cheers, Rodney,' George sighed as he carried the drinks and pie back to the table. He rummaged around frantically in his head and managed to find his smile muscles cowering in the corner of an unused brain cell as he sat down.

'Coo, thanks,' said Candy, picking up the beer with both hands and taking a huge gulp. She pulled a face. She really didn't like it. She was only drinking it to relieve her unhappiness. Then she put it down and attacked the meat pie as though she hadn't eaten anything all day.

'That's alright.' George wiped his sweaty palms on his trousers. He decided against shaking hands.

He watched her, fascinated as she attacked the pie. She actually made growling noises in between blowing the hot meat.

Forcing himself to continue, he said, 'By the way, my name's George. What's your name?'

'Candy,' she chewed.

'Candy? That's a pretty name. What's your surname?'

She swallowed and looked defensive. 'Fosse.'

The penny dropped and George fought hard not to laugh. 'Candy Fosse?'

The girl nodded unhappily. 'Well it's Candice really. Candice Fosse.' Candy said it with an exaggerated French accent. 'My mum thought it sounded French. And she had a craze on them when she was expecting me. Actually apparently she ate all kinds of candies. So she had me Christened as Candice French style and then she insisted on calling me Candy when I was born.'

'And what did your Dad say about it?'

'Nothing. He ran off with the midwife when I was two days old. They fell in love between my mum's legs as I was being born. Apparently he was always running off with other women and then coming back. But this time he didn't come back. I've never seen him. I don't even know where he lives. And I don't care. He's never cared about Mum and me.'

Candy sighed and took a huge sorry bite of the pie while George made genuine sympathetic tutting noises. A drop of gravy trickled down her chin but she didn't notice.

'I haven't seen you round here before. Where do you work, Candy? Is it near here? Can I call you Candy?' He'd winced when he realised that he'd said the word round.

She nodded, sighed and washed down her mouthful of pie with bitter then she pulled a face and wiped her mouth with the back of her hand. 'Call me what you like. Everyone else does. And I don't work there any more. Not after what happened this morning.'

George gently pressed her huge arm down as it lifted the pie towards her mouth. 'Oh dear, what happened this morning?'

She looked doubtful. 'Go on,' he urged, 'You can tell me. A problem shared is a problem halved, as they say.' He forced himself to smile encouragingly. This time he almost meant it.

She let go of the pie. 'I was working at the Prontopay Insurance Company. I've been there for a couple of years. I've always hated it. They've always taken the mickey out of me. Some of them think they're funny, but they're not. They're just cruel. But it was just one thing after another today. The back of my chair broke and I fell over backwards on the floor with my legs in the air and everyone laughed at my underwear. My leggings split as I fell and I didn't know.' She tugged her voluminous top down over her chubby knees. 'So I rushed to the toilets. And it wasn't my fault, it really wasn't! It's stupid the way they make the doors of ladies' loos open inwards. You have to practically stand astride the toilet before you can get out! And then the seat broke, and my foot went in the toilet. And 1 pulled myself free, then I - I got stuck! Oh god, it was awful!' She stared into George's eyes. 'I was jammed between the door, the wall and the toilet for three-quarters of an hour. Connie from Claims found me and told her manager and he called the fire-brigade. They had to take the door off. And when I came out-' She broke off and her eyes filled with tears, '-Everyone was outside in the corridor and they all laughed and cheered, and shouted things like, That must have been in-convenient! and What a loo-ny situation! and Hurry up Candy, or you'll be bog-ged down with work! and, This is definitely your Anus Horribilis! I think that was the worst.'

George put his hand up to his mouth and turned away to suppress his laughter. He shook his head and tut-tutted sympathetically.

Candy continued, 'To cap it all, Mr Warner, my boss was there, and he didn't laugh. He said, Really Candy, this is the limit! It's bad enough having to keep replacing your chair. I hope you're not going to cost us a fortune in toilet doors as well! Everyone roared with laughter and pointed at me and I dashed upstairs to the office and took all my things out of my desk, and my plant, and the ornaments off the top of my computer, and I stuck them in my bag and I rushed out and I'm never going back. Come to think of it, nobody missed me when I was stuck, and nobody tried to stop me leaving. Snobby lot! It was horrible! I've been walking about for hours, and I got lost. I'm not familiar with this area at all. I don't know what I'm going to do. My Mum'll go mad! She finds it hard to manage as it is!' She sniffed, took off her glasses and wiped her eyes with the back of her hand. Then she sniffed again.

George patted her arm, genuinely moved. He passed her a tissue out of his pocket. Candy thanked him and dabbed at her eyes. Then she blew into it loudly and wiped her reddening nose.

He suddenly made a decision, surprising himself. It wasn't often that George felt sympathy. 'Well Candy,' he said, 'I've got a bit of a problem too, and 1 think we may be able to help each other.'

'What's he saying?' whispered Edward, craning forward, as if a few more inches would make their conversation audible across the pub.

'I think they're swapping life stories,' said Rodney, 'Our George is moving in for the kill now. She's shaking her head. Ooh look, he's covered her hand firmly with his. Never fails, the old physical touch! There, she's giggling and nodding with determination. Signed, sealed and delivered. Quick, don't look, they're coming over.'

Everyone had been watching them, trying to eavesdrop while pretending not to. They all jerked their heads away, talking to each other as George and Candy stood up.

George took hold of Candy's hand and stood in the middle of thc room.

'Ladies and Gentlemen!' he called. Immediately he had everyone's attention. (Well, he'd had their attention all the time, which he'd been unaware of, but now it was in the open.) 'I'd like you to meet a young lady who, in twelve months' time will be very slim, very beautiful, and very rich. Miss Candy Fosse!' He said it with a French accent. Then he raised her huge arm in the air, she blushed and giggled, and noise erupted amongst cheers:

'Hooray!' 'Not a chance!' 'She's perfect!' 'She'll stay that way!' 'No she won't!' 'I bet she does!' 'Put your money where your mouth is!' 'I intend to!' 'Candy Fosse?!'

Booky Bill had popped into the Duck and Grouse for his lunch break. He stood up and held his hands out for silence. 'Right,' he said, 'I've been giving this a lot of thought. Here are the rules. You have to get Candy down to less than half her weight. And I'll give you twelve months from tomorrow to do it. She has to be weighed at - Stefan's gym?' He looked at Stefan for confirmation and Stefan nodded. '-in front of witnesses. And she has to wear a bathing-suit or a leotard, so we can see that you haven't cheated and padded her out, or added to her weight. Right?'

Candy placed a hand across her huge stomach, looking nervously around her and holding tightly onto George's hand. She was obviously unhappy about the thought of appearing undressed in public.

'Yeah!' 'Yes!' 'Right!' 'OK!' 'We'll be there!' called the customers.

'Okay, I'll see you all at Stefan's at ten o'clock sharp. And I'll be open for business after that, to take your bets.'

Loud conversations broke out as everyone started to state which way they were going to vote. They all had strong opinions about whether George would succeed or not.

Stefan fought his way to George's side. 'Come on, let's go back to your house and plan our strategy,' he shouted over the noise.

Candy grabbed her coat and the remains of the pie and stood lost and alone amongst all the chaos, undecided about what to do next.

George walked away and left her standing there on her own.

Stefan looked back at her. 'Come on, Candy,' he said kindly.

Obediently Candy trailed behind the four men. She didn't know where she was being taken to and the men completely ignored her.

'See you tomorrow, about 9.45, for the Grand Weigh-In!' Booky Bill called after them over the laughter and the shouting voices.

Luckily the rain had stopped as they left the pub.

***

'So you can pick her up every morning, George. She's free and you're free, so you can entertain her and watch her all the time, can't you?'

'Oh thanks a bundle, Stefan. What's all this You can? What happened to We can?'

'Of course we're supporting you and backing you all the way, old chap,' Edward soothed, 'We're really interested in it, and we're all going to have a bet. But you're the one who's got to work, aren't you? Your Dad said he didn't care what you did as long as you worked. And you can look on this as not just work, but as a challenge as well. That should really impress him.'

'Oh it's a challenge alright,' George muttered, glancing over at Candy.

'You can use my Sweat Shop for free as often as you like. And I'll make all my staff aware to give you all the help and advice you need at any time. They're all well trained in weight loss and other things like dietary needs. Of course, they have clients booked in, but there's usually someone available who you can talk to.'

'Yeah, thanks Stefan, but I'm missing something with all this; I still don't know what I'm supposed to live on - or her. She's not earning anything either.'

They all turned round and stared at Candy, who was spread nervously over two sections of the sofa, nibbling at her pie, then they all bunched together around the dining table again.

'I'll give you half my winnings of course, old chap. I can't win anything without you.'

'That's right, Rodders. And we don't mind paying for your drinks, George. That goes without saying.'

'Yeah, cheers, Edward. And I've got credit at Digby's at the moment with my winnings. But what am I - we - supposed to survive on for a year? It's not exactly a paid job, is it?'

George stood up and took a bottle of 15-year-old brandy and four glasses out of a cupboard. He poured out four generous tots and sat down again. They all sipped silently, thinking hard.

'Good brandy,' said Rodney after a while, examining his glass.

'Yes, excellent! I know, how about sponsors?' Edward suggested.

Stefan slapped him on the back, shooting him forwards. 'Of course! Get the Media interested! Slimming foods, clothes, health restaurants, the Press. They can keep an eye on her progress and get publicity out of it. I have loads of magazines and brochures at the Sweat Shop, and we get inundated with emails. If we go through them we can choose some Companies and businesses to write to. And I've got Reps calling in every day. I'll get a letter drafted and we can email it to everyone.'

'And brochures. Loads of them,' said Rodney.

'And brochures,' Stefan agreed. 'I use a very good printer, and his prices are reasonable too.'

'Will they really pay out, just like that?' George asked.

'Of course,' said Edward, 'If you give them the exclusive rights. Diet stories are always big news, if they're successful. The whole country's obsessed with them, aren't they? I have a good friend in the newspaper world. You've met Justin haven't you? I'll give him a call tomorrow and get some advice. I'm sure they'll pay a lot for a story like this.'

'Hey, how about an Agent?'

'Wow George, that's a BRILLIANT idea!' said Rodney, 'Then they can do a lot of the work for us!'

'I think we need to wait a bit though,' Stefan mused. 'We'll probably have to hang on until we can show some progress. We've got nothing to show them yet and they might lose interest.'

'I've got to go and catch my bus now. My Mum'll be worried.'

They all turned round and stared at Candy. They'd forgotten she was still there.

'Oh, right then,' Rodney said, 'You'll pick her up at a quarter past nine tomorrow morning at her house, won't you George?'

'Will I?' asked George.

'Of course you will, George. The least you can do is give her a lift. Then if anything Goes Wrong-' Rodney put a lot of emphasis into the last two words – 'If her alarm clock doesn't go off, or if she misses her bus, or changes her mind, or ANYTHING, you'll be there to collect her.'

'Oh yes. I suppose so,' George said doubtfully. He glanced at Candy and worried about the suspension in his car.

'Make sure you get her address before she goes. And tell her to be ready on time, with all her gear packed,' said Stefan.

'OK. There's a notebook and pen in the hall beside the front door. She can write it in there so I don't forget it.' George spoke about Candy in the 3rd person, not looking at her. He grabbed the brandy and topped up all the glasses. He was still completely indifferent about the whole idea.

They didn't look up as the front door closed. They were busy discussing sponsors.

TUESDAY 16th NOVEMBER

Reluctantly, George parked his car outside the address that Candy had written down for him. It was an old Council house with a large, untended front garden. He pushed open the broken wooden gate and walked up the weed-infested, cracked path to the front door. There was no visible door knocker or bell, and he raised his fist to thump on the door, but it was opened before he could knock. Candy stood there, wearing a smock top, a pair of very baggy black trousers, and a pair of shapeless black shoes. She held a large, worn handbag in one hand and was clutching a carrier-bag in the other.

'Morning George. Do you want to come in? Mum's gone to the shops.'

No he didn't. 'Morning, Candy. All set? We'd better go or we'll be late, and we'll be in big trouble!' George tried to sound jolly, but his voice tailed off as he suddenly felt guilty realising he'd said Big. He looked at Candy and then looked away quickly. Then he sniffed the air over Candy's shoulder. 'What's that smell?'

'OK, I'm all ready. What smell?'

'It smells like-' sniff sniff, '-Eggs and bacon.'

'Oh, THAT smell! Oh, it was my big celebratory farewell breakfast. Never again though. I'm really determined not to let you down. I'm going to lose weight so that you win your bet, and so that I can be a New Me. So I thought I'd have a final fry-up to celebrate.'

'You stupid-' Her bottom lip started to quiver and George lowered his voice. 'I mean, that was a stupid thing to do. Look, do you realise how many calories you've consumed this morning?'

Candy sadly shook her head. 'No.'

George thought for a moment. 'No, nor do I,' he admitted, 'I've never had to bother with them. We'll have to talk to

Stefan about diets. Come on. Have you got your outfit for the weigh-in?'

She held up her carrier-bag. 'Yes George, but I look terrible in it. I bought it in a sale ages ago for doing exercises in the house, and it was the only one they had in my size. But I've never worn it yet. I've always meant to, but I've never got round to it. And Mum didn't like me jumping around.'

You'd look terrible in anything, dear, he thought cruelly, and I bet the foundations didn't like her jumping around either. But he smiled encouragingly. 'Never mind, it'll give you something to look back on and laugh about when you're slim and lovely. Hurry up, they'll all be waiting for us.'

He walked ahead and opened his car door for her. He winced as the car's suspension protested at the extra weight, then he slammed it shut after checking that Candy was safely on the seat.

Stefan's Sweat Shop was packed with spectators. Word had spread rapidly about George's amazing challenge. A local TV film crew were setting up their equipment, trailing wires along the floor. There was even a small crowd outside in the car-park, watching it live on their phones. The TV Company had linked it all up to Social Media.

The men had come to bet and the women had come to gloat. Candy was a good morale booster for them as she looked far worse than most of them. And if she did start to lose weight, then if she could do it, they'd bet that they could do it too!

'She can get changed in there,' Stefan shouted to George over the din, pointing along the hallway to the ladies' changing-rooms. Candy obediently waddled away, pausing to look helplessly back at George. But he didn't notice as he was talking loudly with a group of Duck and Grouse regulars (including the man who I said was of no importance to this story, but I promise that he won't appear again, except in the background of crowd scenes,) so she carried on forcing her way through the grinning crowd, saying, 'Scuse me. Scuse me. Can I get past please?'

There was a small stage at the far end of the room where aerobics teachers jumped and danced about in front of their class, and where people gave talks on health and beauty. A set of digital scales stood there, waiting for Candy.

The TV crew pushed their way down the side of the crowd, swinging the camera around, filming everyone and holding a microphone under people's noses.

Some people noticed the camera and held their hand up to hide their faces, or to push the mike away. Then the cameraman went back to the front at the side and fixed the camera on a tripod.

Conversations died off and everyone applauded as Stefan walked onto the stage. There were a few whistles and shouts of Woo!

'Ladies and gentlemen,' he began, 'Thank you for coming to Stefan's Sweat Shop today. I've been trying to get some of you in here for years!'

This produced laughter and poking or pointing at each other's stomachs. Some of them breathed in deeply and patted themselves.

'Now we all know why we're here, so I'll just introduce everyone - not that they need introducing! First of all, here's the man who will look after our money and make sure of fair play - Booky Bill!' Applause as Bill stepped onto the stage, '-And you all know who will be helping and encouraging the young lady, and making some of us a lot richer – let's hear it for George Slater!'

Cheers and whistles for George, with shouts of, 'A lot poorer, you mean!' 'Get in there, George!' 'He couldn't get near it!' 'Good luck, George!' 'No chance, mate!' 'He'll use his charm!' 'Charm? He'll need to become a bloody hypnotist!'

George felt a bit like Jonah must have felt just before the whale's jaws clamped shut, imprisoning him inside. And here comes the whale now, he thought cruelly as Candy, her face red with embarrassment and exertion, made her way through the crowd and stepped onto the stage.

'And here's the plucky young lady herself - Ms Candy Fosse!' Stefan announced. The applause and shouts grew louder. Candy stood next to George, clutching a huge floaty, oriental-style dressing-gown tightly around her. She looked close to tears and kept blinking rapidly. She'd removed her glasses and left them in the changing room.

'Ask her to take it off,' Booky Bill told George. Candy inhaled deeply, removed the dressing-gown and handed it to George, who dropped it on the floor.

There was a long couple of seconds of complete silence. Then the room erupted with cheers, wolf-whistles and loud laughter. Mobile phones flashed and Candy tried to smile. George tried not to. She was wearing a black leotard with horizontal yellow stripes. She had black tights and a yellow head-band on. She looked like a giant swollen queen bee. A scattered few in the audience made buzzing noises, but they were quickly shushed as Booky Bill raised his hand.

'Right,' he said, 'Ask her to stand on the scales, will you please, George?'

Complete silence fell again, except for several whispered comments as Candy stepped on the weighing-machine. Stefan, George and Bill stared as the numbers spun around, wobbled, went backwards a bit and finally stopped.

'Let's have a look. It's 236lbs. That's 16 stone, 12lbs. And in metric, it's, um, 107kgs,' Stefan announced to the audience, who all nodded, cheered and clapped for no particular reason.

Most of them had heard the 16 stone, but ignored the metric weight. They were still old enough to think of everything in lbs and ounces.

'Check she's not padded, Bill!' someone called out as Candy stepped off the scales.

'She won't mind, will she?' Booky Bill asked George. Then he gently and carefully poked Candy with one finger in a few areas until he reached her bust. He stretched out a finger, then he changed his mind. Candy stood immobile with her eyes clamped shut and her head turned sideways. Her face had turned a delicate shade of pink.

'She's genuine. It all belongs to her, with no padding!' Booky Bill declared, and everyone predictably clapped and cheered again.

'Right, I'll be open for business in a few minutes to take your bets.' He looked at George, then Candy, tutted and shook his head doubtfully, and walked away briskly, checking his Rolex watch, followed by a group of arguing punters.

Candy picked up her dressing-.gown from the floor, hesitated as though awaiting some instructions, then she silently went to get changed.

George and Stefan stepped off the stage and walked over to where Rodney and Edward were waiting.

'Jolly good show!' Rodney enthused, 'You've really got them all interested! We should be raking in the profits!'

'Yes,' Edward agreed, 'And I loved the queen bee outfit.'

The TV cameraman came over to them, looking down at his camera, followed by his assistant, holding the mike. 'It's going viral,' he exclaimed enthusiastically, 'Look at these stats, and it's still climbing!' He went to pack his equipment away, winding up all the cables and carrying out the lights.

'Have you got a business card?' Rodney asked him, placing a hand on his shoulder to stop him rushing away.

The cameraman rummaged in his jacket pocket. 'Yeah, somewhere. Ah, there you go! Bit crumpled, but still legible.'

'Come on,' said Stefan, 'My staff can deal with this lot now and get rid of them all. They'll direct them to our café, hopefully. Let's go to my office. I've scribbled down some suggestions for sponsors and printed out some letters. I was at it till late last night. I suggest we go to George's to sort them out, some for posting and the rest as emails.' He looked in a plastic file on his neat desk. 'George, here's a booklet of foods and their calorie contents for you to give to Candy, plus some suggested menus, and another copy for you. And I have a chart of exercises that she can follow every day, plus a few online. With her size she can't do anything too strenuous to start with. It could be bad for her heart. But as she loses weight, we'll increase the pace gradually. And at her size she should start losing weight straight away.'

'Oh, that's really good news,' George muttered, 'And the sooner, the better.'

'Okay Stefan, let's get started.' Edward frowned. 'Bad luck with my newspaper pal Justin, I'm afraid. He tried asking his Editor for me, and he said that they're very interested and they'll keep taking photos and publishing snippets with updates if we like, but they won't pay any money until they've really seen some progress and they're sure that there's a story there. They reckon a lot of women start off losing weight, but their enthusiasm quickly disappears and they develop a craving for chocolate or something sweet. I said that George would be looking after her, but they weren't convinced.'

'Oh well, nice try, Edward,' George said, 'And it's something to look forward to. Hey, I wonder if I could get a bank loan on that if I need one?'

'I doubt it,' said Edward, shaking his head.

'Well I don't know do I because I've never needed one before!' George snorted, 'I suppose I can always take out a mortgage on my house if I'm desperate.'

'Just hang on before you do that. Wait and see what materialises,' Edward told him.

'Talking of what materialises, where is she, George?' Rodney asked suddenly, looking around, 'She's taking a long time to get changed.'

George shrugged. 'I don't know! Why does everyone keep asking ME about her?'

'Come on dear, just one more of you trying to touch your toes,' a voice drifted along the corridor, into the office.

'Who's that?' George asked.

'I bet it's that camera guy we saw earlier,' said Edward, 'I thought he was packing up. Come on. He's after a Freebie!'

'Now let's have you on that rowing-machine thing.'

'Oh no!' Stefan groaned, 'Not my new high-tech rowing-machine! That's for fit, sporty people. It's pretty lightweight. We've stuck it in the cloakroom waiting to go back to the supplier because it's faulty!'

He pushed past the others and ran towards Candy. He was too late. As she leaned backwards there was a loud sharp, ominous cracking noise, the back of the seat split and Candy fell over with her feet in the air. A camera flashed four times in quick succession and the TV cameraman bent over her, moving in to film her in close-up.

'What the hell are you doing, you silly great…' George paused as Rodney prodded him from behind. 'I thought you were getting changed,' he said more quietly.

'Sorry George.'

Candy endeavoured to stand up and finally rolled sideways and heaved herself onto her feet, puffing loudly. The men casually watched her while she struggled, but none of them held out a hand to help her up. The thought never entered their chauvinist brains. And Stefan was on his knees, busy examining his broken rowing machine. 'I'll never get a refund now,' he muttered to himself.

'This man asked if he could take a few pictures for the local paper,' Candy continued when she could breathe properly, 'He's writing about me as well. I thought you'd be pleased. And the other guys are filming me for the telly, they said.'

George turned to the reporter. 'And how much are you paying us?'

'Ten thousand pounds' worth of equipment ruined,' Stefan moaned, clutching the broken back of the seat to his chest.

'Badly made, wasn't it?' said Edward.

'Sorry Stefan. I'm always breaking things. I don't mean to. I'll pay you back somehow.' Candy sighed. 'I'll get changed and go home now.' She started walking out of the room.

'Paying you? You're joking mate! I work for the local rag, not one of the Nationals! They've got no spare money at all. I'm lucky I've still got a job. They're making everyone redundant. The machines are taking over! We even have to buy our own coffee! And the publicity will do you good.'

'Candy!' Rodney called, 'Stop her, George! She's upset. She'll go home and eat!'

'Why is it always me?' George complained.

'Oh well it's still under guarantee,' Stefan said, 'Hey, what do you mean, you're not paying us? And you never asked our permission to take any photos.'

'Well she agreed to pose for me. Um, I'd better be going. Get these shots downloaded. For tomorrow's edition. Um, see you. Bye.' He turned and hurried towards the door.

'I'll go and take his camera off him and delete the pictures.' Stefan started to follow the reporter. 'And where's that TV lot gone? I don't want them wandering around, disturbing my clients. We've got privacy rules.'

Edward called him back. 'No Stefan, wait! He's right actually, a bit of publicity at the beginning will probably do us good.'

'Ah, here's George with Candy. You stopped her going home then, George?'

'Yes Rodney. She's coming home with us – well, for a while anyway while we have our discussion and make some plans.'

Candy obediently trailed along behind them, fumbling in her handbag for her glasses, and clutching her carrier-bag to her chest. She looked really miserable. She let out a deep sigh, but nobody took any notice; in fact, nobody heard her.

***

'What you need, George, is someone to pay you regularly for the exclusive rights to Candy as she gets thinner. You need a regular income.'

'I'm well aware of that, Rodney. And I need it quick. How many letters have we got ready to post?'

'Twenty-six,' said Rodney, counting them.

Stefan opened his laptop on the table, switched it on and waited for it to warm up. 'And I've sent 500 or so emails so far. I sent a lot last night. There are thousands of businesses we can contact, just in this country. Imagine how many there are in the rest of the world! You'll be alright if just a couple of them come up with something - sports clothes, exercise equipment, slimming foods and drinks, vitamins. At least it will cut your expenses down. I get Freebies all the time.'

'Yeah, sure, I can live off vitamins and chips.'

'Well, just think how well-off you'll be in a year's time, old chap,' Rodney soothed, 'Loadsa lovely money. All thanks to a woman, your favourite subject, and without needing to be a pimp.'

George pulled a face. 'Pimp?'

Rodney brushed it aside. 'Oh, it was just one of Edward's ideas.'

George glared at Edward, who looked embarrassed and tried to think of a different subject.

'What's she doing now?' Edward asked, 'It's gone awfully quiet.'

'She's still here, isn't she?' queried Stefan.

They all looked round from the dining-area where they were sitting. Candy was on the floor beside the sofa, with her legs stretched out straight in front of her.

'She's not doing anything,' Rodney said, 'Make her do some exercises, George.'

'Sorry George. I'm tired. And I don't know what to do.' Candy sounded really fed up.

George flapped a hand at her. 'What do you mean, tired? You haven't done anything! Well lie down on your back and do something with your legs then.' He turned back to the others. 'Right, who's for a lager and lunch? It's been a mentally exhausting morning. I'm starving.'

'And I'm gasping,' said Rodney as they all stood up.

'But what about…?' Edward nodded towards Candy, who was lying flat on her back on the floor, watching them. She was trying to work out how she was going to get up.

'I don't know!' said George, then, in a louder voice, directed at Candy as though she was hard of hearing, 'We're just going down to the pub to get something to eat.'

Candy heaved herself up to a sitting position. Something about the expression in her eyes pricked his conscience. It reminded him of a badly treated, abandoned ugly stray dog.

'Er, would you like to come with us?' he blurted out, surprising himself, and surprising his friends even more.

Her face lit up and the other three faces fell. 'Not to eat, of course,' he added hastily, 'But you can have a drink. What can she have to drink, Stefan?'

'Slimline tonic, or mineral water.'

'Oh yes, thank you.' Candy struggled to her feet with great difficulty. She had to roll over onto her hands and knees and then haul herself upright, leaning on the sofa. Then she sat on the sofa and struggled to put her shoes on. The effort left her breathless as she grabbed her handbag and trotted after the men, who had already gone on ahead without waiting for her.

'Shut the door after you,' George called back over his shoulder.

***

'Well there's one good thing about old Digby, his food's absolutely marvellous!'

'It certainly is, Rodders. Top quality.' George patted his stomach. 'Cor, that wine went down a treat. Shall we have another bottle?'

Stefan shook his head. 'Count me out. I've got to go to the Sweat Shop later. I've got a couple of important clients to deal with.' And he gave a smile with a lot of meaning in it.

They all made suggestive noises as he pushed his chair back and stood up.

'They wouldn't be mature rich women by any chance, would they?' Rodney grinned. Stefan just grinned back without saying anything.

'Right then,' said Edward, 'Brandies at the bar?'

'Good idea,' Stefan agreed, 'I've got time for that.'

They all stood up and walked round to the other side of the pub.

'George!' Rodney clutched George's elbow and pointed.

George groaned, 'Oh no!'

Candy was clearing crumbs off her plate with a fork. She was hunched over the table, concentrating as she raised the fork to her mouth. She smiled guiltily when she saw them, with crumbs and a blob of cream smeared round her mouth. 'Hello,' she said, 'I've just had some GORGEOUS strawberry cheesecake. And some chips with one of those lovely pies. Aren't I naughty? Digby gave them to me on the house, for free. Wasn't that nice of him? And a couple of gins in my slimline tonic. He said I looked lonely sitting here on my own.' She giggled and raised a hand to her mouth. 'I won't eat anything for the rest of the day now!' She hiccuped and then burped loudly.

'The rest of the week, more like!' George shouted, 'You stupid great… Digby!'

'Sorry George,' Candy said quietly, her smile vanishing.

'You called me, sir?'

'Digby, what have you done?'

'I give in - what have I done?'

'Why did you give her all that food?'

'Well, the poor girl was all on her own, sitting there with her slimline tonic while you lot were scoffing away in there.'

'But all those calories!'

'I know, George, and yet you never put any weight on, do you?'

'Oh, you know what I mean, Digby! You're a cheat, that's what you are!'

'Yeah, we can all guess which way you're voting,' snarled Edward.

'Me?' Digby tried to look innocent. 'Oh, what a cruel thing to say! I'm just a kind, generous, welcoming landlord, that's what I am! I'm deeply hurt, guys, deeply hurt!' He walked to the other end of the bar, laughing.

***

They walked slowly back to George's house with Candy trailing miserably behind them. She kept hiccuping and she held up her hand to try and hide it. Once she let out a large burp and giggled nervously. 'Ooh, I'm not used to drinking,' she tittered.

'No, you're used to eating though, aren't you? We don't stand a chance,' George complained, looking over his shoulder and glaring at her, 'We may as well call the whole thing off right now. Every time we turn our back on her, she's shovelling food in her face! She'd already had a big fry-up this morning before I picked her up!'

'Sorry George,' said Candy, looking really unhappy, and dropping back even further. She slowed down and looked behind her, as though she was looking for a route to escape.

'We do stand a chance, as long as you DON'T turn your back on her again.'

George stared at Stefan in horror. 'What do you mean?' he asked. He knew what Stefan meant. He just hoped it wasn't what he knew it was. It was.

'She'll have to move in with you.'

'Oh no, no way! No no no, no way!' George jerked his head from side to side violently.

Rodney placed a hand on his shoulder. 'Come on, George. Think of the money. With your share of the bets, sponsors' payouts, publicity, etc. in a year's time you could make around a quarter of a million. I've been working it out. Then you can open your boutique. It's got to be worth it.'

'Has it?' replied George miserably, 'Are you sure about that?' He looked in the gutter. Sweeping it couldn't be that difficult, could it? It wasn't actually very mucky. He'd just need to push a broom along in a straight line. He couldn't ever remember pushing a broom along in a straight line or anywhere, but it should be easy to master.

Stefan placed a firm hand on his other shoulder, gently shaking him. 'Yes George, it has. We've already gone so far now that we can't back out without looking stupid. And you don't want to make us all look stupid, do you?'

'No,' Edward agreed, 'A lot of people are expecting us to fail, so we've got to succeed, haven't we, to prove them wrong and show them that we can do it.'

George looked at his friends and swallowed. 'She might not agree,' he said hopefully.

'Of course she will, George, if you ask her nicely. And you will ask her nicely, won't you? I'm sure you can manage to do that with your natural charming ways,' Stefan smiled, squeezing his shoulder. Not very gently. 'And by the way, George, how much have YOU bet on her?'

'Um, well, I haven't yet. I haven't got anything left to bet, have I?'

'Yes you have. What about that three hundred pounds we all gave you yesterday?' Edward demanded.

'That's got to last me a long time. I don't know when I'm going to get any more.' Thank goodness he'd left the money his family had given him at home in his other jacket!

'Perhaps you would be a lot keener to get some more if you had to,' Stefan said, 'If you let us down, Rodney and Edward will have lost a grand each, and I will have lost fifteen hundred - plus all the winnings, of course. At the moment, George, you're the only one who has nothing to lose on this. If it fails, you can always fall back on the washing-up job, can't you?'

'Er, well, I did intend to-'

'Splendid, George!' Edward declared, grasping hold of George from the back and pinning his arms to his sides from behind.

'Hey, what are you…?' gasped George as Stefan blocked his way and then reached inside his jacket and removed his wallet, 'I can't believe it! I'm being mugged by my own mates in broad daylight!'

'Oh come come now, George,' Rodney soothed, 'It's because we are your friends that we're doing this. We gave you the money in the first place and now we're going to invest it for you. Just two hundred pounds I think, Stefan. We'll leave him the rest for his basic day to day needs, shall we?'

'Yes, good idea, Rodney,' Stefan nodded, 'Do you agree, George? Silence? I'll take that as a yes then, shall I? Fine. I'll drop it into Booky Bill's for you as I go past. And I'll take her to the Sweat Shop with me.' He nodded at Candy. 'We've got a Dolores Dailey Dance Class this afternoon. It's quite slow because they're all large or old, and sometimes both. Then she can do some exercises at your place. And you can get her room ready, can't you?'

George looked behind him and walked beside Candy. 'You heard all that?'

'Yes George,' she whispered with her head down.

He tried to sound pleasant and persuasive. 'It's probably a good idea. Just for a while, until you get used to eating less. I'll be able to help you and keep an eye on your progress. And the guys are always popping in, so they'll be able to help us.'

She was doubtful. 'Well, I don't know. My Mum won't be very happy about it. She worries about me. I'm all she's got. I'd be alright wouldn't I? I mean, I'd be safe? There wouldn't be any - funny business would there?'

George stared at the sky. 'I can assure you, and your Mum, from the bottom of my heart, that you'll be perfectly safe. I'll keep all my lustful urges under control and direct them elsewhere.' He walked faster and caught the others up.

'Right that's settled then George,' Rodney smiled, 'You can pick her and her luggage up tomorrow morning, can't you? Wasn't too difficult, was it?'

WEDNESDAY 17th NOVEMBER

236lbs. 16st 12lbs. 107kgs

'So what are you going to feed her on, George?' Digby asked as he plonked down four lagers without spilling a drop.

George glared at him. 'Well it won't be pie and chips.'

'Where's your lady-friend, George?' Frank called out.

George scowled harder. 'Oh very funny Frank. She's at home, unpacking. And she's not my lady-friend, and never will be.'

'I bet she needed a juggernaut to move all her clothes, the size of them!'

'No, she borrows them from Rent-a-Tent!'

The man got an elbow in his ribs from his wife for this comment. 'Don't be so rude! You're no oil painting yourself, are you?'

'Nice to see our George settled down at last.'

The comments and the laughter went on.

'So what ARE you going to feed her on, George?'

He shrugged. 'I don't know, Rodders. I don't know anything about diets. None of my family have ever needed to diet. We're all naturally slim.'

'There's loads of so-called diets,' somebody said, 'And my wife's tried the lot. They're all rubbish. She's been on the Amazing Micro-diet, the herbal diet, the Beverley Hills diet, the high-fibre diet, the honey and vinegar diet, the banana diet, the boiled egg diet - loads of them. She never loses a thing!'

'I did the potato diet once,' yelled Frank's wife, 'And the pineapple diet. That was good. Too expensive though. And it got boring after a few days.'

'They all do,' another woman added, and a lot of people nodded, agreeing with her.

'I followed the milkshake diet,' another woman said, 'I had to replace my main meal with a packet of milkshake mix in a large glass of skimmed milk. Ooh, I did miss chewing though! I lost a load of weight ever so quick, but as soon as I stopped, I put it all back on again, quicker that I'd lost it! Ooh I was upset! What a waste of time!'

'I did the Atkins Diet,' a man called out, 'All that fuss about how marvellous it was, and I never lost a thing. Not a thing!'

'That's 'cos you washed it down with half a gallon of beer!' one of his friends shouted.

'Well I should still have lost weight with me not eating bread or potatoes, shouldn't I?'

'I went to a health farm for a week. My husband treated me to it for our silver wedding anniversary. It was absolutely super. I lost just under a stone in a week.'

'And she put it all back on again in a fortnight,' her husband cut in.

'It wasn't my fault,' his wife snapped, 'I was ever so careful, but it just went back on! And what were you up to while I was away, that's what I'd like to know!'

'Working overtime to pay for it, that's what I was doing!'

'So my neighbour told me. Is that why you took your secretary home with you?'

'Yes it was!' He appealed to the other customers. 'Over a grand wasted, and we haven't stopped rowing about it! We should have gone to Tenerife instead and saved all the bother.' They glared at each other.

The wife appealed to Stefan. 'I was ever so careful, I really was. I know that my calorie intake was low after I got home. I just don't understand it, Stefan.'

Stefan nodded. 'It's the same as when you are ill, with the flu for instance, and you lose a lot of weight rapidly. When you are up and about again, even though you think that you are using up more calories because you are moving around more, the weight almost always goes back on. Rapid weight-loss is wrong. The body fights against it. The best way to lose weight and keep it off is gradually, so that your body can adjust. All the fancy, trendy diets in the world won't work miracles. There is only one way to diet properly, and that is by counting your calories and eating a healthy diet. And it is very important to exercise as well, to keep your body in shape so that you tone up your muscles and you aren't left with a load of hanging flesh.'

George shuddered, picturing a slim Candy with her original fat frame hanging down around her, like a Sumo wrestler. 'So how do we count calories?' he asked, 'It's just a word to me. I mean, I had a look at that booklet you gave me, but how do we know how many calories she can have?'

'There are a lot of books in the shops. Buy a dictionary of calories. Or just look it up online. It will recommend the necessary daily intake of calories for her age, height, etc. It's mainly common sense. You'll get to know what's right and wrong very quickly. But there are some surprises. For instance, a glass of wine and just one ounce of crisps total around two hundred and seventy calories. She would have to exercise violently for over an hour to lose it again. My dietary team will advise her A nice plate of fresh, crunchy salad is very good for you and contains all the vitamins you need. She can eat practically as much as she likes, provided she doesn't add any salt or salad dressings. You'll have to educate Candy on how to eat properly, George, and make sure that she doesn't nibble between meals. And you'll have to educate yourself as well! You haven't left anything interesting in your fridge, have you?'

'You're joking, Stefan. I don't need to lose any weight. I can eat and drink what I like. My fridge is nearly always empty. And I told her not to touch anything of mine. She wouldn't go into somebody else's home and steal their food, would she?'

Stefan sucked in through his teeth. 'You don't know these compulsive eaters, George. They'd practically kill for a bacon sandwich.' He winked at Rodney and Edward, but George didn't notice. He was staring miserably into his lager, picturing a wild-eyed Candy, holding a bread-knife to his throat, and threatening, 'Your bacon sandwich or your life! Gimmee it, now!' He made a mental note not to eat in front of her. He'd have his meals when she wasn't around. Oh, what had he let himself in for? Or rather, what had he been pushed into? Sharing his house with a violent serial eater!

'D'you mean I've got to watch her like I'm a prison guard?' he asked.

Stefan nodded. 'At first, yes, until her stomach has adjusted to smaller meals and she begins to take a pride in her appearance. Then she won't feel so hungry and she won't want to go on eating binges. And if she did, it would probably make her feel sick and bad, like someone who has given up smoking and then fancies a quick puff.'

George drained his lager. 'I'd better go and see how my prisoner's getting on.' He sighed dramatically. 'But it's me who feels like the prisoner!'

'Make her do her exercises this afternoon, George.'

'Yes, Stefan. Thank you for reminding me. See you later, guys.'

'Poor old George, he's really taking this hard,' said Rodney as the door closed, 'We'll have to help him keep his morale up. Three more lagers please, Digby. For OUR morale.'

***

'Ha! Have you read this in the local paper today, Daph? About George and his bet with this fat girl of his?'

'No, not yet, Fred. But Grace told me all about it this morning when we had coffee. Rodney told her he's helping George to win his bet.'

'Bleeding stupid waste of time if you ask me,' Bert sniffed as he cleared away the tea things, 'Course, your George'll win. Always was a charmer with the females, he was.'

Fred put the paper down and Daph picked it up. 'Ooh,' she said, 'They're calling our George the local 'Enry 'Iggins with My Fat Lady. That's a bit rude, isn't it?'

'That's just it Bert,' Fred continued, 'That's exactly why he'll fail. He'll have to charm her into losing weight, flattering and encouraging her **all** the time, and watching her like a hawk. And supposing she fancies him, eh? - which, knowing our George she's bound to do - there's no way he's going to fancy her. What's she going to do when he's out with all his other girls? Wash his socks and clean the kitchen? No, the minute he goes out the door she'll have her poor jealous nose stuck firmly in the biscuit tin.'

Bert sniffed again. 'Well I've got five hundred at Booky Bill's that says he'll do it.'

'And I've got eight hundred,' said Daph, 'I'm sure our George'll win.'

'Daph!' gasped Fred, 'You've never spent anything like that without consulting me first!'

Daph drew herself up straight in her armchair and stuck her chin out defiantly. 'I can do it if I want to. It was my own money, left to me by my Dad.'

'That's not what I meant.' Fred was amazed. 'Course you can spend what you like, luv. But I've put two grand on him losing!'

'Fred!' Daph glared at him, 'Your own son! How could you do it?'

'Now don't get me wrong, Daph. I hope that George manages it, I really do. But I don't think he stands a chance, so I may as well cash in on it. And knowing George - and don't I know George! - he's bound to think of a way to cadge some of it for himself when he's flat broke and comes crawling to us for a loan, in a year's time, or probably before. But I hope I lose the bet. I really mean that. I'd like to see George succeed at something at last, and I'll give him credit, he's having a try and I hope I'm wrong. But I never am though, am I?' He smiled, crossed his long legs and picked up the Financial Times.

***

'Four lagers please, Digby. Oh, and a slimline tonic - without the gin this time.' George had forgotten that Candy was with them.

'There you go, George. Good write-up in the local paper. I loved the photo of the rowing-machine collapsing,' said Digby as he poured the drinks. Oh-oh, don't look now but your icy blonde nympho has just walked in!'

'Oh no!' George's head shot round, an expression of terror on his face.

'George! Why haven't you phoned me? I knew you wouldn't and you PROMISED you would!' She elbowed Rodney and Edward out of the way and grabbed at George. Her hands crept over the front of his sweater and he brushed them off, thinking desperately,

'Let's go back to your place George,' she whispered loudly, trying to stick her tongue in his ear, 'You know I'm crazy about you!'

'Have you seen today's local paper?' he asked, trying to push her away.

She pulled a face. 'No, I don't read that rubbish. I don't read very much.' She tried to attack him again, and he wriggled away.

'Oh good!' He saw Candy hovering behind them. He picked her tonic water off the bar, backed towards her and handed her her drink. He muttered out of the side of his mouth, 'Shut up and don't say a word. I need your help. I'm really desperate!' Then he said to the blonde, 'This is my fiancee. We've just got engaged, haven't we darling?' He tried to smile pleasantly at Candy. 'Let me introduce you girls. Candy, this is, um?' What WAS her name? He struggled to put his arm round Candy's waist. It didn't reach very far. Candy froze with her mouth hanging open and her tonic held carefully out in front of her. Her hand was shaking and she struggled to control it.

'Your fiancee?' squealed the blonde, 'You're joking! You are joking, aren't you? You're not, are you? You - you rat, you! You rat! You seduced me, you did!'

More like the other way round, dear, George thought.

'He seduced me behind your back!' she said, or rather screamed, to Candy, 'He was unfaithful to you. He spent the whole night with me, and he said he loved me! Men are always doing that to me.' She bared her teeth at George; 'And all the time you were engaged to that great big- You're a-a-'

'Rat?' suggested George helpfully.

'Yes, that's what you are, a rat! Oo!' She picked up George's lager before he could stop her, sloshed it in his face, slammed the empty glass down, screamed, 'You - you rat, you! You men are all the same!' Then she ran out, banging the door loudly behind her.

George heaved a sigh of relief and acceptance and moved away from Candy, who was still in her frozen position with her mouth hanging open and her tonic held out in front of her.

Digby handed him a towel. 'Another lager, George?'

'Yes please, Digby.'

'And another drink for your fiancee?'

'I'm never going to hear the last of that,' George groaned, wiping his face with the towel as everyone fell about laughing, 'But it worked. I don't think she'll be back again.'

'So how's it going, George?' one of the customers asked, nodding at Candy.

'Okay. She was at Stefan's this afternoon, exercising. And she's going back later this evening for a workout.' While I have a big, juicy bacon sarny, he thought.

'Any weight loss yet?'

'Not yet.' Not after what she ate yesterday, George thought to himself.

'Better hurry up, George. You've only got three hundred and sixty-four days left!' someone called out. Everyone laughed.

'Oh I've had enough. I'm going. And I need to change these wet things.' George finished his lager and headed for the door.

'Hang on, we'll come with you,' said Rodney.

'Yes, we can send some more emails.' Edward nodded towards Candy. 'Is she going to the gym with you, Stefan?'

'She may as well. I'll see you all later. Come on, Candy.'

'Okay, 'bye, Stefan,' called George with relief. 'Come on fellers, I've got a bottle of old Scotch malt whisky at home that I've been saving for a special occasion. I think this is a special occasion – or special enough. I need some Dutch courage. And there's no point in keeping it is there?' He sighed his martyr's sigh.

THURSDAY 18th NOVEMBER

234lbs / 16st 10lbs / 106.1kgs

How did she get on today, Stefan?'

'Fine, Rodney, fine. She worked hard this morning.'

'Would she like a drink, George? She's probably thirsty.'

'Yeah, why not, Stefan? Get her a mineral water. Is a slice of lemon fattening?'

'Four lagers and a mineral water, Digby.' Stefan threw down a 50-pound note. 'Here, take it out of that. I'm just going to the gents'.'

Digby filled the glasses. 'How's your fiancee, George?'

'Yeah, very funny, Digby. And very predictable. I don't know why I come here. Why do I pay you to get insulted?'

'You come here because of my excellent food and selection of drinks and our great social atmosphere, and because it's the only place where you can still afford to eat and drink! But what are you going to do when your credit runs out, eh?'

'I'll cross that bridge when I come to it.' But he was approaching the bridge fast.

'Hello George, how's she getting on? Any weight loss yet? I've put my money on you winning, you know, so don't let me down, will you?.'

'Cheers, Frank. Yes, a tiny bit. But it should be more noticeable starting from tomorrow, when she's weighed again. Stefan says it should come off regularly now, so I'll be able to collect all my winnings at the end of the year.'

'Oh, stop it! Stop it!'

Everyone turned and stared at Candy.

'What's up with her, George?' Rodney asked.

'I don't know. Why ask me? I don't own her, do I!'

'THAT'S what's up with me! Her! She!' screamed Candy, shaking her clenched fists in the air, 'I'm sick of it! I always was!' She turned and faced everyone in the room. 'Why doesn't anyone talk to ME? I'm just a figure of fun, aren't I? Fat Candy Fosse! I'm not deaf or stupid, in fact I'm pretty intelligent actually. I'm a human being! I may be fat and ugly, but I'm not a lump of meat! I don't fit the expected mould, I'm not a size 10 blonde, but I've still got feelings! I can hold an interesting, intelligent conversation, which is more than a lot of you can do! I'm a bloody woman, you know! Why doesn't anyone care?'

She turned and rushed across the room, wrenching the door open. A gust of rain blew in before Candy slammed it shut behind her.

There were a few seconds of stunned, embarrassed silence.

'Well!' gasped Digby, 'If George upsets many more women in here I'm not going to have any front door left!'

Stefan reappeared. 'What was up with her?' he asked, scooping his change off the bar, 'I could hear her shouting from in there.' He nodded towards the gents' loo.

George shrugged. 'Don't ask me. She just started yelling about nobody talking to her and then she ran out - well, sort of ran.'

'Shouldn't we go after her?' Edward suggested.

'Nah, let her sulk. She'll go straight home. It's a lousy night.' George drank his beer.

'Sure she will, via the nearest corner shop or takeaway!' Stefan made for the door. 'Come on. Any minute now she'll be sinking her teeth into a burger or a bar of whole-nut. That's the first thing women do when they get upset - eat!'

They tried to drain their glasses, then they gave up. Three unfinished halves of lager slammed on the bar and George, Rodney and Edward hurried after Stefan.

'Well,' gasped Digby, 'I've never seen that lot do that before – leaving unfinished drinks!'

There was no sign of Candy in the street.

'She couldn't have reached the end of the road that fast,' said Edward, looking up and down the street, 'Not at the speed that she walks.'

'She must have turned off! Quick,' George commanded as they hunched themselves against the rain, 'Rodney, down to the left, Stefan, down right, Edward, up left and I'll go up right.'

'Okay.' They all splashed away in different directions.

George ran up the road, round the corner and into Norman's Newsagent's. 'Hey!' he shouted as the startled customers stared at him, 'Have you seen a fat girl buying chocolate?' The woman behind the counter shook her head uneasily, automatically reaching one hand under the counter, feeling for the panic button. 'No?' said an old man with an expectant grin on his face, expecting the punchline of a joke.

'Right, cheers,' said George, dashing out again.

'Oy!' called the old man, 'Aren't you going to tell us what's happening?' But George had gone. 'Do you know what he was talking about?' the old man asked the woman behind the counter.

She shook her head. 'No idea. We get some right weirdos in here at night.'

George paddled along the road and into the station. He collided violently with a foreign woman who dropped her suitcase and bag. The bag toppled over and everything spilled out. 'Sorry, um, sorry, can't stop,' George apologised, looking round for Candy and rushing away. The woman and her similarly-dressed companions all waved their arms about and shrieked what was obviously abuse at George. George ran out of the station, expecting a policeman to appear, or some foreign men armed with daggers. He'd prefer the policeman, he decided.

There was a row of shops, restaurants and takeaways. It was a compulsive eater's paradise. George ran along peering in windows but there was no sign of Candy.

The corner shop near his house was open. It usually was. The Asian family who owned it stared at George with worried expressions as he burst in. 'Alright, George? asked the owner.

George ignored him and searched the aisles, shouting, 'Damn it, there's chocolate and cakes everywhere!' then ran out again. Behind him the man locked the door and turned the sign to 'closed' while his wife and daughters huddled together at the back.

They all arrived outside George's house at the same time, soaked and panting.

'It's hopeless,' moaned George, leaning against the wall and gulping in mouthfuls of air and rain, 'She's probably given up and caught the bus home.'

'I expect she's on her third bar of chocolate by now,' said Stefan miserably.

'-Or a giant fry-up. All that work, all that effort,' moaned Rodney. 'Why didn't you stop her, George?'

'Me? How could I have stopped her?' George asked, 'Anyway, she caught me by surprise.'

'You could have said something nice to her.'

'Oh yeah? What about the rest of you, Stefan? Rodney? Edward? When did you lot actually speak to her and say something nice?'

'It's not up to us. It's your project.'

'Yeah, thanks for reminding me, Rodders.'

'All that money we've lost,' added Edward, 'Get that door open, George. I need a drink.'

'Night watchman, that's what I'll do. I'm not emptying dustbins,' muttered George, rummaging in his pockets. 'Where's my bloody keys?'

The door opened. 'What happened to you lot? You're soaked!' gasped Candy.

Four faces lit up.

'Candy! You're here!' shouted George, almost happily.

She looked puzzled. 'Of course I'm here. It's not exactly the weather for a walk is it?'

'And have you eaten anything? Anything at all?' demanded Stefan.

'No, I've just been tidying up. Don't you ever put anything away, George? And I told you I wasn't going to eat a lot now.'

'Oh, good girl!' Edward said.

'Jolly good!' Rodney gushed, 'I say, would you like to clean my cottage, Candy? It's just a small one, in my parents' grounds. I'd pay you, of course.'

She thought for a moment. 'Okay,' she said, 'I need the money. And I've given up my other job. Nothing could be as bad as working there.'

'You haven't seen the state of his house,' Edward told her.

Rodney glared at him. 'It's not that bad. It's just lived in.'

'Well done, Candy!' George said.

'Yes, well done,' Edward agreed.

They all smiled at her and nodded enthusiastically.

She eyed them warily and edged her way to the Victorian fireplace. 'Here,' she said, 'You'd better dry out or you'll catch your deaths.' She switched on the gas fire and the four men huddled in front of the imitation logs, shivering and rubbing their hands together. 'Got any cocoa?'

'You what?' replied George.

Candy sighed. 'I said, have you got any cocoa or anything? I'll make you all a hot drink.'

'Oh yeah.' George nearly smiled. 'I think there's some hot chocolate in the cupboard somewhere. It's years old, so you'll probably have to hammer the lumps out.'

'Right then, I'll go and make it.' She turned and walked into the kitchen. They could hear the sounds of cupboard doors being opened and banged shut.

'Yuck, I'm soaked right through,' Edward complained.

'Me too,' Rodney agreed, standing with his back to the fire and waggling his backside from side to side, 'Even my underpants are stuck to me.'

'Got any brandy to put in the chocolate?' Stefan asked.

'Chocolate,' said George to no-one in particular.

'What?' replied no-one in particular.

George made eating gestures. 'Chocolate. In the kitchen. With lumps in! She's probably scoffed half the tin by now!'

As Candy poured hot milk into the mugs and stirred it, trying to squash the floating lumps, she felt an uneasy sensation of being watched. She turned her head and jumped as she spotted four pairs of eyes peering round the door at different levels, staring at her. Then four faces grinned.

Rodney gave her a little wave. 'Hello Candy, everything alright?'

'Fine?' She said it like a question.

'Oh, jolly good.' Edward strolled in, casually counted the mugs and looked in the tin, then he innocently put his hands behind his back and examined her face for tell-tale signs of chocolate round her mouth. 'Oh, that looks super! You found it alright,' he said, passing the mugs to the others.

'Lovely. Hot chocolate, and with no lumps,' George agreed, pouring a generous tot of brandy in the mugs, 'Well done, Candy!'

'Yes, well done, Candy. Mm, yummy.'

Candy stared up uneasily at the blonde giant smiling down at her. Was she in a Dangerous Situation? 'Er, I think I'll have an early night. Been a long day.' She edged her way out of the kitchen and, glancing nervously behind her, she rushed up the stairs, puffing with the effort, listening for the sounds of pursuing footsteps.

They heard the sound of her key turning in the lock.

'Well!' gasped Edward, 'What's up with her?'

George frowned. 'Really weird she is. I hope I'm going to be safe with her here.'

'I should lock your door if I were you,' Rodney advised him, 'Hell hath no fury like a woman's corned beef, or something like that.'

'Very funny, Rodney – or actually, not very funny at all.'

'Right, I'm off home to change before I catch pneumonia,' said Stefan, placing his empty mug on the table.

'Yes, I'm coming, Stefan. See you tomorrow, George.'

'Yeah, see you, Edward. See you guys. Think of me sleeping down here in an armchair, clutching an axe for protection, won't you?'

'Oh we will, George, we will,' Rodney promised.

FRIDAY 19th NOVEMBER

233lbs / 16st 9lbs / 105.7kgs

What was that strange thumping noise? George opened one eye and pulled the duvet up under his chin. He'd been dreaming about Candy breaking into his bedroom, bursting through the door and leaping on top of him. He could still picture her huge body flying through the air towards him like a life-sized balloon, her arms reaching out for him and her eyes gleaming madly. Then she'd turned into the Ugly Bird Bet with the big nose.

Yes, there it was again, a knocking sound! The door opened and Candy peeped in. 'Coo-ee, only me!' she trilled brightly, 'I've cooked your breakfast.' She placed the tray on his bed, 'It's egg and bacon and things, but I didn't fry it, I grilled it. I didn't have any, of course! And there's your coffee. I didn't know if you took sugar, so I poured some into a bowl. I didn't Hoover in case I woke you, so I'll do it later. I dusted though. Right, I'm off to the gym. See you later, 'bye!'

'Candy!' George croaked.

'Yes George?' Her head reappeared round the door.

'I like my bacon crispier, and my bread toasted.'

'Righty-ho!'

'And I take two sugars.'

'Okay, sorry George, I'll remember next time. 'Bye!'

George stirred sugar in his coffee and dipped a piece of his bread in the egg. Breakfast in bed, eh? Nice and civilised, and he wasn't expected to perform afterwards or say loving things to strangers whose names he couldn't remember!

He picked up the remote beside his bed and turned on the TV, biting on the bread.

THURSDAY 20th NOVEMBER

229lbs / 16st 5lbs / 103.9kgs

There was a tap at the door then it opened and Candy came in, walking backwards to push the door further open and carrying a tray. 'Coo-ee, only me!' she sang.

'Ugh,' grunted George, 'What time is it?'

'Eleven o'clock. Here's your breakfast. I'll put it on the side here.' She sat on the edge of his bed, which creaked and twanged in protest. George grunted again as he bounced up and down a couple of times, then slid downhill towards her. 'I've just got back from Stefan's,' she continued, 'I've done a workout and been weighed, and guess what? I've lost 4lbs, and I haven't been here a week yet! Ooh, I'm ever so pleased! So's Stefan.' She stood up, bouncing George in the air several times. 'Oh, there's some mail for you. And a parcel for me as well.'

'Is it a food parcel from the Salvation Army?' he muttered.

She giggled. 'Oh George, you're so funny! See you later. I'll run your bath and then I'll tidy up a bit. Then I've got to pop over to clean Rodney's cottage.' George grunted once more; with relief this time as his door closed, and he snuggled back under the duvet. 4lbs in a week, eh? At that rate he could be rid of her in four months. Great! He wondered if he was allowed to collect some of his winnings early.

He examined the tray. The bread was toasted and buttered and the bacon was nice and crispy.

Oh well, might as well make the best of a bad thing, he thought, forking the bacon into a slice of toast to make a sandwich, and dipping it in the egg. Then he took a sip of his coffee. Perfect. Two spoonfuls of sugar in it! And even better, she'd gone out so he could take his time getting up. And she said she'd run his bath for him!

A year of this might not be so bad, he thought, tucking in to his breakfast.

Now what should he wear today?

***

'Ah, here's George. Oh, and Candy. Another half of lager over here please, Digby. And a slimline tonic for the young lady.'

'Cheers, Rodders.' George handed Candy her glass and picked up his lager.

'Well,' beamed Edward, 'Hasn't she - haven't you done well? Half a stone in a week, eh?'

Candy nodded and smiled happily.

'Hello George, how's she getting on. then?' Frank asked, then he stared blankly as they all made frantic signs and waggled their heads in Candy's direction.

'Why don't you ask her yourself?' Stefan told him emphatically.

'Yes, I speeka da Eenglish,' said Candy.

Realisation dawned as Frank remembered Candy's outburst. 'Hello Candy,' he said loudly, 'How are you getting on?'

'Very well, thank you,' she shouted back, 'I've lost about half a stone.'

'Very good. I've voted for you, you know,' Frank yelled and walked away.

Candy tapped George on the shoulder. 'George?'

'Yeah?'

She pointed to Frank. 'Is he deaf?'

'No, not that I'm aware of.'

'Then why was he shouting at me?'

George shrugged. 'No idea. Perhaps he thinks you're deaf.'

'-Or stupid,' Candy snapped.

'Had any replies to any of our letters yet?'

'Ah yes, this morning, Edward. One from Harold's Store. They said that every time Candy dropped a dress size, they'd replace her clothes free of charge and photograph her for their in-store magazine. They want a couple of photos now.'

'Ok, not an earner, but a nice one!' Rodney said.

'And Activity, the sports shop.'

'Any good?'

George shook his head. 'Not for me. They've offered Candy a free outfit and trainers on condition that the local paper's there when they give it to her.'

'Not bad,' said Rodney, 'It's a quality shop. But tell them that you'd like a free outfit as well, for when you go jogging with Candy.'

'Me? You must be joking! I'm not going jogging!' George was horrified.

Rodney sighed patiently. 'I know that, but they don't do they? And their stuff costs a lot.'

'No, I s'pose not.' George paused. 'Stefan, what do you know about Sylphie Green?'

Stefan thought for a moment. Then he remembered. 'Sylphie Green? Not much. She's American. Makes slimming foods. Why?'

'We got a letter and a DVD and a load of bumph from her Company this morning.'

'What's it about?'

George shrugged. 'No idea. I haven't watched it, and I probably won't bother.'

'We can all watch it later,' Edward suggested.

'I can't remember hearing the name before,' said George, 'Were they on our list? Did we email them or write to her?'

They all looked at each other, mentally ticking off the letters that they'd sent then they all shook their heads. The name didn't ring a bell.

'Strange,' said George.

'Not really,' Rodney told him, 'We're bound to get loads of junk mail sent to us as word spreads about Candy.'

Stefan racked his brains. 'Oh I remember now. I read an article about her once. Her real name's Sylvia Green and she used to weigh about twenty-five stone. She slimmed down to seven stone and formed her own company, selling slimming foods. She's a multimillionaire now. Then her husband left her for her best friend, who was plump and plain.'

George snorted in disbelief. 'Whatever for? Why would he do that? I don't know how anyone could prefer a woman who was fa...' He glanced at Candy and stopped himself saying it. Candy sipped her tonic and stared around her. She ignored what he'd started to say, even though she'd heard him.

'They often do though,' said Stefan. 'A lot of husbands get jealous or insecure when their fat, placid wives suddenly turn into dynamic beauties and other men start to notice them. Instead of cooking him huge delicious meals, she's often too busy looking in the mirror, or spending their money on clothes instead of food. Then she starts on his appearance and she feeds him salads and fruit instead of potatoes and puddings. So he leaves her for another 'safe' woman who belongs entirely to him, who cooks him the meals that he loves and doesn't criticise his appearance. It happens all the time.'

Rodney shook his head. 'Strange. Oh well, shall we go and watch this mystery DVD?'

***

'Hi! I'm Sylphie Green!'

George, Rodney and Edward whistled and grunted as the woman on the video undulated along the corridor towards the camera. She was pure Hollywood. She was beautiful, her shoulder-length hair and make-up were immaculate and her low-cut, tight, silky dress showed every curve of her perfect body. She paused, placed her hands on her hips and twirled round. 'Not bad for an old lady of forty-nine, uh?' she gushed, then she held a long-nailed polished finger up. 'Ah, but I didn't always look like this.' She paused beside a door with Sylphie Green written on it. The door mysteriously opened on its own and she jerked her head towards the inside. 'C'mon in. Follow me,' she instructed her unknown audience.

At the back of the huge room was a cardboard cut-out of a fat woman with short, dark, greasy hair, wearing a black bathing-suit and eating an enormous ice-cream. Sylphie paused and posed beside it. 'Know who this TERRIBLE woman is?' She stood in front of it. 'It's ME! Hard to believe, isn't it?'

'It certainly is. She's two inches shorter now,' muttered George, sipping his brandy.

'So's her nose,' said Stefan.

'But her lips are twice the size,' Edward added.

'Yes, this is a photo of me when I weighed TWENTY-FIVE STONE!'

'Coo, I'd never let myself get into that state!' gasped Candy. They all stared at her, thinking that she shouldn't have got into the state that she was in.

'-And now I weigh SEVEN STONE - a weight loss of EIGHTEEN STONE! Impossible? Can't be done? It sure can, if you Slim With Sylphie! C'mon with me and hear some of the Sylphie Success Stories.'

The scene changed to a long sandy beach. A man came running out of the sea. He wore skimpy leopard-skin patterned trunks and his body was tanned and muscular. With his shoulder-length blonde hair and gleaming white teeth he could have entered a Tarzan competition.

'Hi! I'm Al.' He rippled his muscles and grinned, displaying all his perfect teeth for a few seconds. 'And this was me two years ago.'

The camera shifted, a bit wobbly, to the right where a huge poster balanced on the sand. It displayed a life-sized photo of a fat man dressed in a pair of Bermuda shorts. His stomach was grotesque.

'I was only twenty then and I weighed twenty stone - a stone for each year of my life.'

'Oh, he can count too!' Edward sneered, 'But he obviously thinks that we can't.'

'All the guys called me Al E Phant. I didn't have any friends. Then one day at the local disco I plucked up my courage and I asked a girl to dance. And do you know what she said to me?'

'Beat it, fatso,' muttered George.

'She said, Beat it fatso. I was so unhappy that I went home and I cried and cried. And I even thought of-' He paused for effect –'ENDING it all! And then it happened. An ad in the paper caught ma eye. It said, Slim With Sylphie. I cut it out, filled it in, mailed it off, and it was the beginning of a new life for me. I made lotsa friends and lotsa money, just by telling everyone about Sylphie.'

The camera shifted to show a palatial house along the beach. Al nodded towards it. 'Yup, that's my home right there. Thanks to Sylphie! And this is my new figure.' He stood with his hands on his hips, flexing his muscles and grinning at the camera. '-Oh, and can you guess what happened to that girl who said, Beat it, fatso, and made me cry?'

'Yeah, you married her,' said George.

'I married her!'

He held out an arm and a petite blonde in a bikini appeared at his side, gazing up adoringly at him. With their arms wrapped around each other and staring into each other's eyes, they strolled up the beach away from the camera and into the sunset which had suddenly appeared, while romantic music played.

The scene changed to a large landscaped garden with a swimming-pool. A couple were standing around a brick barbecue. They were dressed in matching brightly-patterned Bermuda shorts. She wore a white bikini top and he wore a white t-shirt.

'Hi! I'm Wayne.'

'And I'm Mary-Jo. Be right with you! I'm just barbecuing our Sylphie Super Soyaburgers. Have you got that salad ready, Wayne, honey?'

'Sure have, Mary-Jo! And I've tossed it with Sylphie Salad Mix.'

'Oh, COOL!' Mary-Jo squealed. Then she turned on a serious face. 'This was me, three years ago.' She held up a photo of a fat woman with lanky shoulder-length hair.

'-And this was me.' Wayne held up a photo next to it of a fat bald man. 'Pretty awful sight, huh? Huh huh huh,' he chortled.

'So's his syrup,' said Rodney, pointing to Wayne's blonde toupee, which was slightly lop-sided.

'We never got invited anywhere,' whined Mary-Jo.

'No, they probably scoffed all the food,' muttered George.

'We just sat at home and ate.'

'We ordered takeaways every day,' said Wayne proudly, 'Sometimes even twice a day.'

'Until one of our neighbours told us the WONDERFUL news about Sylphie.'

'And we've never looked back. And we've never looked round neither, huh huh huh!'

The scene changed to an enormous building that was like a Western film set.

'Within a year we had won our Double Distributors' Diamond Pin and a week at Sylphie's Reconditioning Ranch. It was real great, wasn't it, Wayne, honey?'

'Sure was, Mary-Jo. Oh look, there's us on our morning jog with all our new friends!' A slightly wobbly video showed them wearing matching tracksuits, jogging along with a group of overweight people, all grinning and waving wildly at the camera.

'-And there we are at the evening get-together. That band sure was great, wasn't it, Wayne, honey?'

'Sure was, Mary-Jo. And there's Sylphie asking me to dance, huh huh huh! I couldn't have managed that a few months ago. I'd have been puffed out!'

Sylphie was holding out her hand to Wayne, who grasped it while he heaved himself out of his chair, and he guided Sylphie onto the dance floor, while Mary-Jo grinned happily, showing all her teeth, and clapping as though her life depended on it.

The camera then showed a close-up of Wayne's hand gripping Sylphie's buttock with her pulling it higher, and went back onto Mary-Jo, whose smile had vanished. She had a face like thunder as she glared up and down Sylphie's back.

'Burgers are ready, Wayne, honey!'

'Be right with you, Mary-Jo! Mm! They sure smell good!'

They both grinned at the camera, their arms wrapped around each other.

Mary-Jo stepped forward, out of his grasp. 'Yeah, Slimming With Sylphie has given us a whole new quality of life, hasn't it, Wayne, honey?'

'Sure has, Mary-Jo.' He stepped forward next to his wife and spoke to the camera, putting on a serious face. 'Why don't you guys come along and join us? It'll change your life! Look forward to meeting you at a Sylphie Star Slimmers' Social!'

'Bye now!' they squawked in unison, waving as the camera backed away.

Another magnificent garden appeared on the screen, this time a front open-plan garden.

A man in his mid-fifties pretended to trim the perfect hedge while his wife pretended to weed the immaculate flower-bed, stopping to examine her perfect nails every few seconds. The man paused and stared over his shoulder at the camera. 'Hi! I'm Bobby!'

'And I'm Betty-Lou!'

They walked towards each other and, hand in hand, they strolled around the garden, pointing at things, while Betty-Lou's voice spoke off-camera.

'We sure look like a perfect couple, don't we? But only eighteen months ago things couldn't have been more different. Bobby came home from work and told me he was leaving me for his secretary. 'I still love you, Betty-Lou,' he said, 'But not physically no more. You sure have let yourself go.' And he was right. I sure had!'

A photo of an untidy overweight woman in a fairground, seated side-saddle on a carousel horse, wearing a denim mini-skirt that displayed huge pink, spotty thighs, and eating a hot-dog, filled the screen. 'Well, I sure wasn't gonna let ma man go, just like that, without a fight! Bobby, sugar-pie, ah said, Stay with me for the sake of our two little ones, and ah swear I'll change, so help me God, as from right now!'

The two of them stopped their inspection of the garden and turned and grinned at the camera.

'So ah said, 'Okay honey, I'll stay for the sake of my two baby darlin's. But things sure had better change around here, and ah really mean it!' said Bobby, pulling a serious face and grinning at the same time, if you know what ah mean.

'And things did change,' smiled Betty-Lou, flashing her teeth, 'Cos we discovered-'

'Sylphie!' they chorused.

At the side of the screen, the camera caught a boy standing frozen, as though he was waiting for a starter's pistol, while a little girl who was a carbon copy of her mother held onto his t-shirt. At the shout of, 'Sylphie!'she let him go and they both ran towards their parents, squawking, 'Hiii Maw! Hiii Paw!' 'We're huuungry!'

Betty-Lou held her hands up and stretched her eyes open in amazement and disbelief, as though her children had just stepped out of an alien space-craft after having been missing for ten years.

'Oh my little Dustin and Madonna!' she gurgled at the camera, 'They sure do have healthy appetites!' She spoke to her little Dustin and Madonna. 'Okay guys, you-all can help yourselves to a-' Face to the camera again. '-Sylphie Super Sesame Snack!'

'Oh WOW!' screamed Dustin and Madonna, as though they'd caught Father Christmas in person filling their stockings. 'What flavour are YOU gonna have, Dustin?'

'Well, I guess I'll have the Sylphie Strawberry Substitute. How about YOU, Madonna?'

'I'm gonna have the Mock Maraschino.'

They both ran to the house, and Bobby and Betty-Lou shook their heads in wonder again. So did George, Rodney, Edward and Stefan.

'Yup, we sure do have a good time,' smirked Bobby suggestively.

'And we've made a load of good friends,' added Betty-Lou quickly, '-Thanks to Sylphie! Oh, look! Here come two of them now!' she squealed.

'Why, it's Dickie and Daisy-May! Hi there!' called Bobby, 'Come on in!'

'Well hi there y'all!' boomed Dickie, waving frantically like a ship-wrecked survivor on a life-raft who's spotted a plane.

'Hi there!' squawked Daisy-May through her nose, not waving because she was carrying something, but she half-curtsied a few times instead.

'Well hi there, Daisy-May!' gushed Betty-Lou, air-kissing her friend on, or rather, beside both cheeks, and making mer mer noises, 'What have you got there, honey?'

'Hi there, Betty-Lou! It's a little bitty gift that I made 'specially for you!'

Betty-Lou gazed at the camera as though she'd just won a fortune, with the palm of her hand on her chest, carefully displaying her long nails. 'A present? For me? Oh WOOOOW, Daisy-May! What is it? I'm just DYING to know!'

'Why, it's one of my home-made Marshmallow Pecan Peanut Pies!'

Betty-Lou turned to the camera again, with both palms on the side of her face and a look of horror, then one hand dropped to her stomach. 'A home-made Marshmallow Pecan Peanut Pie? Heavens, Daisy-May, what about my fig-gure?'

'Huh huh huh,' chuckled Dickie, 'You don't wanna worry none 'bout your fig-gure, Betty-Lou! Daisy-May made your pie with Sylphie Super Pecan-Peanut Filling.'

'And I baked it in one of Sylphie's Super Wonder-Weightless Pie Crusts,' whined Daisy-May happily. Betty-Lou's hand travelled from her stomach up to her chest, with an expression of relief on her face as though she'd just been rescued from a rabid grizzly-bear. 'Oh WOW Daisy-May, you sure had me going then! Now you-all come into the house and I'll fix us some Sylphie Super Waffle-Whizz Mix with Sylphie Super Substitute Syrup. And we'll open a bottle of Sylphie Special White Wine Taste-Alike.'

'Shucks, we sure would love to, Betty-Lou,' boomed Dickie, 'But we're on our way to the chapel to praise the Lord for giving us this wonderful new way of life.'

Bobby held his hand up like a policeman on traffic duty. 'Now you hold it right there for just a minute, Dickie and Daisy-May! Betty-Lou and I would be honoured to join you, with our little Dustin and Madonna.'

'We sure would!' squawked Betty-Lou, 'We sure do have a lot to be grateful for in this wonderful world of ours!'

'Yup, aymen to that!' Bobby added, 'I've seen the error of my ways. I'm a New Man. Thanks to Sylphie. And of course, my wonderful New Wife!'

'Oh WOW!' whined Daisy-May happily.

The camera closed in on Bobby and Betty-Lou, who held hands and gazed at each other with concentrated adoration.

'Yeah, our new life is jest wonderful!' gushed Betty-Lou.

'It sure is - in many different ways!' Bobby winked at the camera as though he'd just shared a dirty joke with the cameraman, 'And it could be wonderful for YOU TOO!' He pointed emphatically at his unseen audience with his arm held out straight, 'If you Slim With Sylphie!'

The scene returned to Sylphie's Reconditioning Ranch. A large group of slim people was assembled on the perfect lawn. All the families who had appeared in the film were there. Everyone wore t-shirts with slogans like, 'Don't just sit there - lose something!' 'Lose weight - gain confidence!' 'I'm a winner - I'm losing with Sylphie!' 'I feel great - I'm losing weight!' 'Chew away a few a day!' and 'Losing weight makes cents!'

'Hiii!' they all trilled in unison, waving and flashing their teeth, 'Come on! What are you waiting for?'

A band marched onto the lawn behind them and everyone started to sing, while marching emphatically on the spot and air-drumming;

Slim with Sylphie! She's The One.
You'll make friends and you'll have fun.
You'll grow rich and you'll grow lean
When you slim with Sylphie Green!

Back to Sylphie's office. She perched elegantly on the side of a desk, displaying a lot of thigh.

'Well, that was just a few of our thousands of success stories. Just ordinary, every-day people like you and me.' A flash of eyes and teeth that said clearly, don't you dare call ME ordinary! 'And while you use the Sylphie products and lose weight, you can make a HEAP of money too, just by telling your friends about Sylphie! And your prospects will tell their prospects. And when their prospects buy our Sylphie products from THEIR prospects, do you know what that means?' George, Rodney, Edward and Stefan shook their heads. 'It means BIG PROFITS for you!'

She pointed a lethal-looking red fingernail at the camera. 'But don't just sit there, taking my word for it - give it a try!'

Her eyes, teeth and thigh flashed and she leaned forward, carefully displaying a large expanse of too-perfect cleavage.

'Oh, we must wind that bit back again,' said Edward.

Then the camera focused on the cutout figure of the original Sylphie once more, before switching back to the Reconditioning Ranch. The band had now been joined by a load of marching majorettes, throwing their poles up in the air and shaking their pompoms.

On cue, everyone cheered, waved and jumped about like demented Muppets on Speed, while the band played Slim With Sylphie. The words Slim With Sylphie appeared on the screen, then it went blank and silent.

They all sighed with relief. George grabbed his remote and turned the TV off, then he took a large swig of his brandy.

'Waal,' drawled Rodney in a mock American accent, 'Wasn't that jest AMAZING, you guys?'

Edward held two fingers in his mouth, clutched his stomach and pretended to be sick on the carpet.

'Huh,' George said, 'That was the biggest load of cra-ooh!'

Stefan had elbowed him in the ribs. He nodded towards Candy. She was sitting upright, gazing spellbound at the screen. They all stared at her and she seemed to awaken from a dream.

'If they can do it, I can do it too,' she whispered, 'That's what they said.'

'Oh no,' groaned George, 'It's a catch, Candy, a scam, a great big con-trick!'

She glared at him, 'How do you know?' she snapped, 'You'd never heard of it before today.'

George glared back at her. 'Yeah, exactly and nor had you!'

'She's right, George.'

George transferred his glare to Edward, 'Whose side are you on?'

'We're all on the same side, you know that. But it's worth looking into, isn't it? Did they send any more details?'

'Yeah, I think so, in the parcel there. Various leaflets and things.'

'Let's see then.' Edward read through them. 'Blah blah blah blah blah blah blah. Ah, here we are - Send £50 for your Super Sylphie Starter Parcel.'

'Oh surprise surprise!' laughed Rodney.

George was horrified. 'Fifty quid? They have got to be joking!'

'Well it's worth it if it works,' Candy retorted.

George snorted. 'And what do you reckon you'd get for your £50, eh? Probably a Slim With Sylphie t-shirt and a couple of packets of cardboard-tasting ready-mix! It's a con I tell you!'

'And I say it's worth a try. I'll lose weight AND we'll make lots of money.'

'Believe that, you'll believe anything. You'll lose money, not weight.'

'Well they did, didn't they?' Candy jabbed a finger towards the television.

'They're different.'

'Why?'

'They're American.'

It was Candy's turn to snort. 'What's that got to do with it?'

George thought. 'Well, they're more optimistic; they'll try anything won't they? We British are more cynical. We analyse and criticise everything. Nobody will believe it'll work, even if it does, and you won't get them to part with their money.'

'Well you're not earning anything, are you? And not likely to from what I can see!'

What had got into her? 'I beg your pardon-' began George.

'Now now children, just leave it for a few days and think about it,' Rodney soothed, 'And meanwhile, we all have more important things to think about - our severe dehydration for instance, so I suggest we all make our way to the Duck and Grouse for some liquid relief.'

TUESDAY 7th DECEMBER

217lbs / 15st 7lbs 98.4kgs

'Coo-ee, only me!'

'Ugh, what time is it?'

'Nearly eleven. Here's your breakfast with crispy bacon and toast as you like it. And your bath's ready, and I've ironed your shirts. And guess what?'

'Ugh?' George wasn't at his best in the morning.

'I weigh fifteen stone seven now!'

George said a happy, 'Ooh, ugh!'

'And I've had another letter from Sylphie.'

'Ugh,' said George, not happily.

'Shall I read it to you?'

'Ugh.' That could mean yes or no. Then he repeated, 'Ugh,' as she sat on the edge of his bed. He bounced up and then slid towards her.

'It arrived in a really important envelope that said, Warning! This envelope has been safety-sealed. Not to be tampered with. Only to be opened by Addressee. Possible penalty of Large Fine, or even Imprisonment!' She unfolded the letter. 'Dear Ms Fosse. Hi there!'

'Ugh.'

'We hope you received your Super Sylphie Introductory DVD, which is yours to keep ABSOLUTELY FREE! If you have watched it, as I'm sure you have, you were no doubt AMAZED at the successful people that it showed, and you must be DYING to be one of them! As you are VERY SPECIAL to us, Ms Fosse, we would like to make you this AMAZING OFFER! We would like to offer you, FREE OF CHARGE, a Super Sylphie Starter Parcel! When you start telling all your family and friends about Sylphie you will see how quickly your Super Sylphie Starter Parcel will pay for itself! And as you Slim With Sylphie there will be BIG

PROFITS for YOU! Hurry! Post your reply in the pre-paid envelope today! And DON'T SEND ANY MONEY YET! Just think, What Have You got to Lose?

'Oh, isn't that marvellous, George? A free Super Sylphie Starter Parcel!'

'Ugh!'

'I knew you'd be pleased. Oh, that's the doorbell!'

'Ugh,' muttered George, feeling motion-sick as Candy stood up and he bounced up and down several times, Who'd be so rude as to call at this unearthly time of the morning? he wondered as she thumped down the stairs. Probably the postman with some more parcels.

Oh dear, not a Sylphie parcel! he suddenly thought.

Oh well, he'd worry about it later.

He hauled himself upright, puffed up his pillows, turned on the TV and lifted the breakfast tray onto his knees.

Perfect. Just as he liked his breakfasts. One thing about having Candy staying here, she was a very good cook!

'Oh!' Gasped Candy with dismay as she opened the front door.

The woman who filled the doorway made Candy look short and slim. The family likeness was obvious, but, where Candy was overweight, her mum was, well, without going into too much detail in case you're eating, wobbly and flabby, and sort of hangy. Not a pretty sight. She was wearing an old double-breasted black and white check coat with part of its hem undone, a permanent scowl, and she grasped a huge battered black handbag as though she was working for Securicor. Her hair was tightly permed in corkscrew curls with a severe side parting and a hairslide, and her fat ankles leaned sideways over her black, sensible-heeled shoes. A thin line of red lipstick covered her mouth as though she'd just eaten someone and her breath emerged loudly and deeply like a marathon runner who's just broken a record.

'Hello Mum, what are you doing here?' asked Candy nervously.

'Well,' snapped Candy's mum, elbowing her daughter aside, 'So this is your little love-nest, is it? Well thanks for not inviting me. I've had to invite myself. I never thought I'd see the day when a daughter of mine would-' She left the unspeakable words unspoken, slightly shaking her head.

'No Mum, I-'

Mrs Fosse collapsed onto George's sofa which complained loudly. It almost sounded like 'Oy!' She sniffed her disapproval of nothing in particular and stared round George's expensively-decorated sitting-room, searching for traces of things that would upset her, like nude paintings, phallic sculptures, bondage objects, girlie magazines. (Luckily, she didn't look under the cushions she was sitting on!) She sniffed again and, running a finger over the small table beside her, she examined it for dust, drugs, etc.

There were sounds from above of bathwater running down the plughole. With a look of panic on her face, Candy glanced up the stairs, wondering how she could get rid of her domineering mother before George appeared.

'Would you like a coffee, Mum?' she asked.

'I don't drink coffee and I never have!' declared Mrs Fosse, 'It's bad for my waterworks.' She silently mouthed the words Waterworks. 'You'd know that if you took any interest in me. It's very bad for your health. I like to look after my health.'

She followed Candy into the kitchen and nosed around, opening and shutting cupboard doors and tutting about nothing in particular; it was just a noise that she often made.

'Well a cup of tea then.' Candy switched the kettle on.

'So where is He? Lover Boy?' Mrs Fosse made He sound like a nasty rash.

'George? Upstairs. He'll be down in a minute. And he's not my Lover Boy.' Candy nervously bit her lip. She was expecting trouble, from both of them.

'Upstairs? At eleven o'clock? I've been up for FIVE HOURS! But some of us have work to do, don't we? We don't just shilly-shally around all day!'

'Oh Mum, please don't start!' Candy handed her mother the mug of tea. She'd only half-filled it to get rid of her mother quicker.

'I'm not starting! What's this, half a cup? And I saw that ridiculous photo of you in the paper, making a public inhibition of yourself. You should be ashamed of yourself! And I hope there's nothing Going On.' She mouthed the last two words as though they were rude.

'No there's not, Mum. He only lets me stay here to help me lose weight for a bet. I don't think he even likes me very much.'

'Course he does, a healthy, good-looking girl like you! And I don't know why you want to lose weight anyway. You can't beat a good meal. You're going to end up ill if you don't eat properly, my girl. And you're not fat. You're just big-boned like all our family. Anyway, you take care, my girl. Things Happen when people are together. Men will take advantage if they're given half the chance. I know we live in a promestuous society, but the neighbours are already giving me funny looks. If you're going to get up to THINGS (More silent mouthing) you make sure you use one of them condiments. You don't want to be lumbered with struggling to raise an illegible child on your own, like I was. You don't know how hard it is, being a single parent.'

Out came the tissue and the tears and she walked over and collapsed on George's couch again, with her legs apart, carefully balancing the mug of tea. This time something definitely loudly snapped.

Candy smothered her laughter. 'Okay, I'll use a- a condiment if the situation arises, which it won't. Um, I know you're busy and you've got things to do, so I won't keep you.'

She heard George coming down the stairs and tried to take her mother's mug of tea off her, but Mrs Fosse clung on tightly. With the other hand, she picked up her handbag and balanced it on her knee, clutching it as though George was a handbag snatcher, or a rapist.

George looked from Candy to her mother and back again, completely shocked. His opinion of Candy mellowed instantly. Fancy being brought up by a woman like that!

'George, this is my mother,' said Candy unhappily, worried about the growing expression of horror on his face.

'Yes, I can see the likeness.' George remembered his manners and nobly forced a smile on his face and reluctantly held out his hand. 'Mrs Fosse! Delighted to meet you.'

To his relief she didn't take it. He'd imagined her squeezing it into pulp. Instead, she regarded it as though he'd just come out of the loo without washing his hands.

'Well,' she declared, 'So you're HIM are you?'

'Mum!' muttered Candy, smiling apologetically at George. 'Sorry George,' she whispered.

'No, I'm me,' replied George, trying to smile brightly. He failed.

'Huh,' snorted Mrs Fosse meaningfully, not really knowing what she meant.

'Oh Mum!' Candy repeated miserably, afraid to meet George's eyes again.

'Right I'm off down the pub,' said George, 'I'll leave you two ladies alone so you can talk in peace. See YOU later, Candy.'

Mrs Fosse's face lit up, which was as equally unattractive as her scowl. 'The pub? We'll come with you. I haven't been in a pub for years. I wouldn't dream of going in one unaccompanied, unlike some people I could name. I have my pride.' Another dig at Candy. 'And I want to TALK to you.'

'Oh, um, er, you wouldn't like it,' George stammered, backing away, 'It's, er, very crowded and, um, ever so loud. You'd have to stand.'

'I'm not afraid of a bit of standing,' declared Mrs Fosse, 'A bit of standing never hurt anyone. Don't you worry about me.'

I'm not, I'm worried about me, George thought, picturing everyone's faces and the comments as he walked in with Candy and her Mum. I'll go away to one of my Dad's villas abroad until people have forgotten about it, he decided.

Storming along the icy road with Mrs Fosse puffing and blowing loudly behind him as she tried to keep up, and Candy following miserably behind him, George increased his pace.

'Will you stop hurrying and WAIT FOR ME!' she ordered in between gasping for breath. George ignored Candy's whispered attempts to apologise.

'It's not my fault, George,' she pleaded, 'I didn't invite her, honest!'

'I believe you,' George snapped, glancing behind him.

He'd just decided to walk straight past the Duck and Grouse and go to a pub where he wasn't known when inspiration struck. And the holly wreath on the door and the sounds of laughter wafting out of the window were so inviting! And he couldn't afford to go anywhere else. And it was his Local after all!

Winking at Candy, he waited for Mrs Fosse to catch up and he took hold of her massive fleshy arm, trying not to recoil from the feel of it. He led her to the side of the window and flashed her a genuine warm smile, his thoughts elsewhere.

'You probably know that Candy's becoming a bit of a celebrity around here, Mrs Fosse,' he said. She nodded cautiously, not pulling away from him. 'And as her mother, you'll be a celebrity as well, of course.' He smiled charmingly.

Mrs Fosse nearly blushed. 'Well I don't know about that,' she cooed, patting her hair into place, 'Although my Grandad always said I'd got star quality…'

George smiled even more. 'Oh yes Mrs Fosse, it's true. So I'd like you to make a great big entrance.'

That's the only entrance you can make with a figure like yours, he thought, keeping the smile clamped on his face. He slid along the wall like a detective in an old film, and peered through the window. Yes, Rodney, Edward and Stefan were all standing in their usual places. George hissed and beckoned to Mrs Fosse. 'See that bloke over there?' he asked, pointing to Rodney. Mrs Flosse nodded eagerly. Rodney was very good-looking and obviously rich. 'Well when he scratches his nose like this-' George gave a demonstration of Rodney scratching his nose, '-You come in through the door, okay? I'll have announced you by then.'

'Ooh, I don't know if I could,' gushed Mrs Fosse happily.

'Course you can, Mrs Fosse. Now you stand there, where you can see through the window but no-one can see you. I'll give you a great big build-up.' To match your size. 'And you come in on the signal, okay?'

'Okay,' giggled Mrs Fosse, clutching her handbag.

'Right - signal, and -in! See you in a minute.' He gave a little wave and went inside, followed by Candy, who looked up at him and wondered what he was up to.

The atmosphere was becoming very festive. The room had been decorated and a large tree with lights was standing in a corner.

George pushed through the crowd to his usual spot beside the bar. 'Hello there, George. And Candy. Hello Candy.'

Rodney raised his arm to call Digby, but George stopped him.

'No, wait. Listen, Rodney, when I step on your foot, do me a favour and scratch your nose, will you?' Rodney looked surprised, but he never questioned a request from a friend.

'Certainly, George old chap. Anything to oblige. What are you up to?'

George raised his finger. 'Wait and see. You can call Digby now.'

'Digby! A pint of your excellent lager for George. Oh, and a slim-line tonic for the young lady.'

George leaned casually on the bar. 'I feel lucky today,' he said to Digby, 'I bet you - um, let's see, twenty quid on who's coming through the door next. We haven't played that for ages.'

'Right, you're on,' nodded Digby, slapping the drinks on the counter.

George stared at the ceiling. 'I bet it's - a woman!' He stepped on Rodney's foot and Rodney scratched his nose.

Candy clutched at George's sleeve and pointed. 'George,' she said as the door opened and two men came in, laughing and joking.

Digby roared with laughter. 'Right, that's twenty quid you owe me, George! Shall I knock it off your credit?' George glared and Candy backed away. Then Mrs Fosse burst grandly through the door and paused, as though she expected to be greeted with loud applause. Everyone stared at her.

George marched up to her. 'Where were you?' he snapped, 'Why didn't you come in on the signal?'

'I was fixing my lipstick,' she snapped back, 'I don't like to look a mess. And I know it's early but I'll have a brandy and coke to celebrate if you're buying. After all, it's nearly Christmas. No, make it a double; for mecidinal purposes; as protection against the cold.'

'Really? Mecidinal?' George was amazed at her cheek.

'Sorry George. I'll pay you back,' Candy said miserably as her mother spotted a group of people preparing to leave.

Mrs Fosse elbowed everyone out of the way and went to claim their table.

'Are you leaving? Oh good, we'll have it then,' she ordered, beating another couple to the seats who had been patiently waiting. 'Come on, over here!' she ordered, beckoning to the men.

'Ooh, she makes me so mad!' Candy continued as her mother sat down and beckoned to them again, 'She's so bossy! She really embarrasses me the way she orders people about!'

'I'll get the drink,' said Edward, 'Digby! A double brandy and coke for Candy's charming mother, please.'

Digby poured it out and smirked at George. 'Brandy for the Mother-in-Law is it, George?'

'I can't wait for all the corny jokes later,' George muttered to his friends, 'I'm going to make sure I leave before they start.' Then he carried Mrs Fosse's drink across to her and turned to go, but she leaned forward and grabbed hold of his jacket and patted the seat beside her.

'There, we didn't have to stand at all!' she declared triumphantly, 'Sit down, I want to have a talk with you, young man.'

George obediently sat down. Actually, his knees collapsed and he fell into the chair.

Candy trotted over and perched miserably on the seat opposite her mother.

Warily, George wondered what Mrs Fosse wanted to talk about. He was sure that it wasn't going to be a cosy, friendly chat. Mrs Fosse was obviously one of those people who never managed to say anything nice. Oh dear, she was smiling. It really was worse than her scowl as her narrow red lips parted.

'Now George - it is George, isn't it?' George agreed that it was George. 'I think it's quite nice what you're doing for my Candy, even though she doesn't need to lose weight,' George thought it best not to disagree. 'And I don't approve of her living in your house, even though it's a nice house.' She held up a hand for silence, even though George had no intention of speaking. 'So I'll tell you what I've decided to do.' She patted her huge stomach. 'I could do with losing some weight as I've got a bit of a spare tyre myself lately.' Spare tyre? More like a full set of juggernaut wheels, George thought. 'So I'd like to diet with my Candy. I thought I'd kill two birds with one stone, so to speak, and you can help both of us at the same time.'

I know a couple of plump birds that I'd like to kill, thought George with a fixed smile on his face.

'I've decided to move in with you both for a while,' continued Mrs Fosse, 'So's I can keep an eye on the two of you and make sure you're eating properly. Now isn't that a good idea? It means that none of us need to spend Christinas on our own! You can pick me up tomorrow morning, nine o'clock sharp. None of this eleven o'clock business! Half the day's gone then.' She held her hand up again. 'No, you don't need to thank me. I'll do it for nothing, out of the kindness of my heart!'

George tried to stand, but his legs wouldn't let him. He vaguely noticed that Candy was trying to attract his attention by opening and closing her mouth like a fish with no words coming out, her eyes pleading for forgiveness, although his vision seemed to have gone fuzzy, with red dots floating about.

As Mrs Fosse didn't speak very quietly, everyone had been able to eavesdrop easily. Rodney, Edward and Stefan stared helplessly with an expression of sympathetic horror on their faces. Digby grinned.

Then George recovered the use of his muscles. This was no time for politeness, he decided. Attack was the best form of defence. He had to go straight for the jugular; or the juggernaut.

'Mrs Fosse,' he said firmly, 'Your daughter is living temporarily under my roof in a separate bedroom. And she's old enough to do what she likes. But if you don't like it, you can take her home with you. I couldn't care less! We don't need you to look after us, thank you very much. I'll decide who lives in my house. No, you can NOT move in. It's my home, not a bloody charity health farm!'

Digby stopped grinning and started groaning as Mrs Fosse heaved her huge frame upright.

'Well!' she said to Candy, breathing out loudly, 'So this is the sort of person who you've chosen to spend your life with and to co-inhabit with, is it?'

'No Mum, he's-'

'To think that you'd abandon your own mother for - for HIM!'

'Mum, I-'

'Well, I shall at least expect you home for Christmas, my girl. If you think I'm spending it all alone while you cebrelate with - with HIM, you've got another think coming! I've been saving up with the Christmas Club all year to give you a nice Christmas! Oh, after all I've sacrificed for you!'

Cue tissue and tears. Then she threw her drink down her throat in a couple of loud glugs, wiped her mouth on the back of her hand, leaving a red smear there, and stood up, slamming down the glass.

Digby covered his face with his hand and shook his head dramatically as she charged towards the door, like a bull towards a matador's cloak. When she banged the door shut behind her, the windows rattled and the glasses danced on the bar. 'My foundations,' he moaned, 'She's loosened my foundations! This is a listed building. It'll be listing sideways soon, if George upsets many more women!'

George re-joined his friends, with Candy trotting behind him. 'Sorry George, it's not my fault,' she begged with tears in her eyes, 'I didn't know, I really didn't. I didn't know she was coming today and I didn't know she was going to say that, I swear I didn't!'

'Digby, give George a whisky,' said Rodney, 'He looks positively ill.'

Digby had regained his confidence. 'How'd you fancy having her for a mother-in-law, George?' he asked loudly.

'Oh, shut up Digby,' snapped George, while everyone laughed. He picked up the whisky and drained it in a couple of gulps. Was it time to retire to the villa now? he wondered.

He turned and saw Candy. 'Please George, I'm sorry,' she began.

'Look, just go home,' he said, trying not to bite her head off, 'I'll see you later.'

'What, to your home or – or to mine?' she asked nervously. But he didn't answer. He'd turned back to his friends.

He hardly noticed as she left. Stefan had just handed him another whisky. 'I don't want to stay here,' George said, 'I'm fed up with Digby's stupid jokes.'

'Let's go and have a curry,' Edward suggested, 'We haven't done that for a long time.'

'Good idea!' everyone agreed.

As they walked out into the cold air, they saw four girls staggering towards them, in fits of laughter, obviously the worse for wear. They were very underdressed for the weather.

George brightened up. 'Good afternoon, ladies,' he called, 'Where are you off to?'

'We're going to the pub,' one of them said, 'We've had our office party this lunchtime, and we've got the rest of the day off.'

'Cos we're not fit to work,' one of the others added, rather obviously.

They all giggled.

'Would you like to come for a curry?' Rodney suggested. They all giggled again.

'Okay,' said the first girl, 'If you're paying!' More giggles.

'Of course we are!' Edward told them, 'It's our treat. You're our guests!'

'I'll have the one in the blue,' said Rodney out of the corner of his mouth.

***

George and the girl were leaning against his wall, locked in a passionate embrace. 'Oh, Laura, Laura, Laura!' yelled George, sliding his hand up her skirt. He was determined to remember her name the next morning. 'Laura, Laura, I hope you're not a snorer!'

Laura shrieked with laughter, then went, 'Shshsh!' holding up a finger in the area of her mouth and nose.

George struggled to fit his key in the door, then Laura collapsed against him, the door flew open and they both fell in through the door and fell over at the foot of the stairs in fits of laughter.

'Shshsh!' said Laura again for no particular reason. She took her shoes off and carried them as she staggered, crab-like up the first couple of stairs. George followed, half on his knees, with his arms out in front of him. They helped each other halfway up the stairs, then they slid down again. They sat at the bottom, laughing too much to move.

'Upsadaisy, Snorer,' George mumbled and they crawled up again, padding up the stairs, George pushing Laura's backside. They burst through George's bedroom door and collapsed on the bed, in fits of laughter. Then the laughter stopped as George kicked the door shut and they ripped each other's clothes off.

Candy was awake, trying not to listen. She pulled the pillow over her head, but George's bed was thudding against the wall and Laura kept yelling, 'Oh George! Yes! Yes!'

Candy, couldn't stand it any longer. She got up, dressed in baggy trousers and a huge sweater, tiptoed down the stairs, and opened the front door. She gasped as an icy blast of air hit her, then she shut the door and walked along the road.

The supermarket was open all night. It was empty except for several members of staff stacking shelves and manning the till and a few people buying things that they couldn't live without until the next day. Two men wandered around, jingling their car keys and loudly cracking jokes to each other, and selecting crips and cans of beer.

Another man dressed in tracksuit bottoms, a tee-shirt and a jacket rushed in and dashed past her carrying two jars of gherkins and a king-size bar of chocolate.

'When's it due, Andy?' a woman stacking shelves asked him.

'In four months' time. I reckon it'll look like a gherkin the way she's getting through these jars!'

A man in a suit was carrying a basket filled with some dusters, a tin of sardines, a packet of frozen bubble and squeak, and an aubergine. Why? Wondered Candy.

Several groups of identical lads walked round, shouting 'Oy, over 'ere mate! and waving at the security cameras. They bought a couple of budget four-packs of lager which, after half a can, would turn them into demented Don Quixotes with a hatred of inanimate objects like shop windows, cars and bus shelters.

Candy loaded her basket with bars of chocolate and bags of sweets and paid at the checkout. She ripped one of the chocolate bars open and she was halfway through the second bar of chocolate before she was out of the door - or rather, it was halfway through her!

'Blimey, look at that! She looks WELL stupid!' said a young lad with five earrings in one ear and one in his nose, baggy jeans with dirty, deliberately-frayed bottoms, ripped at the knees and pulled down to his thighs, showing all the back of his Mickey Mouse underpants, a cheap copy of a designer tee-shirt, an enormous oriental tattoo on his scrawny right arm which, unknown to him, said, I am Very Stupid and Gullible, and produced outbursts of suppressed laughter from passing members of the Chinese community, his hat on back to front, and a can of lager in his hand which he sipped when his friends weren't looking because he didn't want them to know that he didn't really like lager and preferred a cup of tea.

'Yeah, fancy shagging 'er!' said one of his clone-like pals, who'd have given anything to shag anyone for the first time, but for all his big talk, had never had the courage to ask any girls, 'You'd need an effin' ladder to get at it! Effinell, I'm WELL pissed!'

'Oy darlin', fancy a gang-bang? You could fit us all on top at once!' called his mate, bellowing loudly at his own joke.

A Mars Bar hit him on the forehead, bursting an over-ripe zit. 'Ere, you wanna watch it!' he shouted at Candy, 'That effin' 'urt!'

One of his friends laughed, then a Walnut Whip whacked him on the nose, making it bleed, followed by a Milky Way.

A Snickers Bar landed on another lad's chin. 'Quick, run!' he said bravely, 'I don't hit birds. And she's bigger than the four of us put together!'

Candy swung her carrier-bag of remaining sweets and chocolate bars round her head like a biblical sling and let it fly through the air after the departing heroes. It caught one of them on the back of the head and she thought she heard him crying.

Her anger and frustration had faded - almost. So had her craving for chocolate. With a sigh she headed home, hoping that George and Snorer had fallen asleep.

WEDNESDAY 8th DECEMBER

215lbs / 15st 5lbs / 97.5kgs

Candy entered George's house and quietly closed the door. She'd been to the gym at 8 o'clock and put herself through a punishing workout to try and get rid of her extra calories before anyone noticed. Then she'd been shopping to postpone going home and meeting George and the girl.

George appeared at the top of the stairs in his dressing-gown, clutching his stomach, his hair tousled and a growth of stubble on his chin. 'Morning, Candy,' he muttered, letting out a large burp. Curry and several bottles of red wine weren't a very romantic aid for his insides in the morning.

'Mermer,' she muttered back, not looking at him.

'Candy?'

'What?'

'Any chance of some breakfast?'

'There's always a chance,' she snapped.

What was wrong with her this morning? he wondered. 'Good girl. Er, make it two, please.'

'Oh, Snorer still here is she?' Candy snapped again.

Ah yes, that was her name - Sn - Laura! 'Thanks Candy!' he said and went back to bed.

Candy kicked on his door, walked in and plonked the tray on top of George and Laura.

Laura peered bleary-eyed over the duvet. She had a massive hangover. 'Who's the fat girl?' she asked, 'Does she live here?'

George didn't reply.

'Is she your sister or something? Or your housekeeper?'

'Um, yes, sort of my half-sister,' George bluffed, trying to lift the tray off them without spilling the coffee as Candy banged the door shut behind her. God, she was in a strange mood this morning! Must be her time of the month or something. He felt a metaphorical weight lifted off him when he heard the front door slam, and he turned towards Laura and kissed her. ‘Morning, Laura,’ he said. Yes, he’d got her name right. Good old Candy! Then he had to rush out of bed and into the bathroom.

Oh, Candy hasn’t filled my bath, he thought when he’d lifted his head up from the toilet.

MONDAY 13th DECEMBER

196lbs / 14st / 88.9kgs

George turned the key in his lock and pushed the door. But it wouldn't open more than a few inches. Something was blocking it. Then Candy's head and part of her body appeared in the small gap.

'Hello George, um, come in,' she said, smiling strangely.

'Thanks, I will come in, considering it happens to be MY home.'

He pushed the door open another millimetre and Candy squeezed through the gap and stepped outside, flapping her arms up and down. 'Er, have a nice time at the pub, did you?'

'Yes thank you. Could you get out of the way please?'

She didn't. 'Rodney and Edward there, were they?'

'Surprisingly enough, yes they were.'

'And Stefan?'

'Yes, and Stefan too.' George tried to squeeze past Candy, but she didn't move.

She leaned one hand against the doorframe, then she started flapping her arms again. 'I saw him this morning at the gym. Did he tell you I'm fourteen-eleven now?'

'Yes, he did.'

'I've lost just over two stone already. Isn't that great?'

George stood still. 'Yeah, fantastic! Candy, will you stop flapping about like a sealion guarding her pups and tell me what you don't want me to see in there?'

His heart suddenly felt as though it had come loose and dropped down into his stomach. Four pints of lager grumbled in protest. 'Oh no, it's not your mother! Tell me it's not your mother!'

Candy almost looked relieved. 'No, no, it's not my mother.' She chuckled shyly, 'It's-' She stood aside.

George walked into his sitting-room and let out a long, ‘Ooooooh!’

‘-It’s my Super Sylphie Starter Parcel. And they sent me a Super Sylphie Selection as well. Wasn’t that nice? The lorry arrived just after you went out.’

‘How convenient,’ George muttered, ‘Hiding round the corner were they? Did you tell them to wait until I left the house?’

‘It’s all free, well, on credit,’ Candy continued, ‘I just pay for the first lot and then the rest as I sell them, George. George?’

George was unable to reply. He stared with mute horror at the hundreds of cardboard boxes stamped Slim With Sylphie that lined the hall and the walls and covered the carpet and most of the furniture. Then he let out another, ‘Oooooh,’ and dragged himself up the small pathway of stairs that was free of boxes.

‘I left the banister side clear. I thought it was safer,’ Candy called hopefully from the bottom of the stairs, ‘And there aren’t any boxes in your bedroom. I thought you’d be annoyed.’

George’s vocal chords regained their power. ‘Annoyed?’ he squeaked as he picked his way carefully down the stairs. Candy backed away across the lounge, through the narrow lane between the boxes, followed by George.

‘Annoyed?’ he bellowed in her face, ‘I’m bloody furious! Look at my house! Look at it! It looks like a bloody warehouse!’

‘Sorry George,’ Candy replied, ‘I didn’t know there’d be so many.’

He took several deep breaths and spoke in a quieter voice. ‘Right, I won’t say any more. I’m going out for the afternoon, and when I come back I want to find this lot gone, do you hear me? Gone!’

‘What shall I do with it, George?’

'I don't know and I don't care. Sell it, dump it, give it away to the poor, or eat it, but get it out! Out! All of it! Aaagh!' He fell over a box, picked himself up, yelled, 'Out! I mean it, out!' while jabbing his finger at the front door. Then he squeezed through to the front door and slammed it shut behind him.

***

'It's no use Rodney, she's got to go. She's driving me up the wall!' George slumped miserably in an old leather armchair in Rodney's cottage and stared into the fire. The spitting and crackling of the logs was relaxing him a bit. So was Rodney's brandy.

'Cheer up old chap and have a refill of this excellent brandy.' Rodney topped up their glasses and sat down in the other armchair.

'She's driving me nuts! She's taking over my life! My home! It's horrible! I can't stand it any more!' He gulped his brandy down and gasped as it hit the back of his throat.

'But she does all your washing and cleaning for you, doesn't she?' Rodney said encouragingly, 'I should have thought that was a very big plus since you had to sack your cleaning lady. And she cleans in here really well. I'm so relieved at not having to do it myself any more.'

George sighed one of his sighs. 'There's not much of my home left to clean now. It's been converted into a Super Sylphie Storeroom. I'm sure they dump all their goods into people's homes so they don't have to pay to rent a warehouse. She's got to go, Rodney. She can move back with her Mum.' He shuddered as he pictured Mrs Fosse, 'After all, the diet's going well. She's following it seriously. She doesn't need me any more- And I certainly don't need her!'

'I don't think you should do anything hasty, George. It's early days yet. We're not sure how she'd react if she wasn't supervised all the time. And I dread to think what that awful mother of hers would feed her on. Leave it for a while, eh? There's a lot at stake for all of us.'

'Yeah, my reputation for one thing, and my home,' George moaned, holding his brandy glass out for a refill.

***

George was seething. 'I thought I told you to get this lot out of my house before I got home!' he shouted.

Candy knelt on the tiny remaining area of floor space, a pen gripped in her teeth, rummaging through a pile of paperwork. She flapped a hand at him without looking up. 'Ssh,' she told him.

Could this be truly happening? Had he really been openly defied and then told to shut up in his own home? 'I beg your pardon for speaking,' he said politely, 'But I would be extremely grateful if you'd kindly clear this load of rubbish out of my house, and then clear yourself out with it.'

Candy removed the pen from her mouth and stared directly up at him. 'You told me I could sell it George, and I have been. I think I've made about £150 profit so far, but I can't cope with all these forms.' She began to search through the paperwork again.

George swallowed. 'Did you say £150?'

'Yes I did.'

'£150 profit?'

'Yes.'

'This afternoon?'

'Yes George, I think so. It could be a bit more than that.'

George squashed himself onto the carpet beside her. 'Well if we're going to do this thing, we've got to do it properly. Have you got any instructions?'

Fred would have been proud of his son if he was a fly on the wall (which of course, he wasn't.)

Candy smiled gratefully at him and resumed her search through the papers. 'Yes, they're all here somewhere. I saw them just now.'

'So who's been buying this load of - this lot?' asked George, genuinely interested now.

'Digby.'

'Digby?' George sat up straight. 'What, OUR Digby? Who bet against us winning? You're having me on, aren't you?'

She shook her head.

'No. He ordered four cases of Sylphie Special Wine Taste-Alike and ten boxes of assorted Sylphie Super Sesame Snacks, and six boxes of Sylphie's Adorable Animal-Free Flavoured Mock Potato Crisps. And he wants them all as soon as possible. I've got some here, if I can find them, that he can have for a start before the others are delivered.'

'That's absolutely brilliant, Candy! Unbelievable! How on earth did you manage to sell it to a cynical sod like Digby?'

'I told him that, in this health-conscious society of ours it was his duty to offer an alternative choice of low-fat, low-calorie foods and alcohol-free drinks to his customers. And it would increase his profits by up to twenty percent per week, or even more after Christmas, when everyone decides to go on a diet.'

'That's amazing! How did you think of that?'

'It's on page three hundred and twenty-two of the Sylphie Super Sales Manual, in the How to Sell to Bars and Restaurants chapter.'

George checked his watch and stood up, 'Come on, it's only six-thirty. Let's load my car up and sell some more to places that I go to regularly, before everywhere gets busy for the evening. Fancy anyone buying this stuff. I'm pleasantly surprised. And Digby as well! I can't believe it! And I don't need to sell my car now, either!'

He paused, jingling his car keys in his hand. Er, Candy,' he said,

Yes George?' asked Candy, staggering along, carrying three boxes.

'You'd better drive - you can drive, can't you? I've had a couple of brandies today.'

'And the rest,' she said to the boxes.

FRIDAY 24th DECEMBER

196lbs / 14st / 88.9kgs

'Well, goodbye, George. I'm off to catch my bus home. See you next year.'

'Yeah, see you, Candy.' He gave her a little wave over his shoulder without bothering to turn his head from the television. Eight days without her. Eight days with the house to himself - plus whoever he decided to entertain, of course. Great!

'Um, George?'

'Yeah?' Hadn't she gone yet? She was standing beside his chair. He looked up. She was holding out a packet wrapped with Christmas paper with snowmen on it.

'Merry Christmas, George,' she said shyly.

'Oh!' He took his feet off the Slim With Sylphie box and sat up straight. 'Thanks, Candy. You shouldn't have bothered.' George hadn't bothered. He hadn't given it a thought.

'Aren't you going to open it?'

He smiled up at her. 'Shall I? Or shall I wait till tomorrow morning?'

'Yes, go on. Open it now.'

He tore the paper off and held up a brown sweater. 'Oh Candy, that's really nice!' he exclaimed. He meant it too.

'Do you really like it?'

'Yeah, it's great! My colour too. And I love the pattern.'

She blushed. 'I knitted it myself, when you weren't here, and sometimes in my room at night.'

George stood up and pulled it over his head. 'It's a perfect fit,' he said, 'In fact I think I'll wear it tonight!'

Candy was pleased. 'It's a sort of thank you present as well, for all you've done for me.'

George kissed her on the cheek. 'And that's a thank you from me.'

She blushed again and giggled nervously. 'Well, I'd better go or I'll miss my bus.'

'Okay. And you watch your diet. Don't go overeating just because it's Christmas, will you? Don't let that mother of yours pile roast potatoes on your plate.'

'No I won't. I'm just having turkey and veg. I'm fifteen five today.'

'Oh good. Bye now!'

Candy picked up her heavy suitcase and bag. George opened the door for her and an icy gust of wind blew in. He hadn't even considered offering her a lift.

Candy staggered out onto the freezing pavement and he shut the door behind her, then he rubbed his hands together. Hee hee, freedom! And he had money to spend, thanks to Sylphie's overpriced rubbish. He didn't need his father's charity after all. Right, time to meet the gang. Yes, he was really looking forward to this Christmas after all!

***

Candy tramped along the icy road towards her house. She fought back the tears, blaming it on the freezing wind. But she knew that it wasn't just the cold December gale causing it. She was dreading spending Christmas with her mother. She'd rather be tolerated or ignored by George and his friends than be blamed and nagged at and criticised - and fed - by Mrs Fosse.

She stopped outside her front gate and put down the heavy suitcase and bag. She saw the net curtain twitch and took a deep breath. Then she picked up her things again and held her head firmly high.

'I won't put on weight, I won't put on weight, I won't put on weight,' she chanted as she walked up the path, dragging her luggage along.

SATURDAY 25th DECEMBER

Where was he? What had happened? George woke up feeling very confused and disorientated. He was sprawled amongst a pile of Slim With Sylphie boxes in his lounge, at the bottom of the stairs.

He disentangled himself, stood up, trying to stretch his muscles, examined himself in a mirror to check who he was, then wished he hadn't. It wasn't a pretty sight. How had he aged 10 years overnight? Where had those bags under his eyes appeared from? They weren't there yesterday!

Hauling himself up the stairs, he ran a hot bath and delicately lowered himself into it, vowing to Oswald the duck that he was definitely teetotal starting from today.

He opened his wardrobe and chose a pair of casual beige trousers and a check shirt from the row of shirts, all neatly ironed by Candy. And he finished it off by pulling on Candy's sweater. Yes, it looked good, he thought examining himself in the full-length mirror on the wardrobe door and hooking out a pair of brown suede shoes.

Then he went downstairs into the kitchen and made toast and black coffee. Feeling a bit more like homo sapiens again, he smiled as memories of the night before became clearer.

It had seemed like the answer to their prayers when four more giggling girls on their way from their office party had walked unsteadily into the Duck and Grouse.

'I love these Christmas office parties,' said Edward.

'You've never been to any in your life,' Rodney told him.

'No,' Edward agreed, 'I just wait for them to come to me! Go on, George.'

'Why me?' asked George.

'Because you're so good at it, old chap,' Rodney flattered, 'And you've got your house to yourself. Go on, you can have first pick. We'll follow you.'

'The tall atheletic-looking blonde will do me nicely,' Stefan claimed.

'I'm not bothered which one I get. They're all acceptable,' Edward said happily.

George eyed up the other three. 'Um, I think I'll have the ginger one. Should make a nice change. Yes, she'll do for me!'

And it had. What was her name now? He was sure he could remember if he concentrated. Think of word association. Something to do with cakes. Ah yes. Madeleine Battenburg.

They'd all drank a lot of Champagne, then moved on to Madeleine's flat and drank a lot more.

Yes, all in all it had been a good night. And he was seeing her again on New Year's Eve when she returned from her parents' house. Roll on New Year's Eve!

How had he got home? he wondered. Then he shrugged. He couldn't remember.

He'd have to spend the night at her place. He couldn't bring her back here with all these boxes everywhere, he thought, staring at what used to be his lounge.

George inspected himself in the mirror one more time and groaned at the bags under his bloodshot eyes, then he piled his family's Christmas presents into two carrier-bags and delicately drove to his parents' house.

He'd left all his shopping to the last minute as usual, so he hoped they'd all like their gifts that he'd chosen for them.

***

'Late as usual, I see.'

'And a Merry Christmas to you too, Bert. Here's your present.'

'Huh,' sniffed Bert happily, taking the package from George, 'Waste of bleedin' time if you ask me. I'd better get on with the dinner. I've been at it since early this morning.'

'GEORGIE! YOU'RE HERE!'

'Hello Suzie, Merry Christmas. Give your big brother a hug! But not too tight. Hello, Dad. Hello, Mum, Grandad.' George hugged and kissed the women and hugged and shook hands with the men and gave them all a present out of his carrier-bags.

'Oh, how nice,' said Fred in a sarcastic voice, 'Sylphie Special White Wine Taste-Alike! Yum yum! I can hardly wait to try it!'

'Fred!'

'Sorry luv. Oh well, it's the first present you've ever bought me that I haven't paid for, son.'

'Oh, Fred! Don't you be so mean!'

'Sorry luv. Just kidding.'

'GEORGIE! CHOCOLATES! HOW SUPER!'

'Sylphie Super Mock-Chock Chewies,' Daph read out, looking at her own present, 'Oh, how nice, luv! Mm, I'll look forward to eating them.'

'And they're all low in calories,' George said.

'Oh great! We can all watch our figures now! Well, your Mum's so plump!'

'Fred! Behave!'

'Sorry, luv. I was only joking.'

'Thanks, George.' Fred Senior held a large bottle of Sylphie Special Sugarless Stout Taste-Alike. 'I'll have a drop of this at bedtime.'

'So tell us, we're dying to know, who or what is Sylphie?' asked Fred, handing his son a sherry, 'You obviously think a lot of her products.'

George kept a straight face. 'It's my new job,' he smirked proudly, 'I'm a Sales Manager.' Well it wsn't a lie. After all, he managed Candy.

'GEORGIE! HOW MARVELLOUS!' gasped Suzie encouragingly.

'You?'

'Freeeed!'

'No, I wasn't knocking him, luv. I'm delighted. And what a good choice! I presume they're all slimming products?'

'Yeah,' said George.

'That's the ideal job for a ladies' man like you, son. Most women are permanently on diets and you shouldn't have any difficulty in charming them into buying something.'

'I'll have some, George.'

'Daph! That's cheating, buying from your son. You don't need to lose any weight and you know it.'

'Well you know I like to look nice for you, Fred.' Daph regarded him coyly. 'It won't do me any harm to lose a pound or two after Christmas.'

'Nor me,' Suzie agreed, 'I'll have some as well, Georgie. I have to keep my weight down for my horse-riding.'

Daph opened a Sylphie Super Mock Chock Chewie, bit into it and pulled a face. 'Er, have you got anything else?' she asked.

'Sure, we've got loads,' George told her, 'I'll bring the list tomorrow.'

'And speaking of diets, Professor Higgins, how's My Fat Lady getting on?' asked Fred.

George pulled a face. He didn't want to think about her for a while. 'Very funny, Dad. She's getting along fine. She's losing weight regularly. She's lost over two stone already.'

'I bet she puts on weight over Christmas though,' said Fred hopefully, 'I heard about her dreadful Mum.'

'I don't care at the moment,' George replied, 'It's nice to have my house to myself for a few days. Nice and peaceful.'

'When are we going to meet her, George?' Daph asked.

'Oh yes Georgie, WHEN?' Suzie added.

George was surprised. 'I don't know. I never thought about it. Do you want to? I'll bring her round here one day.'

'Good. I'll look forward to that,' said Daph.

‘Ooh yes, so will I,’ echoed Suzie, ‘I bet she’s EVER so nice, Georgie!’

‘She must be to put up with you lot bullying her about all the time.’

George pulled a face. ‘I don’t bully her. She’s a volunteer. She can give up any time she wants to.’

‘Well I think it’s a real noble thing you’re doing, son, real noble,’ Fred Senior told him.

‘Yeah,’ George sighed, ‘So do I.’

‘Dinner!’ Bert called, ‘’urry up before the Queen’s speech starts!’

FRIDAY 31st DECEMBER

206lbs / 14st 10lbs / 93.4kgs

'So my food's not good enough for you any more, isn't it?'

'Yes Mum, it's lovely, but I've had enough!' And I'm sick of turkey, roast potatoes and Brussels sprouts, she thought, looking down at her unfinished meal.

Out came the tissue. 'I've been looking forward to our Christmas together. I've been saving my stamps every week in the Christmas Club so's you could have a nice Christmas with all the trimmings, and you just waste it! I may as well throw it all in the bin! It's become an obsession with you, this eating lark. If you're not careful you're going to end up anorexical, my girl!'

'Ooh!' Candy struggled hard to control her simmering anger. 'Okay, I'll have some more turkey! Mm, it's delicious! Really tender!' And nearly a week old. She was pretty sure that she'd never eat any turkey again as long as she lived.

Mrs Fosse reached over with her fork and speared four more roast potatoes onto her plate, then she speared three onto Candy's plate. 'There you are. You always said you loved my roasties. You can't eat turkey on its own without roast potatoes!' She poured gravy onto both plates.

Candy pushed her plate aside. 'I don't WANT any potatoes, Mum. I don't WANT them! I'm not hungry, and I'm bloated with overeating!' She burped loudly with her hand over her mouth. 'And there's not much chance of me becoming anorexic is there? I weigh over FOURTEEN STONE, Mum! FOURTEEN STONE! And I bet I weigh more now. I'm fat! I'm overweight! I'm a freak! I'm twenty-four years old and I've got no friends and I can hardly move I'm so bloated! You're killing me! I can't stand it any more! I'm going back to George's!'

She stood up and rushed to her room, packed her bag and suitcase and, walking down the stairs, she grabbed her coat off the hook by the door.

Mrs Fosse stood watching her with her hands on where her hips would have been if she'd had any.

'That's right, run back to your fancy man!' she shouted.

Candy opened the door and shouted back at her mother. 'A, he's not my fancy man. He'd never fancy me in a million years! And, B, I can't run back to him because I can't bloody run!'

She shut the door, picked up her case and staggered angrily along the path.

***

Eight-thirty, time to meet everyone. George had slept off the effects of his lunchtime celebrating, and he'd freshened up for the long evening ahead. He checked his appearance in the mirror. He was wearing his free sports gear from Activity, the sports store. He'd chosen a pale blue ensemble and white trainers. He thought the sporty look might impress a lot of girls.

'Oh yes, very nice,' he told his reflection, 'The lovely Madeleine's a lucky girl, George my boy! Oh hell, what's that?' Someone was opening his front door.

'Oh!' he said in dismay as Candy walked in, 'Candy! What are you doing here? You're not due back for another couple of days!'

'I know,' she sighed, plonking her bags on top of the boxes, 'But I just couldn't stand my mum any more. When she wasn't feeding me she was nagging me. I'm sure I've put on weight again, I feel so bloated, but eating was the only way to shut her up! I'll work hard to get rid of it again, I promise. Oh George, it was awful! She's driven me up the wall!'

He made sympathetic noises, then walked past her. 'Well I'm off down the pub. See you later.' Or hopefully not, he thought.

'Okay.'

'Well it's New Year's Eve.'

'Yes, I know that, George.'

'And I've got a date.'

'Oh. Right.'

George looked at her. It was no good, he couldn't leave her on her own all night, especially after the terrible Christmas she must have had.

'Oh, come on,' he said. Her face lit up. 'But you'll have to sit in a corner and behave yourself,' he added.

'Yes, George. Sorry George. I'll be as good as gold. And as quiet as a mouse. And thank you.'

***

Ah, this is how a New Year's Eve should be, thought George, glowing warmly from Digby's home-made mulled wine. Everyone had just sung 'God Rest Ye Merry Gentlemen,' while someone played the piano; not very well, but mostly in tune. Then George and Co had sung 'If you want my Body and you think I'm Sexy come on Baby let me know it,' with what they thought were sexy movements, followed by 'We're Walking in the Air' from The Snowman, sung in falsetto voices, waving their arms about which the four girls found very funny.

Now a slow tune was playing and George was just preparing to go into a passionate smooch with Madeleine when be felt a tug on his sleeve.

'George?'

'Huh?' He'd forgotten that Candy was there. She'd sat quietly in a corner all evening like he'd told her to.

'George, I want to go home. I'm going to have an early night. Can I have your keys please? I've forgotten mine.'

'Oh yeah, sure.' He let go of Madeleine and took the keys out of his pocket.

'Who's that?' asked Madeleine, swaying slightly. She'd had quite a lot to drink.

'Only Candy.'

'ONLY Candy?'

'She's George's fiancee,' shouted Digby.

'Oh shut up Digby!' George gave Candy the keys and tried to put his arm round Madeleine again but she wriggled free.

'Is it true?'

'No it's not!'

'But she lives with you?'

'Well yeah, but it's not like-'

'You swine! No wonder you had to go home early on Christmas Eve!'

'I was drunk. I was-'

'You certainly were! Got an open relationship have you? Rich heiress is she?'

'No, I-'

'Think you can use me and then go home to your fiancee do you?'

'Fiancee? No, she's not-'

'Swine! Men always use us girls and then marry big fat ugly women!'

'Ugly?' squeaked Candy, who had stayed to listen to the row.

'You've made a right fool out of me, haven't you?'

'No, really, I – it's just Digby's joke! Tell her, Candy.'

'I'm staying out of it,' said Candy.

'It's a joke alright!' She turned to Candy. 'You can keep him, the no-good, two-timing swine! Ooh!'

'Oh no, here it comes,' Digby moaned as Madeleine grabbed George's lager.

'Swine!' she screamed, throwing it in George's face. Then she marched to the door, opened it and slammed it shut. Two decorations came unfixed from the ceiling. One floated down and landed on George's head.

'Sorry George,' said Candy, hiding a grin behind her hand.

'Happy New Beer, George!' shouted Digby, handing him a towel and another lager.

'Oh very very funny, Digby,' George snarled, 'Thanks for ruining my love life!'

He wiped his face with the towel while everyone laughed unsympathetically.

Digby placed another pint of lager in front of him.

Someone started counting the seconds to midnight and everyone joined in.

They all linked arms and sang Auld Lang Syne, then everyone kissed everyone else.

George noticed Candy standing on her own. Ruefully he kissed her on the cheek. 'Happy New Year, Candy,' he said. I doubt if it will be though, he thought.

Then everyone else kissed her. She smiled happily. 'Happy New Year, George.'

FRIDAY 7th JANUARY

201lbs / 14st 5lbs / 91.2kgs

'I never thought I'd see the day when I'd enjoy working,' declared Edward.

'No,' Rodney agreed, I never intended to work at all, whether I enjoyed it or not - and voluntarily too. This stuff is so easy to sell that it almost makes me feel guilty when I take their money! By the way, has anyone, apart from Candy, that is, actually tasted this stuff?'

George pulled a face. 'No thanks. It all looks extremely unappetising!'

Edward took a Sylphie Wonder Wafer out of a box, unwrapped it and bit into it. 'Oh, yuck and super-yuck!' he grimaced, spitting it into the wrapper and peering into the packet. 'Just checking that I wasn't eating the cardboard instead of the biscuit. It's absolutely revolting! Completely tasteless!'

'We'll take your word for it,' George said.

'Oh, they're one of my favourites!' declared Candy, 'And I'm still losing weight, aren't I Stefan?'

Stefan nodded. 'Steadily, about a pound a day. I'm very pleased. We've nearly got her back down to what she was before Christmas.'

'I'm really sorry about that,' Candy sighed, 'I really couldn't help it. My Mum kept loading me with food. She's such a bully!'

'Well you just need to make sure that she's kept well away from Candy in the future, George,' Stefan warned.

'I'm not sure how I can manage that. But I'll try. I'll get extra locks fitted on the door! What I can't understand though,' said George, looking around him, 'Is how, even though we've sold loads of these boxes, they never seem to get any less. In fact, I'm sure they're multiplying when we're not here!'

The doorbell rang. 'I'll get it,' Edward volunteered, putting down his brandy glass on the table and following the narrow trail between the boxes into the hall. He reappeared, walking backwards, with an expression of horror and dread on his face.

'Oh hello Mrs Fosse,' said George warily, 'To what do we owe this pleasure?'

What now? He thought. It was bound to be trouble.

'Sorry George,' Edward whispered, sounding just like Candy, 'She just barged her way in before I could stop her! She nearly knocked me over! She didn't even say hello.'

'So THESE are them,' snapped Candy's mum, glaring at all the boxes, 'Well, I've never seen anything like it in my life! What a mess!'

'Hello Mum, what do you want? Everything alright?' Candy inquired nervously.

'No it's NOT alright, my girl! I'm ASHAMED of you, trying to con your own mother! I suppose it was HIS idea!' She scowled at George.

Candy looked puzzled. 'What are you on about, Mum?'

'I mean THESE!' Mrs Fosse swept a huge majestic arm towards all the boxes. 'You told me I'd lose weight. Huh! I've had fifteen Sylphie Substitiute Meals – FIFTEEN! And I haven't lost a THING! Not a THING! – except for my money, that is.' She glared at George again.

'Fifteen?' George gasped, 'You like them then?'

Mrs Fosse scowled at George even harder. 'No I DON'T like them! I ate them to lose some weight after my dinner! FIFTEEN I've eaten and I haven't lost an ounce!'

'But Mum,' Candy wailed, 'You only got them yesterday! You're supposed to eat one a day instead of a meal, that's all!'

'Am I?' Mrs Flosse was taken aback for once and struggled to think of a retort. Then she snapped, 'Well why didn't you say so then? You should have told me, shouldn't you?'

'I did tell you, but you never lis-'

'If I'd have been properly informed of all the reverent facts I'd have known, wouldn't I?'

'It explains clearly on the packet, Mrs F-,' George told her – or tried to tell her.

'Packets?' she snapped, 'I haven't got time to waste my time sitting around reading PACKETS! Some of us have got work to do!'

'And you got a free tee-shirt, Mum.'

'Oh yes, you mean THIS?' She undid her check coat, pulling it open and thrusting out her huge chest. She was wearing a tweed skirt that must have contained a record number of pleats. And printed on a tightly stretched tee-shirt across her huge bosom was I'm a Super Sylphie Slimmer. Every Day I'm looking Trimmer. The letters were stretched so far that they were almost illegible.

It was no good. George just couldn't control his laughter. Nor could Rodney and Edward. Stefan was used to overweight women so he didn't laugh as much as the others.

Mrs Fosse glared at all of them. 'Something funny?' she asked. They all spluttered and shook their heads, unable to speak.

'There's them as laughs at other people who should take a closer look at themselves first,' Said Candy's mum ominously.

'Give it time, Mum, please,' Candy pleaded, 'It's working really well for me. And you could make lots of money too, if you – if you would talk nicely to people.'

'TALK NICELY? I always talk nicely! I was taught to have PROPER RESPECT for people, not like SOME that I could name.' She sniffed meaningfully. 'And you can give me a box of them Strawberry Substitute things while I'm here.'

She snatched the box off Edward and said, 'I'll see myself out, thank you. I won't put you to any bother. I'm not one to outstand my welcome.'

She waddled down the hall, the front door slammed and they all relaxed and let out simultaneous sighs, then collapsed in uncontrollable fits of laughter, including Candy.

'Your mother should be a very successful sales lady,' Edward said to Candy in between his laughter.

'Why's that then?' Candy asked.

'Because nobody would dare say no to her!'

'You're telling me,' Candy sighed, and they all started laughing again.

'Shall we all mosey on down to the pub?' suggested Rodney, 'No offence meant, Candy, but your mother always makes me very thirsty!'

'No offence taken. She has the same effect on me,' Candy agreed, 'And unfortunately, she makes me hungry too!' She grabbed a Sylphie Pineapple Pitstop and bit into it hard while they walked along the road. She had to because it WAS hard.

'And here we are at the Duck and Grouse,' said Edward.

'And here's the old grouse himself. Digby! The usual, please!' Rodney called.

'No,' Candy interrupted, 'Let me. Digby! Four pints of lager please, and a glass of Sylphie Special Red Wine Taste-Alike for me.'

She smiled happily as Rodney said, 'Our Candy's quite at home here now.'

'Yes, she's really one of the boys,' George agreed. Candy stopped smiling.

They all turned round as the door opened and a voice squealed, 'George!'

'Penny!' gasped George. They ran towards each other and he picked her up and swung her round. Her arms entwined his neck, her legs wrapped round his waist and she kissed him passionately.

'When did you get back?' he asked when they emerged for air and he put her down.

'An hour ago. I went home, then I rushed straight over here. I knew I'd find you here! I've got a week's holiday. My au-pair job's really great, but, oh, I did miss you, George!'

They kissed passionately again. 'Do you want a drink or shall we go straight back to my place?' George emphasised My Place.

'Oh, straight back to your place.' She giggled and they kissed again.

'And guess where you'll be spending your nights,' George whispered in her ear.

Penny acted innocent. 'I give in. Where?'

'At my house of course. With me. Oh, and Candy. You haven't met Candy, have you?'

Everyone groaned. Penny froze. Then her handbag collided with George's head.

'Oh, you, BASTARD!' she screamed. 'I'd heard rumours, but I didn't think it was true! I've come home and caught you out, haven't I?' She gestured at Candy. 'Do anything for you, would she?'

'Well yes, she-'

'Puts up with all your two-timing ways, does she?'

'No, she's not-'

'Into threesomes is she? I suppose you think you can have the two of us at once don't you, you – you – pervert, you!'

'No Penny, I don't-'

'You think you can make females do anything you want, don't you?'

'No honestly, it's not like- give me time to explain.'

'I don't want to hear your stupid excuses!' She grabbed George's lager and tipped it over his head. 'Ooh, Mummy was right about you!' she shrieked, 'Oh, how COULD you?'

'Penny, stop, I'm-' George protested lamely as she ran, sobbing, towards the door.

Digby covered his face with his hands as the door slammed shut and the building shook. Then he handed George a towel.

'One thing about my lager, George, it certainly goes to your head quick,' he said, refilling George's glass. Then he added, 'And guess who's paying my next year's buildings' insurance policy? That's if I've got any building left standing to insure!'

'But what did I do?' George appealed to everyone, holding his hands out.

Old Gubbins just examined the inside of his pipe and laughed.

SATURDAY 8th JANUARY

200lbs / 14st 4lbs / 90.7kgs

'George?'

Sigh.

'Here's a sandwich.'

Grunt.

'George?'

Sigh.

'Why don't you go round and see her?'

Sigh.

'Look George, you've been really quiet all day. Go and see her! I'm sure if you went round and told her why I'm here and explained things to her and said that you could – you could never fancy me, everything would be alright again. I'm sure she'd understand.'

George sighed again, but he looked interested. 'Do you think she'd listen?'

'Well it's worth a try. She obviously fancied you, the way she wrapped herself round you. And it's better than moping around here, isn't it?'

'Yeah, I suppose so. Thanks Candy.'

He turned the TV off and went upstairs to shower and change, and returned, dressed in a brown suit with a white shirt and a tie on.

'Oh, very smart!' said Candy as he handed her a clothes-brush.

'Brush my shoulders will you? This suit shows up every speck of dust.'

As she brushed him, George watched Candy in the mirror. Then he said, 'Candy.'

'Yes?'

'You're a girl, aren't you?'

She sighed and stopped brushing him. 'Yes George, I am,' she snapped, 'Well how observant of you to notice!'

Her sarcasm was lost on him. 'Well, do you think I should take her a present? Would you appreciate it if I did something like that to you?'

'Oh yes, I'd be ecstatic!' She handed him back the brush.

'Well go on, what should I get her? What would you like if it was you?'

'I don't know. I'm hardly an expert am I? How about some flowers?'

George thought for a moment. 'Yeah, that'll do. I'll get some at the stall outside the station. I can park there and grab them quick. Wish me luck.'

'Good luck.'

'Right, I MIGHT see you later. Then again, HOPEFULLY I might not! Will you be alright here on your own?'

'Course I will. I've had enough practice.'

'You won't get bored and eat, will you?'

'No, I'm past that stage, I think. It's been hard to shift the weight that I put on over Christmas.'

'Okay, 'bye then.' He hesitated, then he kissed her on the end of her nose, gave her a little wave and left.

With a sigh, Candy switched the television on and sat down. Football. She pressed the remote. An opera. She pressed it again. Halfway through an old film. A boring documentary. Some stupid fly-on the-wall programme with future one minute wonder stars making complete fools of themselves. A bit like me, Candy thought, switching it off. Maybe one day I'll be invited onto some of these programmes for forgotten celebs who nobody remembers.

She stood up and walked round the boxes. She took a Sylphie Super Choc-Chip Crunch out of a box. Tearing it open, she bit into it and pulled a face. Edward was right, it did taste like cardboard.

Wandering into the kitchen she threw it into the bin and then washed up the few things in the sink. She reached up and opened a corner cupboard door. Chocolate digestives! Real ones, hiding in the back! Nearly a whole packet!

She slammed the door shut, then she opened it again. The packet seemed to glow in the dark corner. She was sure she could hear a little voice squeaking Eat me! Eat me!

Just one wouldn't hurt! Surely she was entitled to a little reward for all the hard work she'd done. She'd put in an extra half an hour at the gym.

Oh the ecstasy! The heavenly taste of that chocolate melting in her mouth! And the delicious oaty contrast of the biscuit!

She was on her third one when she heard the front door shut.

***

George bought a bunch of assorted carnations. He buried his nose in them and sniffed. Lovely! Guaranteed to melt the most hard-hearted female!

He parked his car outside Penny's house.

Candy was right; he only had to explain everything and Penny would fall about laughing. Imagine him with Candy! What a stupid idea! And imagine him with Candy and Penny together! There wouldn't be much room in the bed, would there?

Personally, George wasn't into threesomes. It was too much hard work. And the rest of the night was really uncomfortable. Women took up so much room in bed!

Silly girl, she must have been tired last night, after her journey from Switzerland. Tired and touchy.

Clutching the flowers, he walked up the path and rang the bell.

Penny answered the door at once, wearing a short pink dressing-gown, a towel wrapped round her head. Ah good, she must have been looking out for him! There he was at home thinking that she didn't want to see him any more, and all the time she was waiting; hoping that he'd come along and sweep her off her feet. The poor girl!

George grinned lecherously. 'Hello Penny,' he smirked, holding out the bouquet, 'I've brought you a present, to say sorry for your little misunderstanding yesterday.'

'Fuck off!' she yelled and slammed the door, slicing the tops off the flowers and leaving him clutching a handful of stems.

George stared down at them, then he opened the letterbox. 'You might as well have the rest of it!' he shouted, then he posted them through the door, stuffed the wrapping paper after them and stormed off down the path, his wounded pride slightly repaired.

He fumed with anger all the way home, and he was still fuming when he pushed his key in the door and opened it.

He thought he heard a cupboard door bang shut in the kitchen and Candy appeared. He briefly noticed that she had a guilty expression on her face.

'Hello, you're back early,' she said, 'How did it go?'

'I don't want to talk about it,' he snarled, pushing past her in the narrow lane between the boxes. 'The stupid bitch!' he added, going into the kitchen, 'And your flowers idea was rubbish!'

'Well I told you that I'm no expert,' Candy said, walking upstairs.

Vaguely, George thought that she definitely looked a little bit guilty. Perhaps because she'd given him the wrong advice.

He turned the kettle on to make a coffee and reached into the cupboard for his secret store of digestives. Funny, he could have sworn that there were more of them in the packet... Candy! Oh no! She was getting cravings. He'd have to watch her more carefully. Bloody women. They're all trouble, he thought as he drank his coffee and crunched on a biscuit, feeling sorry for himself. Then he went to the drinks cupboard and poured himself a brandy, tipping some of it in his coffee cup.

***

She woke up. She'd been dreaming that she was playing Gretel in a pantomime, wearing a floral dress and with two long blonde plaits. But the gingerbread house had been real. And she was chewing on the window-sill. Oh, she could still taste it! If only she could just nod off and carry on with the dream! All that lovely food, and with no calories!

It was no good, she just couldn't go back to sleep. Her stomach was rumbling too much. She was starving and she kept picturing those delicious chocolate digestives downstairs, hiding in the cupboard.

What was that noise? It sounded like that tiny voice, calling her name; 'Candy! Oh, Candy! We're here, waiting for you!'

Candy closed her eyes. She could see the packet of biscuits. It had a pair of red, glowing eyes and two biscuits formed a mouth.

'Ooh, Candy,' it said, 'Bite me! Suck me! Lick me! Taste me! Feel that chocolate oozing between your teeth! Crunch those crumbs, baby!'

Just one more, that was all she wanted, just one more. And a glass of cold milk, sliding down her throat. She'd work harder at the gym tomorrow. Nobody would know that she'd strayed off her diet. Surely a couple of biscuits couldn't do any harm!

Candy heaved herself quietly out of the bed. Her voluminous nighty billowed around her like a hot-air balloon. She tiptoed barefoot along the landing to George's room and listened outside the door. He was snoring gently. Good, he was flat out. She tiptoed back to her room, put on her slippers and her oriental dressing-gown, and tiptoed back along the landing towards the stairs. And bumped straight into George.

It was impossible! A few seconds ago he was unconscious to the world, and now he was standing at the top of the stairs, dressed in his boxer shorts, grinning at her with his arms folded.

'Going somewhere, Candy?' he demanded.

'Um, er, yes. I just couldn't sleep, so I thought I'd go downstairs where I wouldn't disturb you, and, er, have a glass of water and do some exercises to help me to relax and make me tired.'

'Oh, good idea,' said George sadistically, 'Well I can't sleep either, so I'll come down and have a coffee and give you a bit of encouragement.'

'Oh, um, good,' said Candy.

SUNDAY 9th JANUARY

202lbs / 14st 6lbs / 91.6kgs

'So I'm through with women. Finished completely with them.'

'Does that mean that now I don't need to buy a reinforced, slow-closing front door after all, George?'

'Yes it does, Digby. Women are nothing but trouble. They always think you've said something that you never said at all – that's if they take the time to listen!'

'Yes, and they twist your words round to give it a completely different meaning to what you originally said. But they never admit it!'

'Quite right, Rodders. I'm sick of it. Women are just too much hard work. My Dad was right. I'm going to remain completely celibate now and concentrate on work that earns me a living. As from now I'm totally dedicated to the Candy Campaign.'

'Are you sure about that, George?'

'Yes Stefan, positive. Why, what's wrong?'

'How long did you leave Candy alone for yesterday?'

'An hour, more or less. That's all. Why?'

'Her weight's up again this morning. I'm keeping her at the Sweat Shop all day, and I've got my staff giving her the full works – exercise, massage, a swim, and more exercise. I think she's reached a fed-up stage, or a plateau. She mustn't be left alone again, not for a minute. She must have got upset or bored when you went out.'

'I had a suspicion that she was up to something while I was round at Penny's,' said George, 'I think she may have helped herself to some of my Chocolate Digestives while I was out.'

'Perhaps she's fallen for you, George and she was jealous,' Rodney suggested helpfully.

'Oh no,' George groaned, 'That's impossible!'

'Why?' added Edward, 'Because she's overweight? She's still a female with feelings, you know. And they're the most dangerous.'

'And she's developing into a lovely girl,' Stefan said.

George groaned again. 'Well she's never given any signs of fancying me, thank God!'

'Would you have noticed if she had?' asked Stefan.

***

'It's absolutely amazing how this stuff keeps selling,' laughed Rodney, filling in the paperwork.

Edward nodded. 'I sold fifty quid's worth of Sylphie's Pasta Joke to Ricci's Ravioli Bar this afternoon, plus six cases of Sylphie Special Wine Taste-Alike and I could hardly keep a straight face while I explained it!'

Stefan agreed. 'I have it in Reception, and nearly all my clients buy something on their way out, to nibble on the way home. We've become a nation of nibblers!'

George handed the men another can of lager each and sat on a pile of boxes. 'This is dead cushy. When I think of how my poor old man flogged himself for years!' He raised his can. 'Here's to work!'

'To work,' they all chanted and clinked cans.

'-Well, to easy work,' Rodney added.

They hardly glanced in Candy's direction as she squeezed past them and said, 'Just going for an evening jog. Won't be long.'

'That tracksuit from Activity's a bit loose on Candy now,' Edward commented, 'You'd better ask them for another one.'

'Does she usually go for an evening jog?' Stefan asked.

George nodded. 'Sometimes, I think, when there are crowds of them pounding the pavements. About eightish, before all the muggers come out for the night. Why, what's the time now?'

'Nine.'

'Well she's been acting a bit erratic lately,' said George, 'I think she might feel guilty for scoffing some of my chocolate digestives last night.'

They all looked at each other and raced for the door.

They rushed outside, reached the corner and spotted Candy running along the pavement.

'Candy!' George yelled.

She glanced back and increased her pace. The four friends hared down the road, but even the overweight Candy could easily outrun them. None of them were used to running. They couldn't narrow the gap at all. In fact, she was getting further ahead.

'No, don't!' they all yelled as she turned left, crossed the road and disappeared into Happy Micky's Meatyburger Bar.

By the time they caught up she was coming out of the door, raising a Mightyburger up to her mouth. Alarm crossed her face when she saw them. She sank her teeth in the burger, trying to chew fast and run away at the same time.

George leaped at her, grabbing her round the knees in a rugby tackle, and they both fell over on the pavement.

'Spit it out!' he ordered her desperately, cupping his hand under her chin and trying to pull it down as they wrestled on the pavement.

'Urg, ook!' she spluttered, trying to chew and wriggle free.

A police car slowed down, glanced at them and then drove off.

'Her nose! Grab her nose!' Stefan urged.

George did. 'Give! Spit it out!' he yelled.

A smart, elegantly-dressed middle-aged lady stepped daintily over the two wrestlers' legs, completely ignoring them as though she saw sights like that every night. Her white French poodle walked up their bodies and down the other side.

Candy struggled to breathe and chew as a lad on a skateboard leaped effortlessly over them.

A small crowd had gathered on the other side of the road, watching the fight with interest.

'Grab her bun,' Rodney encouraged.

'Her what?'

'Her bun George, grab her bun.'

'Oh.' George grabbed it. 'Give!' he panted, 'Drop it!'

He wrenched the burger free from her hand and threw it in the gutter as a jogger vaulted over them, the heel of his shoe landing on George's ankle. A camera flashed.

George yelped with the pain and Candy spat chewed-up burger in his hand. Then he yelled again.

'What are you yelling about, George?' Edward asked.

'She bit me! Look, she's drawn blood!'

What am I doing here? He thought miserably, watching a stray dog sniff at the burger and reject it in disgust. I'll probably get rabies now, he thought, examining his hand.

Candy pummelled the pavement with her fists and feet. 'I want a burger!' she sobbed, 'I want a burger! I HATE Sylphie Substitutes and salads! I want a big, juicy burger!'

The camera flashed several times.

'Let's get her out of here,' Rodney urged, 'Come on George, stop lying on the pavement. Get up.'

Stefan pulled Candy to her feet almost effortlessly, put his arm round her and led her back to George's house with Candy still shouting, 'I want a burger! I'm hungry!'

The camera flashed again.

'I bet she's done wonders for our Sylphie trade,' George complained to himself as he trailed miserably along behind.

***

Sleep was impossible. She was too wound up. Every time she closed her eyes she could picture that big, juicy Mightyburger, and almost taste the flavour.

Her stomach was gurgling like bathwater going down the plughole. She just wanted to eat something small. Anything would do, even a Sylphie Super Soyaburger! Yes, she'd stick one of them in the microwave. That wouldn't do any harm, surely? After all, it was hours since her last meal so she'd probably digested that. She hadn't swallowed any of the Happy Micky Burger. She hadn't had time. Just chewing couldn't add any calories, could it?

Candy slid out of bed and tiptoed along the landing to George's room. He'd left his door slightly ajar. Good, he was sprawled on his back with his mouth hanging open. He was out cold to the world.

She tiptoed back to her room and then changed her mind about putting on her slippers and dressing-gown. So she glided along the landing again like a fat white ghost – and bumped into George.

How did he do it? He'd been completely unconscious a few seconds ago!

Candy didn't fancy a repeat performance of the night before when George had made her exercise for over an hour while he drank coffee and watched the television.

'Feeling tired now?' he'd asked maliciously when his TV programme had finished and she'd collapsed on the carpet.

Thrusting her arms out in front of her and almost closing her eyes, she tried to walk past him down the stairs as though she was sleep-walking. But George took hold of her nose and twisted it round, turning her face back the way she had come. 'Ow!' she yelled, 'Dat 'urt.'

'Oh dear, I hope I haven't woken her. It could be dangerous,' George said sarcastically as she walked back to her room, still holding her arms out in front of her. 'Goodnight Candy, sleep well,' he called after her loudly, giving a cartoon-like chuckle.

She ignored him, trying to keep up the pretence of sleep-walking. George followed her and closed her door behind her.

What was that funny noise outside her door?

'Just to make sure you don't do yourself an injury sleepwalking, I've tied some string to your door handle and attached it to my half-open door,' George called, 'So if you open your door in the night, mine will shut. Nighty-night Candy. Sweet dreams – low calorie ones, of course!'

WEDNESDAY 2nd FEBRUARY

184lbs / 13st 2lbs / 83.5kgs

'Coo-ee, only me! Here's your coffee. Your breakfast's waiting downstairs.'

'Ugh.'

'I've been for my workout with Stefan. He's not always got time to spend with me as he's got all his other personal clients. But he tries to see me several times a week.'

'Ugh.'

'One of his staff will always keep an eye on me.'

'Ugh.'

'We've got lots of mail today.'

'Ugh. Sylphie suing us yet is she, after your public performance and newspaper write-up last month? I've been expecting some reaction from them.' George lifted himself onto one elbow and reached for his coffee.

'No, they've written and said, Dear Super-Special Sylphie Slimming Sales Person,'

'Ugh.'

'Hi there!' Candy said it with a mock-American accent.

'Ugh.'

'Thanks to your Amazing Sylphie Publicity Stunt, our Sylphie Sales have increased in your area.'

'Ugh.'

'Yes, apparently lots of people have contacted the paper, inquiring about Sylphie. Isn't that great?'

'Ugh.'

'So we're sending you a Super Special Selection of Sylphie Foods at an Unbelievable Reduced Price so that you can offer Amazing Bargains to your Customers. Just pay for them as you sell them!'

'Ugh.'

'And they've enclosed a list of all the interested people who've contacted them, for us to call on. There's loads of them! Isn't that kind of them?'

'Ugh. Well they've got no-one else around here to do it for them, have they?'

'And I've had a letter from Heads You Win, the expensive hairdressers and beauticians in the High Street. They've offered me a free hair-do and make-up every week and on special occasions if they can take photos. That's good, isn't it?'

'Ugh.'

'And even better, Cuddles Boutique for Large and Little Ladies, sizes 8-28, have offered me free clothes, plus the loan of expensive outfits for special occasions, if I model for them. That's really exciting, isn't it? Nothing fits me any more. Do you realise that I've lost over three stone?'

'Ugh!' That was a happy Ugh.

'And you'll enjoy this one – Happy Micky's Meatyburger Bar has named a burger in my honour – The Amazing Low-Calorie Candyburger. And they've said that we can eat there, free of charge, every week. And they've offered me £500 to advertise for them. They want a photo of me eating a Candyburger to promote their new health-conscious range of meals.'

'Ugh.' A slightly interested Ugh this time.

'I think I'll call round there and sell him some low-calorie drinks and some Super Sylphie Substitute Snacks. I'm sure he'll be interested.'

'Ugh!'

'Oh, and there's a free jar of multi-vitamins from a health company. You'd better have them. You look as though you need them.'

'Ugh.'

'Oh George, I wish you'd show some interest! After all, you need the money too, don't you?'

'Ugh.'

THURSDAY 10th FEBRUARY

178lbs / 12st 10lbs / 80.7kgs

'Bye, see you later George. Cheerio, Candy.'

'Yeah, get the lagers lined up ready for 6ish, Rodney.'

'Close the door quietly now, Candy, or Digby will have a heart attack!'

'Yes Edward, I will.'

'See you this evening, fellers.' George strolled along beside Candy, then he stopped. 'You're doing well lately, aren't you?' he asked.

'Yes, very well. I'm 12 and a half stone today!'

'Come on,' he suggested, 'Let's go mad. Forget your Sylphie lunch. Let's go to Happy Micky's and get a couple of free burgers for our lunch, shall we? After all, they said we could have one freebie a week, and we haven't bothered yet.'

Candy's face lit up. 'Ooh, yeah, I'd like that! But how will they know who we are?'

George took hold of her elbow and steered her along. 'Don't be silly. We're famous, aren't we? Of course they'll know who we are – especially after your well-publicised demonstration of your love for their food outside their premises!'

They did. They recognised them at once. George ordered a double Mightyburger with chips, and Candy was presented with a Candyburger as though it was an Oscar.

All the staff asked her for her autograph, and photographed her with their phones, proudly holding up her Candyburger.

'You'll have to practise your signature,' George said as they walked home.

She giggled. 'Yes, I'll do lots of twirly bits.'

Candy fetched two plates out of the kitchen. 'Look, no sauces for me,' she said.

'That looks even more unappetising than this does,' he commented, biting into his burger. 'Fetch me the ketchup, will you?'

Candy picked her bun up off the plate, examined it happily and bit into it. The whole lot exploded in a cloud of crumbs, leaving her holding a thin layer of soya mince with a pickle on the top.

'Christ,' said George, staring at the mess, 'No wonder it's low-calorie!'

They both burst out laughing.

TUESDAY 9th MARCH

166lbs / 11st 12lbs / 75.3kgs

'Now come on Candy, eat your salad.'

Cupping her chin in her hand and resting her elbow on the table, Candy flicked a chickpea across the room. She sighed loudly. 'I'm fed up,' she said.

'Now don't be like that. We're in this together, aren't we? I'm suffering just as much as you are. Okay, I've got chips with my salad. And a steak. But apart from that, we've both got exactly the same meal, not counting the salad cream, and my bread roll. And my lager. And I don't need to diet, do I? I'm only doing it to keep you company.'

Candy flicked another chickpea; and another.

'Oh, come on Candy, don't be like that. You've only got to clear it up later, haven't you?'

Another chickpea went flying, hitting George on the nose.

'Sorry George,' she sighed, not looking sorry at all.

'What's up with you? What's wrong?'

Candy sighed again. 'Oh I don't know. I'm just disillusioned. I'm not losing weight so rapidly any more and- well George, it's not fair on us both, all this tension. Why don't we just forget about all this? You can have your house back. After all, you didn't want me here in the first place.'

That's true, he thought, thinking of having his home to himself again. He mentally ran through the list of jobs that he'd have to choose from. But what could he do? Then he remembered what Stefan had said in the beginning.

'Watch her until her stomach has adjusted to smaller meals. Then she wouldn't feel so hungry and she won't want to go on eating binges. And if she did? It would probably make her feel bad; like someone who has given up smoking and then fancies a quick puff.'

Would it work? Well it was worth a try.

He smiled and leaned over the table to Candy, grasping her hand. She looked confused but she kept still.

'I'll tell you what we'll do,' he said.

'What?' she asked, tensing with suspicion. But she didn't pull her hand away.

'As a special mid-diet treat, tomorrow you can have a complete break and you can eat absolutely anything you fancy.'

Her face lit up. 'What, anything?'

'Yes, anything.'

'Really? Are you sure?'

'Yes, really. I'm quite sure.'

'Ooh George, I promise I'll work extra hard afterwards!'

'I'm sure you will.'

'Can I have a fry-up? I've really missed them.'

'If you like.'

'A big one?'

'If you must.'

'And a lager?'

'Sure, why not? Let's go the whole hog, as they say.'

'A pint?'

'Two pints if you like. Hey, I didn't think you liked lager!'

'I don't. I didn't. but I really fancy one now. It must be because I've seen you lot enjoying it so much!'

I hope this works, George thought, keeping his smile on his face. He let go of her hand. 'And now you'd better clear up all these chickpeas.'

WEDNESDAY 10th MARCH

165lbs / 11st 11lbs / 74.8kgs

'How do you like your eggs in the morning?'

'Sunny side up please. Why are you singing it, George?'

'It's an old American song; by Dean Martin, I think. My Dad used to play it.'

'Who?'

'Dean – oh never mind. Unbroken? Sunny side up?'

'Yes please. Unbroken. But not too runny. And fried bread. And beans. And squidgy tomatoes. Ooh, I can hardly wait!' Candy banged her knife and fork up and down in anticipation.

'Bacon?'

'Of course. Not too crisp though.'

'How many slices would Madame like?'

'Two. No, three. Just this once, eh?'

'Oh yes, just this once.' George piled everything neatly onto a plate. He'd chosen a small one to make it look full up. Then he poured out the lager into a pint mug. He placed it in front of Candy and then looked away in disgust as she hurled salt, pepper and tomato sauce over everything.

Then she paused, knife and fork clutched in her hand. 'Why aren't YOU eating anything, George?' she asked suspiciously.

'Oh I'm not hungry at the moment,' he replied, sitting opposite her to await the results of his experiment.

I hope this works, he thought, taking a swig from a can of lager.

She rubbed her hands together. 'Ooh, what shall I have first? A little sippy, or a munchy-poos? A little sippy, I think.'

George agreed that a little sippy would be nice.

Candy picked up the glass with both hands and took a long gulp of the lager, then another one. 'Oh, heaven!' she gasped with her eyes closed and her head thrown back, 'I might get to like lager! Right, eyes down, and in we go,' she said, putting the glass down on the table.

She carved a slice of fried bread, speared egg, bacon and tomato on her fork, balanced some beans carefully on the top and levered the lot into her wide open mouth.

'Oh, oh, yummy!' she spluttered, spraying chewed-up food in George's direction, 'Yummy yummy and yummy again! Oh, what have I been missing? Oh, this is WONDERFUL!'

A trickle of egg yolk ran down her chin but she didn't notice.

George watched her with morbid fascination. He'd never seen anyone climax on a fry-up before. He hoped that he didn't look like that when he was having sex.

Candy swallowed and gulped some lager again, then she chewed on some more egg and bacon.

Her movements were definitely becoming slower. She looked down at the plate, sipped some more lager and put some more food in her mouth. She didn't look so happy any more. In fact, she looked a bit pale.

Suddenly she stood up and put down her knife and fork and dashed to the downstairs loo, while George called out, 'In a hurry aren't we?'

He listened with satisfaction to the loud retching noises coming through the door.

Candy returned, wiping her mouth with a tissue, her face a definite light green hue and she sat down. staring at her plate.

'Had enough?' asked George politely.

She glared at him weakly. 'You knew that would happen, didn't you?'

George shrugged.

'You knew I'd do that, didn't you?'

George shrugged again, trying not to smile triumphantly.

'Yeah, go on, laugh. Fatty Fosse makes a fool of herself again! I'm just a fat, greedy, ugly cow and you think it's funny, don't you?'

She stood up and rushed up the stairs, sobbing unhappily and slammed her bedroom door.

George shrugged again, listening to the muffled sounds of crying from above his head. Why were females such hard work? If he didn't give her what she wanted it was wrong and when he did give her what she wanted, that was wrong too and she still wasn't satisfied.

He picked up Candy's plate from the table and scraped the remaining food into the bin.

FRIDAY 21st MAY

149lbs / 10st 9lbs / 67.6kgs

'Could you guys do me a big favour?'

Rodney nodded. 'Of course, old chap. That's what friends are for, as they say.'

'Could you let Candy spend the day with you tomorrow? It's Grandad's 66th birthday.'

They all stopped smiling and looked at each other uneasily.

Edward spoke first. 'Oh George, of course we would normally. But we met three gorgeous girls a couple of nights ago after you'd gone home, and we're all off to Paris for a positively filthy weekend. Sorry to let you down and all that, but we really can't take her with us, can we?'

'Any other time though, old chap. As you know, we've all become rather fond of Candy,' Rodney added hastily.

'Yeah sure, thanks.'

'Why don't you take her with you, George?' suggested Stefan.

'What, to my parents' house?' George was horrified.

Stefan just shrugged and picked up his lager.

'Well everyone knows about her,' said Rodney, 'She's no big secret is she?'

'But Dad's throwing a surprise party. He's invited several of Grandad's old dealer friends and their families, and some of our Romany relatives. I've never met most of them. It's going to be great fun – or it was.' He sighed dejectedly.

'Well there you are then,' Edward smiled at him encouragingly, 'You'll hardly have to speak to her, will you? And I'm sure you'll both have a lovely time.'

'And I'm sure WE will, too,' Rodney added.

'Yeah, but just think of all that tempting, high-calorie buffet?' George protested weakly, 'I can't watch her all afternoon, can I?'

Rodney slapped him on the shoulder. 'Cheer up old chap and stop worrying. Don't forget that your family all have bets on her – except your father. I'm sure they'll keep an eye on her and make sure that he doesn't try to tempt her into eating, or drinking. So take her along with you and have a jolly good time.'

'I don't seem to have any choice, do I?'

'Oh I do feel frightfully rotten about letting you down, George,' said Edward, looking suspiciously frightfully un-rotten-feeling, 'You know that any other time we'd be glad to help you. Digby! What's this, a temperance meeting? We're all suffering from lager withdrawal symptoms over here!'

SATURDAY 22nd MAY

148lbs / 10st 8lbs / 67.1kgs

'Ooh, it was ever so nice of you to invite me, George. I've really been looking forward to meeting your family.'

'Ugh,' grunted George concentrating on his driving.

'Do I really look alright?'

'Mm,' he said without looking.

'Do you like this suit?'

'Mm.'

'I do too. I thought it was a bit of a tight fit for my figure. And a bit short with my legs. But Marie at Cuddles said it has a really good slimming effect. And after I tried it on I agreed with her. I think she's right. Don't you?'

'Ugh.'

'I love polka dot dresses, don't you? I've never dared to wear one before.'

George had never thought about it. He was always more interested in what was underneath, and how easily they undid.

'Ugh.'

Candy was wearing a navy blue fitted polka-dot dress, belted at the waist, with a matching navy jacket. She had a white carnation in the buttonhole. George had gone right off carnations since Penny had rejected him and his bouquet.

'Does my hair and makeup look OK?'

'Ugh.' George stared in front of him.

'Stevie at Heads You Win coloured it a bit lighter, and he's cut it quite short. And then Marlin did my makeup. When he'd finished and made me look in the mirror, I thought it was a bit too much at first, but then I looked again and I loved it! I couldn't believe it was me! There's not much makeup on, but it's really clever how he did it. You shall go to the ball, Cinders, I thought.'

'Ugh.'

'Ooh, I'm so excited to see what everyone thinks of me! I've spent most of my life hiding in the background, and now I want everyone to look at me! Funny that, isn't it?'

'Ugh. We're here.'

'Is this your parents' house? Oh wow, it's GORGEOUS! And so big!'

'Ugh.' George had never thought of it before. All his friends' parents had big houses.

He blasted his horn and the gates slowly opened.

'Oh you're 'ere then,' snapped Bert happily, 'Better late than never.' Then he looked Candy up and down as she stepped out of the car. 'I thought she was meant to be fat,' he said approvingly, 'Looks alright to me.'

He spoke to Candy and jerked his head towards George. 'You watch yourself with 'im. Don't know how you put up with 'im. Always was a right one, 'e was. You watch your back, luv, and make sure you keep your bedroom door locked. And talking of locks, I've got to lock all the doors. I know some of the shifty characters your Dad's invited!'

'Oh Bert, surely nobody would nick anything from my Dad!'

Bert shuffled along in front of them. 'They might not nick anything, but they'd have a jolly good nosy round the 'ouse if they had the chance. Everyone's out the back,' he said, pointing with his thumb.

The sounds of music greeted them as they walked through the house and into the garden.

Fred had ordered a marquee, professional caterers, portaloos and a group who were playing middle-of-the-road music quietly. Some guests were already dancing, with a small group of childen running around the field, playing chasing.

George took a glass of Champagne off the tray being held by a waiter, and checked to make sure that Candy didn't take one.

Another waiter held a tray of orange juice and sparkling water. Candy carefully took a glass of water. 'I don't want to spill anything on my dress,' she giggled nervously.

'GEORGIE! YOU'RE HERE!' squealed Suzie.

'Hi Sis, you look stunning!' George said, kissing his sister on both cheeks. She did. She was wearing a flouncy white dress with a small pale blue fascinator balanced on top of her blonde curls.

'Oh, and you must be CANDY!' she gasped as though Candy was a famous celebrity. 'Oh Georgie, I'm SO glad you've brought her! You look absolutely FABULOUS!' she informed the blushing Candy, taking hold of her arms and staring up and down admiringly, winning a fan for life. 'What a BEAUTIFUL suit! Come on, everyone will be DYING to meet you! Oh I'm SO glad you're doing well! Charles and I have bet an absolute FORTUNE on you, and we've been following your progress with GREAT INTEREST! Haven't we, Charles?'

'Yes,' said Charles.

She linked arms with Candy and led her towards the marquee, chatting to her as they walked.

'So when are you and Suzie going to get married?' George asked Charles as they tailed behind Suzie and Candy, carrying their Champagne.

Charles looked baffled. 'Married? Whatever for?' he replied.

George frowned. 'Well, you've been engaged for five years, and engaged couples are supposed to get married, aren't they?'

Charles's face slowly lit up. 'I say! Yes, I suppose they are! I hadn't thought of it. I say, what a marvellous idea! I'll go and suggest it to Suzie.'

Then his face fell. 'Oh dear.'

'What's wrong now?' George inquired. What could possibly be wrong?

'I don't know how we can fit it in, what with Epsom and Ascot and Henley, and the Summer fete here, and Hickstead of course.'

'Well you could get married in the autumn, couldn't you?'

'Oh yes,' cried Charles, looking happy again, 'I never thought of that! Jolly good idea!'

'Well well well, it's young George! Long time, no see! Cor, don't you look like your Dad?'

A slimmer version of Fred Senior spoke. He stood next to George's Grandad. Both men wore shirts with dark navy striped waistcoats over the top, and had flat caps on their heads. And both of them had a bottle of Brown Ale.

'George, here, you remember Tinker Tom, don't you? He taught me all I know about the scrap metal trade when I was just a boy.'

'Course I remember him, Grandad! How are you, Tom?'

'Can't complain, Son, can't complain. So where's this large lady that everyone's bet on?'

'Over there, with Suzie.'

Tom lifted his cap up and scratched his forehead. 'Cor blimey, I thought she was fat! She's a bit of alright if you ask me! What do you think, Fred?'

'Yeah, she is! So we have the honour of meeting the young lady at last, do we?'

Daph and Fred the Younger joined the group. 'So that's Candy is it?' said Fred.

'Oh George, she's lovely!' said Daph, I must go and say hello to her.'

'Yeah, and I must go and show her our delicious buffet,' Fred added.

Daph turned round and waggled a finger at her husband. 'Oh no you don't Fred Slater. I'm watching you very carefully!'

George helped himself to another glass of Champagne and walked around to see who was there. He vaguely remembered some faces, but he couldn't recall who they were.

Candy went to inspect the lavish buffet. Out of the corner of her eye, she saw George leading a girl out of the marquee.

'So you're living with our George I hear,' said Tinker Tom, gently guiding her hand away from the vol-au-vents.

'Yes,' she admitted, 'But only for a while, until I finish losing weight.'

'Well you watch yerself with Lover Boy there.' He jerked his head at the departing George, 'Always was a randy little sod, he was.'

Candy laughed. 'No fear of that for me!'

'Why not?' asked Tom, genuinely surprised.

'Well, look at me,' said Candy, holding her arms out.

'So? I'm looking at you, ain't I?'

'Well I'm a bit on the large side, wouldn't you say?'

'So?' repeated Tom, 'A man wants a bit of meat to hug when he gets home, not a bleedin' bone! Give me something to get hold of, that's what I say, not one of them scrawny, half-starved stick insects they call fashionable today! Half of them have bigger lips than waists! Come on, let's boogy, baby!'

Putting down his bottle, he placed his hand round Candy's waist and grabbing her hand, he whirled her round in circles to the music with a bit of rock 'n roll thrown in. Candy could hardly keep up with him as she was laughing so much.

Everyone else stopped dancing to watch them, and they all laughed and clapped them. Then they started dancing again.

Gradually there were shooshing noises as Fred held his hands up for silence.

'Hello everyone, I'll keep this short-'

'Thank goodness for that!' someone called out and everyone laughed and nodded.

'It's great to see you all here today for my Dad's birthday. It's our way of showing our appreciation of everything he's done for us. In fact, he's the 2nd best Dad in the world.'

'2nd best?' asked Fred Senior.

Fred looked at his Dad. 'Well of course, I'm the best, aren't I?'

'Yeah, Suzie's lovely. Shame about George!' shouted Bert.

'George? Where is he?' Daph asked as a sheepish George appeared with lipstick on his face, followed by the girl he'd disappeared with earlier.

'Nice to see you, George!' Fred called out ruthlessly, 'Good of you to join us.'

Everyone looked round and stared at him, laughing.

'Anyway,' Fred continued, 'Please raise your glasses and drink a toast to my Dad. To Fred.'

'To Fred,' they all chanted together, drinking their Champagne.

One of the caterers came in with a cake covered in lit candles, and everyone sang Happy Birthday to you.'

'Cor, bugger me,' said Fred Senior, wiping his eyes with the back of his hand, spilling Brown Ale down his waistcoat.

Daph wiped his front with a napkin. 'Happy Birthday, Dad,' she said, kissing him on the cheek, 'Come on, blow out your candles.'

Fred made a mighty effort, and succeeded in blowing them out with several breaths. Everyone clapped and cheered him.

The group began playing louder. Some guests started dancing again, and others lined up to say goodbye to the family. They had travelled a long way to get there and had a few hours' journey home. The rest sat at tables, eating their cake or wandered around talking to old friends.

'Your son seems to have taken a fancy to my Delia, Fred.'

'My son would take a fancy to any attractive young girl, Knocker.'

Delia Dawson was one of Knocker Dawson's ten children and she was dragging George around the marquee by the hand.

Knocker Dawson had made his fortune by what was looked on in the antiques business as the lowest method of all. He'd knocked on doors and asked if they had anything to sell.

'You're a rogue, Knocker,' Fred used to tell him regularly.

'Yeah, but I'm an honest rogue,' Knocker would reply.

'How much did you pay for this clock?' Fred had asked him once as he'd paid Knocker £200 for it in his shop.

'I won't lie to yer, Fred, I paid twelve pounds fifty for it.'

'Twelve pounds fifty for this? Off some little old lady, I suppose. You ought to be ashamed of yourself, Knocker!'

Knocker acted hurt. 'Why should I be ashamed of meself? I said I'd give 'er a tenner cash for it and she said she'd bin told it was worth a lot more. Nah luv, I tells 'er, Not wiv that bit missin' off the corner. 'Oo told yer that rubbish then? 'Avin' yer on, they was. And then 'er face lights up all crafty like, and she says, Give us fifteen and yer can 'ave it. Tell yer what I'll do, luv, I says, Cos yer reminds me of me dear old departed Mum, bless 'er 'eart, I'll give yer twelve pounds fifty but I'm cuttin' me own throat and deprivin' me Missus and the kids. Done! She says, snatchin' the money out of me 'and. So she finks she's diddled me, don't she? We've all got a bit of the rogue in us, Fred. And I always leaves 'em 'appy, wiv a bit of a joke, like. And it all goes towards bringing me kids up well, know what I mean?'

One of Knocker's well-brought-up kids was tugging George out of the marquee again. He looked round to see if anyone had noticed, then they both hurried away.

Candy had noticed. She went to see what she could eat.

'Hello,' said a voice. She looked up. A man in a white coat stood watching her. He held his hand out. 'I'm Nigel, the catering manager. Well actually, It's my business. You seem to be studying the buffet carefully. Are you looking for anything in particular?'

'Oh,' replied Candy. 'It all looks delicious. But I'm wondering what I can eat that doesn't have too many calories in it.'

'I can fix you something. It'll just take about five minutes,' said Nigel.

'Are you sure? That'd be great, if it's not too much trouble. I am quite hungry now. But I'm not allowed to eat anything that's on here.'

Nigel shook his head. 'Don't you worry about that. I have to cater for all dietery needs nowadays; vegeterian, vegan, ovo-vegetarian, lacto-ovo vegetarian, pescetarian, glutein-free, wheat free, dairy free, nut allergies and a great long list of other food allergies, low calorie, low fat, coeliac, Kosher, Halal-'

'Oh dear, I never knew there were so many! And have you got anything round the back there that would suit me?'

'Leave it to me. I'm always prepared for anything,' Nigel winked, disappearing out the back to the catering marquee that was attached to the main marquee.

He was back in five minutes. 'Here you are,' he said, 'A lentilburger with lettuce instead of bread. Try it. I made it myself, and they really are delicious, though I say so myself.'

Candy took a bite, and closed her eyes with pleasure. 'Oh that's really yummy!' she gasped, 'And so juicy. It's not dry like a lot of low-calorie stuff.'

Nigel watched her with interest. 'You're that girl who everyone's been betting on to guess if you'd lose weight or not, aren't you?'

Candy nodded, unable to speak.

'Well you're looking great now!' Nigel said, eyeing her up and down, 'I think I'll have a bet on you tomorrow!'

SUNDAY 23rd MAY

150lbs / 10st 10lbs / 68kgs

'Coo-ee, only me! Here's your coffee. I thought you'd like it black this morning. And I've made you some toast.'

'Ugh,' groaned George, as usual. But this time he meant it. What had happened to his head? There was a strange thundering noise inside it and his neck muscles couldn't lift it off the pillow. He gave up trying and collapsed backwards.

'Oh, wasn't that a WONDERFUL party?' Candy gasped, 'I danced with loads of people and had a long chat at about food with Nigel, the caterer.'

'Ugh.'

'And then everyone was singing all those old songs, Roll out the barrel, The Okey-Cokey and Knees up Mother Brown. Just think, a few months ago I couldn't have got my knees up! Ooh, I had a LOVELY time! And your family's so nice. Your Mum and Dad made me ever so welcome, and Suzie took me round to meet EVERYONE!'

'Ugh,' said George. Was it his imagination or was Candy sounding like Suzie, being SO ENTHUSIASTIC about EVERYTHING?

'Pity you collapsed and passed out.'

'Ugh?'

'I haven't been to a party since I was a child you know, and not many then. Only if someone's Mum felt sorry for me. But the other children NEVER wanted to play with me or let me join in their games. Fatty Fosse they called me. Fatty Fosse. I used to cry a lot. In the end, I just said no and didn't bother going.'

'Ugh,' said George kindly.

'And I'd never danced with anyone in my life, until yesterday. Oh it was GREAT!'

'Ugh.' George felt sorrier for himself than he did for Candy at the moment. Then a thought managed to fight its way into his fuddled brain. 'How did I get home? I can't remember a thing!'

Your Dad and Bert loaded you into the back of your car and I drove us home. Oh, you were hard to get indoors. You kept stopping and talking a load of rubbish.'

Another thought surfaced as he lifted up the covers. 'Who undressed me?'

'I did. I thought you'd be more comfortable, and less likely to choke to death. Don't worry, I left your pants on and I didn't peep at anything.'

He peered at her out of one eye. She was getting very sure of herself lately. He rubbed his feet together. Oh good, she'd taken his socks off!

'Oh, and I've just read yesterday's mail. I've had an email from the TV. They want me to appear on the Paul Morgan and Sally Rhodes Breakfast Show. Isn't that FANTASTIC?'

'Ugh.'

Good, I knew you'd be pleased. Oh, I'm so EXCITED, and nervous too! Just think, me on the telly! I don't know what to say!'

'Ugh.' Why couldn't he move?

'I'm going down the gym now, for a couple of hours because it would be a miracle if I haven't put on a few pounds. Then I'm going to meet Marie at Cuddles. I spoke to her on the phone and she's opening the shop specially for me as she wants to spend time with me without being interrupted. She wants to choose something really special for me to wear.'

'Ugh. Mm.'

Right, I'll run your bath, if you can stagger that far. Don't go back to sleep and forget it or you'll have a flood. Bye!'

***

'Ugh,' said George later, emerging from the bathroom and rubbing his hair dry with a towel. Who was ringing his doorbell on a Sunday morning? It couldn't be Candy back already, and she never forgot her key. And was it his imagination or had the bell got louder?

He pulled on his tracksuit bottoms and went down the stairs to open the door as the bell rang several times again.

'Ugh,' George gasped as he opened the door and Delia Dawson burst in, flung her arms round his neck and gave him two loud kisses, which felt as though she'd punched him in the face.

'What are you doing here?' What was her name?

Delia wiggled past him and into the lounge.

'You invited me here for the day, don't yer remember, George? Oo, why've yer got boxes all over the place? Are yer moving?'

'Ugh,' George replied, tempted to say yes, he was moving today, in a few minutes, when the lorry arrived. But the words wouldn't form shapes and come out of his mouth.

'Shall we go upstairs?' Delia shrieked, grabbing hold of his hand and pulling him. 'It was fun yesterday, wannit?'

'Ugh,' groaned George, shaking his head and wishing he hadn't. Funny, he'd thought she was really pretty yesterday at his grandad's party. He hadn't noticed her loud, nasal voice then. And common! He wondered if she was a distant cousin. Was that classed as illegal?

'Where's yer bedroom then? You promised you'd show it to me yesterday.'

'Did I?'

'Yeah, don't yer remember?'

'No. And I don't feel well. In fact, I've got to go. And quick.'

He dashed up the stairs and locked the bathroom door. Then after he's thrown up he closed the lid and sat on the toilet with his head in his hands. He felt terrible, and his stomach ached.

Delia was waiting right outside the door. 'Oo, yer did have to go, didn't yer? Are you alright now? Shall we go ter bed?'

Had she been outside while he was on the loo? Well she'd know that he was genuinely ill then, wouldn't she?

George unpeeled her hands, shuffled into the bedroom and collapsed on the bed. Delia tried to fall on top of him and he turned sideways just in time. 'Look, go home now. I'm really ill,' he begged.

'Oh George, I bet you'll be alright in a minute,' she wailed. 'I'll make yer feel better!'

No he wouldn't be alright in a minute. He wouldn't be alright for a long time. In fact, he might never be alright again.

George did something that he never did with females; he shouted at her.

'Get out!' he croaked loudly, wishing that he hadn't as it hurt his head. 'I'm ill. I'm suffering. Now get out and leave me alone!'

Delia stood up and pulled her skirt down, which wasn't very far as it was so short. 'OK I'm going. I know when I'm not wanted. A girl has her pride, you know.'

And she left, slamming the front door behind her.

George sighed with relief. Then he got up quick and rushed into the bathroom again.

'No more! Never more!' he groaned, opening the bathroom cabinet and taking out the Paracetamol. 'It's time to clean up my act before I die. It's just not worth the agony.' Then he went back in the bedroom and climbed into bed.

***

'Aah, that's better,' George sighed, relieved. A couple of hours' sleep had cleared his head. His stomach still felt a bit delicate, but it was more under control.

He had a cool shower, got dressed and decided to go to the Duck and Grouse. Rodney, Edward and Stefan were still in Paris, so he'd just stay for a short time. He'd enjoy a quiet hour there before coming home and going back to bed.

It was drizzling with rain, but George still opened the hall cupboard drawer and took his sunglasses out. He thought the bright daylight would hurt his eyes.

Digby poured him a lager without being asked.

'No, I-' George began, about to order a soft drink instead. But then he thought a hair of the dog would be refreshing, and help to clear his head.

'Good party was it, George?' Old Gubbins asked, staring into his pipe.

'Apparently so.' George tried to remember it, but it was all a blur.

'Yeah, Candy told us it was,' said Digby.

'When did she do that?' George asked, 'She's been out all morning.'

Surely he hadn't slept the clock round had he? It was still Sunday, wasn't it?

No, she's over there,' Digby replied, nodding across the room with his head.

George glanced behind him, then he did a double take that Tom and Jerry and Homer Simpson would have been proud of. His sunglasses dropped into his lager but he didn't notice.

Candy was sitting at a table, deep in conversation with a man. He had his arm draped over the back of her chair.

What was going on? And what was she drinking?

George stormed across, picked up her drink and sniffed it.

'What's this? Wine?' he asked.

'Of course not,' Candy retorted, 'It's a Sylphie Spritzer. George, this is Nigel-'

'Is it? And have you been eating? Has he been trying to feed you?'

'No he hasn't! He's put on a bet that I'll win. And he's got a lovely range of low-calorie food. And some good recipes too.'

'So where did you meet him? George continued.

'He was the catering manager last night.'

'Oh, was he?' George looked at Nigel for the first time. 'Well, Mate, I don't know what you put in your food, but I've had food poisoning all night.'

Nigel was furious. 'Well I can assure you that you didn't catch it from my food. What a cheek! I'm well-known for my cleanliness, I'll have you know!'

'Perhaps it was something to do with all the alcohol you consumed, George,' Candy said.

'What do you mean? I hardly drank a thing! I was too busy socialising.'

'Yes, I saw you lead her outside,' Candy shouted. 'And that was in between all your glasses of Champagne and wine. And you even had a bottle of your Grandad's Brown Ale before you collapsed.'

'That wouldn't have upset my stomach like that. I've really suffered, thanks to your food!' George yelled at Nigel.

Everyone in the pub was watching them and listening to the row.

Nigel stood up. 'Look, I'm going,' he told Candy. 'I'm not staying here having my food slagged off like that. My food's really high quality and carefully sourced locally. I've got a very good reputation, and I'm not having it ruined by HIM.' He pointed a finger at George.

'Oh, Nigel!' Candy protested, 'Don't take any notice of what George says!'

'Sorry Candy, I'll call you. And YOU'll be hearing from my solicitors,' he said to George. And Nigel left, slamming the front door.

'Ooh, look what you've done!' Candy stood up and spoke through gritted teeth with her fists clenched at her side.

'It's for your own good, Candy.'

Good? What do you mean, good? We were just having a CONVERSATION, and I don't have many of them, do I?'

George looked genuinely puzzled. 'Course you do. We hold conversations every day!'

'Yeah, right. Ugh, ugh, ugh.' Candy leaned forwards with her arms bent in front of her like a gorilla.

'That's very unfair, Candy. I've made you a welcome guest in my home-'

'Oh rub it in, why don't you? YOUR home. You never wanted me there in the first place. And that doesn't give you the right to dominate my life!'

'Dominate your life? Me? I don't know what you mean!'

Candy shook her head. 'You just don't get it, do you, George? You never have.'

'Get what? What are you on about now?'

'Oh, I give up. I'm going home – or rather, I'm going back to YOUR home. I haven't actually got a home any more, have I?'

Digby placed his hands over his ears and groaned as Candy marched to the door. But she closed it quietly behind her.

George addressed the room. 'What have I done now? Honestly, I just can't win!'

'Well you don't try very hard, do you, young George?' Old Gubbins said to his pipe.

'I don't know what you mean! I've been trying hard ever since my Dad cut off my allowance!'

Old Gubbins looked at George. 'She's a lovely girl, and you should be nicer to her or you're going to lose her if you're not careful.'

'Lose her? What do you mean?' George asked.

Carefully, Old Gubbins drained the tiny drop of beer at the bottom of his glass. 'Right, I'm off to milk the cows or they'll all be waiting for me and complaining.'

'That's women for you; always complaining,' sniggered George, trying to lighten the conversation. Old Gubbins looked at him, tutted, shook his head and waved goodbye to Digby.

George fished his sunglasses out of his lager and drank it.

'Another, George?' Digby asked, picking up a clean glass.

'No thanks. I'd better go home and get sulked at!'

'That's right, you go home to the Little Wife,' said Digby. Everyone laughed.

'She's not my wife and she never will be,' George snapped, 'Honestly, I don't know why I bother coming in here.'

'Well don't stop coming, George,' Digby shouted, 'We'd miss the entertainment!'

***

George opened his front door and paused. He could hear sounds of movement upstairs in Candy's bedroom.

He stood still and listened, suddenly feeling a bit apprehensive, wondering if he'd pushed her too far.

'Candy! Candy! Come down and talk, will you?' He hesitated, waiting for a reply. 'Candy!' he called again.

She came down, carrying two suitcases.

'Going home to Mother are you?' George sneered.

'Yes,' she snapped, 'YOUR Mother.'

'MY mother?' Blinking cheek, he thought.

'Yes. My mum would wreck the whole thing. She'd keep saying I told you so! Then she'd try to cheer me up by feeding me great big helpings of puddings and things. Your mother said I could stay with your parents until I find somewhere permanent to live on my own. She said they've got plenty of room. Goodbye, George.'

She squeezed past him and all the Sylphie boxes and staggered along the hall, dragging the cases.

'Candy, wait! You don't need to go.'

Candy turned, resting the cases on the ground. 'No George, I've been nothing but a nuisance to you. I'm sorry, and grateful for all the things you've done for me, even though you didn't really want to do it. I'll find somewhere to store all the Sylphie boxes tomorrow and I'll still pay you your share. So you can have your home back now.'

'Candy-'

'Aah, here's my taxi. Goodbye George.'

And she'd gone.

WEDNESDAY 2nd JUNE

145lbs / 10st 5lbs / 65.8kgs

'Right you lot, I've got a load of bacon sandwiches ready for sale, and free tea and coffee set out in the other bar.'

'Did I hear Digby say Free?' someone called out.

'Yes I did, and don't be so cheeky! And those of you who want a drink at the bar, you've got 10 minutes to come and get it and settle down before it starts. I've never opened up so early in my life!'

The Duck & Grouse was packed. Everyone had come to watch Candy on the TV. They could have watched it at home, but the atmosphere in the pub was more fun.

There were three large televisions in different parts of the bar fixed high up on the walls so that everyone could have a clear view. They were used for important sports events or to watch the news sometimes. Digby didn't allow them to be on all the time. He said it spoilt the atmosphere.

As the ads came to an end there was lots of shooshing and everyone found a seat or somewhere to stand where they had a good view and didn't block anyone else's view.

'Why weren't you invited, George? Rodney asked.

George shrugged. 'I don't know. I wouldn't want to be on the telly anyway.'

His friends sucked in through their teeth, not believing him.

'Well it's true,' George continued, 'Imagine what time I'd have had to get up! Anyway, I expect Candy will mention my name.'

The theme tune played and Paul Morgan smiled at the camera. Sally Rhodes was sitting beside him.

'Right then,' he said, 'And now we have an interesting guest. She has to lose half her original weight to win a bet, and she's been doing very well so far. But can she keep it up? Or down, I mean? Let me introduce Miss Candy Fosse.'

Another camera showed Candy, and all the customers gasped. She'd been professionally made up and had her hair done. She was wearing a black silk dress with pink roses that lightly skimmed her body.

'Blimey, is that our Candy?' Frank gasped, 'She looks like a celebrity!'

'She IS a celebrity!' someone else called out.

'Welcome to the studio, Candy,' Paul continued.

Candy smiled slightly nervously. 'Thank you,' she said.

'So tell us your story. How did all this start?'

I'm not quite sure,' Candy replied, thinking, 'I'd just walked out of my job, and suddenly I became the subject – or rather, the object of a bet.'

'Why did you walk out of your job, Candy?' Sally asked.

Candy stopped smiling. 'Everyone was laughing at me, as usual. They were either laughing, or they just ignored me. I was their figure of fun again. Often cruelly. So I walked out.'

'You mean, your figure made you a figure of fun?' Sally added

'Exactly.'

'Let's see what you looked like at the beginning of this bet,' said Paul. A large photo of the old Candy appeared on the screen and everybody in the invited audience gasped.

'Well you look absolutely amazing now,' Sally said.

'Had you tried to diet before? Paul asked.

Candy shook her head. 'Not really. I loved my food too much. And I used it as an escape when I felt miserable.'

'Did you drink at all?' Sally asked her.

'No, I never fancied alcohol. I drank fizzy drinks with my food. You see, it wasn't my size that bothered me. I just wanted to be treated like a human being. I hated being ignored.'

'Did being obese affect your health much?' Sally said.

'No, not at all. I'd hardly been to the doctor in my life! I never missed a day's work, but some of them went sick if they broke a nail!'

There were sounds of laughter in the studio.

Candy continued. 'I was good at my job, but a couple of them were promoted when they weren't half as good as me! One of them was often invited on overnight trips to meetings with the Director.'

'Oh was she?' grinned Paul, looking at the camera.

'Well I think it's terrible how badly women are still being treated and passed over for promotion in their jobs, no matter how good at it they are,' Sally said angrily.

Paul held his hands open and looked at the camera. 'You see, the trouble here is, we men just can't win. If we chat women up, we're in trouble. And if we don't, that's wrong too!'

'Oh Paul, it's not like that at all!' Sally protested, 'It's completely unfair that women are promoted for their looks over unattractive women - if you don't mind me saying that, Candy - who are much better at their jobs!'

'Well there's no fear of that now,' Paul said, hastily changing the subject. 'You're looking marvellous, Candy.'

He stared into the camera. 'Stay with us. We'll be back after the break to talk some more to Candy Fosse, who has lost a lot of weight for a bet and completely transformed her appearance.'

Everyone began talking at once. A lot of them headed for the bar. Some of them went to get a free cup of tea or coffee.

'Quick, four lagers over here, Digby, for the Management Team!' called Rodney.

The shushing started again as the adverts stopped and the theme tune began playing.

'Welcome back,' said Paul Morgan, 'Today we have a very interesting guest, Miss Candy Fosse, who, like 'Enry

'Iggins and Liza Dolittle, is the subject of a bet. Candy's bet is that she can or can't lose half her weight in a year.'

'Candy,' Sally asked, 'Would you mind telling us how much you originally weighed?'

The camera switched to Candy.

'Well, on Tuesday 16th November last year, I weighed 236lbs, or 16st 12lbs, or 107kg.'

And what do you weigh today, Candy?'

I weigh 145lbs, that's, um, let me think, 10st 5lbs, or 65.7kgs.'

Sally glanced at Candy and then the camera. 'That's a total loss of 6st 7lbs. I can't work it out in kilos.' She looked aside. 'Can anyone help me with this?'

'Just over 41kgs,' someone off-camera called out.

'And is there an 'Enry 'Iggins behind your success?' asked Paul.

'Oh yes-' Candy smiled.

George grinned and lifted his lager in a salute to the room.

'-In fact I've got four of them!' Candy continued.

Rodney, Edward and Stefan all elbowed each other in the ribs. George just stood there.

'What do you mean, you've got four of them?' Paul said.

'Well, George is the main one, with the help of his friends Rodney, Edward, and Stefan, who runs the gym where I work out every day. They all keep an eye on me, and they've kept me on the straight and narrow, so to speak.'

'And of course, they've all bet on you to win,' Paul laughed.

Candy nodded, smiling.

'Do you think working out is very important, Candy?' asked Sally.

'Oh yes, especially when you lose as much weight as I have, or I'd have rather a lot of excess skin! With exercise I've been getting in shape as well as losing weight.'

'How much more have you got to lose, Candy?' Paul asked her.

'Just over two stone.'

'And do you think you'll manage to do it? You seem to have plenty of time left.'

'It seems like it, but my weight loss has slowed right down now. And I am eating a little more, to get me adapted to eating normal meals.'

Sally looked concerned. 'Do you think you're pushing yourself too hard, Candy, and your body's protesting now?'

'Oh no. It's natural to slow down at this stage. And I'm still a bit overweight for my height and bone structure, so losing a bit more won't do me any harm. Some of my fat is turning to muscle. And I eat healthily and of course I have plenty of exercise.'

Paul put on his serious face. 'But what comes next, Candy?'

Sally glared at him. 'What do you mean?'

I mean, when she reaches her target weight and everyone collects their winnings. What will you do when it's all over, Candy?'

Candy shook her head. 'I'm not sure yet. I've had several offers for modelling jobs. I'm going to wait and see. I've still got time to think about it. Maybe I'll write a book about my experiences. I'll need to get an agent for that.'

'Well thanks for coming in, Candy, and we wish you all the best,' said Sally.

'Yes,' Paul agreed, 'And I bet you'll never be ignored again!'

SATURDAY 12th JUNE

140lbs / 10st / 63.5kgs

'Morning Bert.'

'Hello Bert, old chap.'

'Bert.'

'Hello Bert.'

Bert sniffed. 'That's five pounds each, please.'

George was horrified. 'But Bert, I live here!'

'No you don't. You live in town.'

'Well it's my family home.'

'And this is the Summer Fete. Five pounds or you don't come in.'

Rodney took a 20 pound note out of his wallet. 'Here you are Bert, take this for all of us. Are my parents here yet?'

Bert pointed. 'Bin here since six o'clock this morning, running about like maniacs. Which is more than can be said for some people I know.'

Rodney patted Bert on the shoulder as they passed through the gate and into the field. 'Well it's only half-past ten. That's not bad going for us, is it?'

Bert just gave one of his disapproving sniffs.

'Have YOU paid, Bert?' George called when he was safely out of range.

'Go on, git out of it!' Bert growled, shaking an elbow at him.

'I say, I love these fetes, don't you?' Edward exclaimed happily as they wandered past all the stalls, selling everything from ethnic food to tractors.

'Yes, great fun,' George agreed, 'And it's a lovely day too.'

'Thank goodness. I hate wading through mud,' said Rodney.

'Right, I'm off to find our stand,' Stefan told them. 'I'd better make sure the staff are pulling their weight, so to speak, demonstrating what we do to everyone and selling subscriptions. I'll see you guys later. Where will you be?'

'Oh Stefan, Stefan, Stefan, where do you think we'll be? In the beer tent of course!' Rodney declared, 'We'll see you there at oneish, okay?'

Stefan nodded and went to find the Sweat Shop stand.

'I'd better try and find Suzie,' George said, 'She'll be down the bottom of the field with her horses.'

'With brother Charles, of course. I'll come along and say Hi,' Rodney added, following him.

It took them a long time to reach the end of the next field as they kept meeting people they knew, and trying free food and drink samples.

By the time they found Suzie and Charles they were wearing baseball caps and carrying balloons and bags full of leaflets and special offers.

Suzie looked up from grooming her horse. Charles was leaning on the door, watching her. 'GEORGIE!' she squealed as though she hadn't seen him for months.

'Hello Suzie.'

'Hi there, Suzie. You look gorgeous as usual, even in jodhpurs and a shirt,' said Edward.

'Do I?' Suzie opened her large eyes even wider. She patted her horse and came out of the stable, bolting the door behind her.

'You certainly do,' Rodney agreed, kissing her on both cheeks, 'I shall enjoy having you as a sister-in-law. You're a lucky man, Charles.'

'Yes,' agreed Charles, adjusting his check cap.

'Oh, we've got some REALLY IMPORTANT news to tell you, haven't we Charles?'

'Yes,' said Charles, nodding and smiling.

'We're getting married in September. Isn't it EXCITING!'

'Yes,' agreed Charles.

Suzie, that's great!' gasped George, 'We never thought you'd get round to it!'

'And guess where we're going to spend our honeymoon!'

'We can all guess that!' Edward laughed.

'Can you?' Suzie opened her eyes even wider. 'I thought it would be a BIG SURPRISE!'

George put his arm round her. 'Go on, tell us where you're going. Edward was only teasing.'

'Was he? Oh. We're going pony trekking through Morocco, for a WHOLE MONTH! Oh it'll be SUCH FUN! Won't it, Charles?'

'Yes,' agreed Charles.

The other three glanced at each other, unable to believe what they'd been told.

'Sounds like great fun,' Edward managed to say.

'Especially for a honeymoon,' George added dryly.

'That's what we thought. We're really looking forward to it SO MUCH, aren't we darling?' Suzie gasped, smiling at Charles.

'Yes,' said Charles, smiling lovingly back at her.

'Won't you have sore bums?'

'Georgie! We're used to riding for ages.'

Everyone bit their lip and avoided making eye contact.

'Oh!' squealed Suzie, grabbing hold of Charles's hand, 'It's the children's races! We're judges. We'll see you later for lunch. Must hurry! Bye-ee! Come on, Charles.'

'Yes,' said Charles as she dragged him along.

The three friends trecked slowly uphill back to the upper field, sampling more food and drinks on the way.

'Good gracious, look over there!' gasped Edward, pointing.

'My word, it's Candy!' Rodney exclaimed, 'Doesn't she look a picture?'

Candy was strolling ahead of them. She was wearing a pale cream floral dress, belted at the waist and slightly flared. On her head was a wide-brimmed straw hat with a ribbon round the brim.

'Candy!' called George as Rodney and Edward were accosted by two promotions girls and led into their woodburning stand, where they were fed sparkling wine and smoked salmon sandwiches.

She turned and slowed down. George caught her up. 'Hello,' he said, smiling at her.

'Hello,' she replied, smiling back.

They ambled along together in silence for a while.

'It's nice here.'

'Lovely day.'

They spoke together and laughed.

'Go on, you first,' invited Candy.

'No, you. Ladies first.'

She smiled up at him. 'I was just saying it's nice here, with all the stalls and events and things. Go on, now it's your turn.'

'And I was just saying what a lovely day it is.'

'Yes, it is,' she agreed. They strolled along together in silence again.

'Candy.'

'Yes?'

'Where are my grey trousers? I can't find them anywhere.'

Candy looked ahead of her again. 'I took them to the cleaner's. You got them filthy when you collapsed at your Grandad's party. The ticket's in the drawer by the front door.'

They paused as they were handed a free newspaper.

'Candy.'

'Yes?'

'Where's my grey Paisley shirt?'

She sighed. 'In your wardrobe on the right-hand side, next to your pink one.'

'Oh, thanks.'

They reached the end of the row of stalls. A giant oak tree cast a welcome shade in front of it and they both stopped, enjoying the coolness.

'Candy?'

'Yes George?'

George gently took hold of her shoulders, pulling her towards him. She looked up at him queryingly, her lightly made-up face haloed by her hat. He gazed into her eyes. She gazed back. 'Oh Candy,' he whispered huskily.

She looked up into his eyes. 'Yes George?' she breathed.

George paused and looked down at her. 'Oh Candy, please come back. I can't find a bloody thing!'

Her eyes shot daggers at him. 'Ooh!' she snarled, wrenching her shoulders from his grasp. She stomped away angrily without looking behind her.

Spreading his arms out wide, George addressed the tree. 'Christ, what's up with her?' he demanded of the wise old oak. But the tree didn't reply.

'I say, what's this, some pagan ceremony?'

George spun round. 'Oh hello, Edward. You made me jump. No, it's that Candy. Honestly, I don't know what's up with her. She can be so moody sometimes.'

Edward shrugged. 'Well what can you expect? She's a female, isn't she?'

'And how did you two get on?' George asked them as they aimed instinctively for the beer tent, 'Did they sell you any woodburning stoves?'

'No,' Rodney smirked, 'But they were completely bowled over by our charm. We're meeting them both in the beer tent.'

'Yes,' Edward added, 'I need to discuss wood burning stoves with Stacy in private. I've been thinking about getting one fitted in my cottage.'

'Since when?' George snorted in disbelief.

'Since she said she'd come round and have a look at my flu.'

'I bet she gets to see more than your flu,' George laughed.

They passed Candy, who spotted them and turned away, pretending to be engrossed in examining dog leads on a stall.

'Oh hello Candy. Come and have a drink.' Edward grabbed her round the waist and half-dragged her along with them, while she glared at George over her shoulder. But George didn't notice. He was talking to Rodney about woodburning stoves.

'Ah, the layabouts have arrived. Three more lukewarm lagers please. And you'd better make them pints. It takes so long to get served here!'

'Hello Dad,' said George.

'Hello Son. And what would you like, Candy?'

'Gin and slimline tonic please.' She glared defiantly at George as she talked to Fred.

'Candy, do you think you should?' asked George.

She tossed her head, slightly dislodging her hat. 'I'll do what I like. It's a free world,' she snapped, tugging her hat back into place.

'You're in a right mood today, aren't you?'

'No I'm not. It's you.' She sipped her gin and pulled a face, then she sipped it again.

Rodney put his arm round her waist. 'Tell us what George has been doing to upset you now, Candy,' he soothed.

'Me?' wailed George, 'Why does everyone always blame everything on me?'

'Because it's always your fault, George!' Fred shouted over the noise in the tent.

'Fred!'

'Well it's true, Daph, isn't it?'

'Yes, but you don't need to say so.'

'Mum!'

'What's the matter, son?'

'Oh what's the use? Shall we get some food?'

Everyone queued up at the buffet and loaded their paper plates with chicken legs, dainty sandwiches and slices of gateau.

Nigel spotted George and walked behind the buffet table until he was facing George.

'I'm watching you,' he said menacingly, pointing a finger at him, 'There's absolutely nothing wrong with my food, and don't you dare say there is!'

'No,' George agreed, 'It all looks very nice. Excuse me.' And he hastily kept on walking.

'I'll pay for this lot,' Fred told the woman on the till, 'Don't know why, but I will.'

George began to eat, and then he spotted Candy across the marquee. She was talking to a man in jodhpurs and he was handing her another gin and tonic. There was nowhere to put his plate down, so George stormed across to her, tripping in a hole in the grass and staggering the last few yards, colliding with the man.

'I say,' said the man.

'Candy!' he snapped, ignoring the man.

'What?' she snapped back.

'Give me that gin at once. You've had enough to drink.'

'I will not!'

'I say-' said the man again.

'You keep out of it!' George told him. The man quietly walked away.

'Give me that glass!' George ordered Candy.

'Mind your own business.' She raised the glass to her lips and had a sip. She pulled a face, but she had another sip.

'It IS my business! Give me it!' George shouted, pulling it away from her.

'Get off, George!' Candy pulled it back and George pulled harder, wrenching it out of her grasp. Gin and tonic shot all down the front of his pale blue shirt, and a slice of lemon peeped out of the top of the shirt.

He groaned and Candy put her hand up to her mouth. Reaching in her handbag, she took a tissue out and dabbed at his shirt, removing the lemon slice. She undid a couple of buttons and wiped his chest while he held his shirt open.

'Oh,' sighed George, 'as if I haven't got enough washing to do!'

'Sorry, George,' grinned Candy. Then they looked at each other and burst out laughing.

'Please move back home Candy, won't you?' George pleaded.

'Alright then,' Candy smiled, 'I'll come back if you really want me to. But only until I reach my target weight. Then you'll win your bet and I'm going off to do something with my life. Agreed?'

'Agreed. Here, have a chicken leg.'

THURSDAY 17th JUNE

138lbs / 9st 12lbs / 62.6kgs

'Coo-ee, only me.'

'Ugh. Morning.'

That surprised Candy. Two words, in the morning!

'Here's your coffee,' she continued. Can I borrow the car? Your Dad said I could store the Sylphie boxes in one of his sheds.'

'Ugh,' Which meant yes.

'There aren't many left as our customers usually give us their orders now so we don't need to have many boxes; just a few for samples for new customers.'

'Ugh.'

'Then I'm going to the gym, so I'll see you in the pub later, after I've got changed shall I? Unless you've got other plans – ha ha!'

'Ugh.' Oh she was getting sarky sometimes now!

***

'Hi everyone.'

'Hello Candy. What can I get you? A Super Sylphie Sherry substitute?'

'No thanks Digby. I'll have a lime and soda.'

Digby put her drink on the bar. 'And can I say how lovely you're looking? Am I allowed to say things like that any more? You have to be so careful nowadays!'

'Digby, you can call me lovely any time.'

Candy was wearing a plain royal blue Summer dress which just skimmed her hips.

'Yes, we all think you're lovely, Candy, don't we George?'

'Yes, Rodders.' But George wasn't looking at Candy. He was watching as the front door slowly opened and a head peeped round it.

It was a weaselly-looking head with greasy, slicked-down black hair with a side parting and a long, pointed nose under small, beady eyes.

George knew that you shouldn't pre-judge people on first impressions; especially since he'd known Candy.

But his first thought was that he'd never buy a second-hand car from this person.

The rest of the body followed the head round the door and into the pub and a rather short man stood looking around him.

He spotted Candy and, with a relieved smile forced on his face he walked towards her.

'Candy! Aah good. There you are!' he called, as though she was an old friend that he'd arranged to meet in the pub.

Suspicious, Candy moved closer to Edward. She looked at the four men, checking their facial expressions.

She really hoped that they hadn't planned anything as cheesy as a Kissogram. The thought of this horrible little man stripping off in front of her wasn't even funny; it was repulsive.

But they all seemed to be as confused as she was.

'Excuse me, but who are you?' she inquired.

The man forced a laugh. 'Of course you don't know me, do you?' Candy shook her head. 'I'm your father! I'm your Daddy, Darling! I've come to make the acquaintance of my lovely daughter!

'My father?' gasped Candy.

'Her father? gasped George, Rodney, Edward, Stefan, Digby and half the pub.

'Yes. I saw you on the telly and I was so proud of you, and so ashamed of myself-' He lowered his head for a posed moment- 'that I thought I'd find you in here and make amends for my inexcusable absence in your life, my darling.'

He patted his chest. 'By the way, could one of you lend me twenty quid for a drink and something to eat? I seem to have left my wallet at home.'

'Oh dear, so have we,' said Rodney. He patted his jacket and so did the other three men.

Candy reached for her bag, but George grabbed it before she could take her purse out. He knew what she was going to offer to do.

The man waited expectantly, then as it was obvious that nobody was going to give him any money, he decided to introduce himself.

'By the way, my name's Colin. Colin Fosse,' he announced, holding out his hand. But nobody took hold of it to shake it, so he shrugged and lowered his arm.

'So where have you been hiding all these years – Colin? Rodney asked.

Colin was obviously relieved that someone was speaking to him. 'I'm a shoe salesman. I've been travelling all over the country.'

'Lost your way home did you?' added Edward.

'No, it was just impossible for me to live there any more,' replied Colin, who was obviously completely thick-skinned. 'Oh Candy,' he continued, 'Haven't you got lovely feet? I think I've got some shoes in my car that would really accentuate your ankles.'

He bent down, about to reach out for Candy's foot. She lifted it up and kicked him hard between the legs.

Colin collapsed, clutching his nether regions. He tried to laugh. 'Ooh, you have got a hard kick, Candy. You should have been a footballer!' Nobody laughed.

'Don't you touch me, you little creep!' Candy snarled between her teeth, 'My Mum brought me up on her own without getting a penny from you! So don't you come in here, trying to get round me as though nothing's happened. Go on, piss off!'

'Isn't it funny that you've decided to make an appearance now that Candy's a celebrity,' Stefan snarled, lifting Colin up by the back of his jacket, 'Come to pay your bill for all those missing years, have you?'

'No, I-' Colin spluttered.

'Well as Candy said, go on, piss off – or would you like some help?' Stefan added, looming threateningly over the little man.

'Candy?' Colin pleaded to his newly-discovered daughter. But she turned her head away and picked up her drink. 'The door's over there,' she said.

'Okay, I know when I'm not wanted,' said Candy's dad, backing towards the door.

He turned and hastily disappeared. And that's the last time that anyone ever saw him.

SATURDAY 10th JULY

134lbs / 9st 8lbs / 60.8kgs

'Coo-ee, only me.'

'Ugh.'

'Oh George, you look so funny in the mornings!'

'Ugh.'

'Here's your coffee.'

'Ugh.'

'I'm off to the gym for an hour, then I've got an appointment at Mother Nature Knows Best, that health food shop in town.'

'Ugh.'

'They want an article about me in their monthly magazine that they give away in their shop, so we're going to discuss the price they're going to pay me.'

'Ugh.'

'I'm not doing any of these things for free any more. They know now that if they want me, they've got to pay me.'

'Ugh.'

'I'll tell you what happens later, in the pub.'

'Ugh.'

'Right, I'll run your bath and cook your breakfast.'

'Ugh.'

'Don't you think you should lay off the fry-ups? You're getting a bit of a beer belly.'

'Ugh.' Beer belly? I am not, he thought.

'Maybe you should have a bowl of meusli instead.'

'Ugh.' And he meant it.

'Okay, how about a couple of poached eggs on toast then?'

'Ugh,' George agreed.

'Right, that's settled then. See you later. Bye!'

'Ugh.'

***

'Aah, here's Candy. Four more of your delicious lagers, Digby, and a White Wine Sylphie Substitute for the young lady.'

'There you go, Rodders. I-'

'What's the matter Digby? Have you had a fit?

'No George, it's-' and Digby nodded towards the door.

'Yoo-hoo Candy! Coo-ee boys!'

They all turned and stared with their glasses still untouched on the bar.

'That's your mother – isn't it?' muttered George.

Candy gawked. 'I think so.'

It was. A completely transformed Mrs Fosse. Her hair had been cut very short and tinted pink at the edges, she wore huge dangly hoop earrings and pink lipstick, black calf-length leggings clinging desperately to her legs, stretched to straining point, she balanced on very high stiletto heeled shoes and she wore a low-cut tee-shirt with a glittery picture of a Beryl Cook-type voluptuous female in a scanty bikini, sprawled on a sun lounger, sipping a large cocktail with a parasol in it through a straw, a huge sun hat and pointy sunglasses, and one large leg crossed over the other with a stiletto-heeled sandal dangling off her foot. Underneath was written Big is Beautiful.

But Mrs Fosse's appearance wasn't the only shock; she was clutching the arm of a very good-looking man, at least 10 years younger than her, and three inches shorter, due to her high heels.

If this was a film, it would now turn black and white, and everyone would be frozen with their glasses halfway to their lips and their mouths hanging open.

What really happened was, the usual loud noise slowly dropped to a murmur and then silence as everyone gradually became aware of her presence. And then they all froze with their glasses halfway to their open mouths.

‘There’s my daughter,’ Mrs Fosse informed her companion, dragging him across the room.

‘Hello Mum,’ Candy managed to say.

‘Hello Candy. Hello boys. I’d like to introduce you to Grant, my fiance.’

‘Fiance?’ gasped Candy, George, Rodney, Edward, Stefan, Digby, and some of the nearest customers in unison.

‘Well I’m blowed!’ said Old Gubbins to his pipe.

‘Yes, isn’t he COOCHY?’ Candy’s mother pinched his cheek. ‘Ooh, that Sylphie diet certainly worked wonders for me!’

‘But Mum, you haven’t lost any weight!’ Candy wailed, completely confused.

‘I know, but who cares? You don’t, do you, Granty-wanty?’

‘Of course I don’t, Flossy-wossy,’ he replied with his arm halfway round her waist, squeezing a handful of flesh, ‘You’re my big cuddly-wuddly girly-wirly, aren’t you?’

‘Oh, hoo hoo!’ Candy’s Mum giggled coyly.

‘So where did you two meet?’ Rodney asked.

Candy’s Mum giggled again. ‘Grant moved next door a couple of months ago. We got chatting in the garden, and he bought a load of Sylphie products off me.’

‘You don’t actually need to slim, Grant, do you?’ said Stefan, looking at his thin frame.

‘No,’ Grant agreed, ‘But I was too shy to ask her out, even though it was love at first sight.’

Everyone checked his eyes for defects.

‘So Grant kept buying more and more Sylphie products until I asked him why he wanted them all!’

‘And then I admitted that I was in love with her-’

'-And we've been together ever since!' Candy's Mum held her left hand out and flashed her large engagement ring, that had obviously cost a lot of money.

'What do you do for a living, Grant?' Edward asked. It was obvious that Grant wasn't short of money.

'I'm in the property business. My Grandfather started it, my Father enlarged it even more, and now I run it. We build houses, we rent property, and we sell it too.'

'So what will we call you after you're married, Mrs Fosse?' Rodney inquired.

Candy's Mum giggled again. 'I'll be Mrs Winterbottom. But Grant said he'll still call me Fossie. He said he likes calling me that.'

'That's right. You'll still be my Fossie-wossie, won't you?'

'Ooh, you are a one!' giggled Fossie again, slapping him on the chest.

'When are you planning on getting married?' Stefan asked.

Fossie and Grant gazed at each other. 'We're going to the Seychelles, aren't we, Granty-wanty?'

'Yes, we fancy a really romantic wedding.'

'And I'm going to wear a floaty white dress.'

'It'll definitely float!' George muttered.

'Sorry you can't be a bridesmaid for us, Candy. But we'll have a little party when we get back. I promise. Okay?'

'No, that's fine, Mum. I'm going to be a bridesmaid at Suzie's wedding in September.'

'You are? I didn't know that,' said George.

'Right, I'll get the drinks. You get that table in the corner there, Fossie and I'll bring them over. Two halves of lager, please, Landlord, and two packets of tortilla chips. And whatever these good people want,' said Granty-wanty.

'I always like a man who offers to buy the drinks,' said Edward as Digby poured the lagers and Candy's wine.

'He seems like a decent guy,' George reluctantly admitted, watching him carry the drinks over to the table where Fossie was blowing him kisses and patting the seat beside her.

'Strange taste though,' said Candy, voicing what they'd all been quietly thinking, but were too polite to say it aloud.

The two of them whispered and loudly laughed together. Then Mrs Fosse placed a tortilla crisp between her teeth and Grant nibbled it until their lips met and they kissed with lots of mmm noises.

Then it was Grant's turn. And this went on for two packets of crisps.

Everyone felt relieved when they finished the second packet. Grant screwed it into a ball and they both stood up to leave.

Mrs Fosse went over to her daughter. 'Bye-bye Candy,' she said, 'And you finish that diet. I've got a big bet on you!'

Candy was completely amazed. 'What? I thought you said I was wasting my time!'

'Don't be silly. Of course I didn't really think that! Did you honestly believe I'd bet against my own daughter?' Mrs Fosse placed a hand on each of her daughter's cheeks and gave her a big kiss on the lips.

'You're looking lovely and I'm very proud of you.'

'You are?'

'Yes I am. Bye everyone. See you after the wedding!'

'What shall we do this afternoon, Fossie-wossie? Shall we play our version of Hunt the Thimble?' suggested Grant.

'Ooh, you naughty boy, you!' replied Mrs Fosse, gently slapping him on the arm.

And Granty-wanty and Fossie-wossie left, both giggling like schoolchildren.

SATURDAY 18th SEPTEMBER

124lbs / 8st 12lbs / 56.2kgs

'Well, the Big Day's arrived at last. Cheers Daph.'

'Oh Fred, we shouldn't be drinking this early!'

'It's only a small sherry. And it's nice being here, just the two of us, celebrating alone, before everyone arrives.'

'Do I look alright, Fred?'

'Course you do, luv. You always look smashing. You could be the bride's sister instead of the bride's Mother.'

'Oh Fred!' Daph dabbed at the corner of her eye with a pink tissue.

'Now now, you're not getting all emotional already, are you, Daph luv?'

Daph shook her head. 'No, I was just thinking about when we got married. We were only kids. And we'd got nothing. And just look at us now.'

Fred smiled. 'Go on, we'd got an awful lot. We'd got each other. And a new baby to look forward to. I loved you then, Daph Slater, and I love you just as much now, if not more.'

'I love you too, Fred.'

'Come on, give us a kiss, Gorgeous.' Fred put his glass down, pulled Daph towards him and kissed her as the door burst open, making them both jump.

'Oh, this is where you're hiding, is it? And with the door shut?'

'Hello George,' said Fred resignedly, 'Want a sherry?'

'What, bit early for drinking, isn't it?'

'You don't? Right, fine.'

'I didn't say I didn't want one. I just said it was a bit early. Cheers.'

'Cheers,' said Daph and Fred.

'Just think, in a couple of hours my little sister will be married to a Rt. Hon! She was only a scrapdealer's daughter-'

'George!'

'It's alright Mum. I was just going to say, She was only a scrapdealer's daughter, but we all admired her mettle.'

'Very funny. Actually, yes, that is funny. I think I'll use it in my speech!' smiled Fred.

'Where's Candy?' George asked, 'She'd gone when I woke up. And she didn't wake me! I had to make my own breakfast and coffee.'

'Aah, what a shame! Where is she, Daph?'

'Upstairs, getting ready with Suzie. They've been up there for ages!'

'She was 8st, 12lbs yesterday, Dad. So who's going to lose his money, then?'

'Perhaps I'll gain more than I lose,' suggested Fred

'What do you mean?'

'Well, she's a pretty girl now, son.'

'Is she? Yeah, I suppose she is. So what will you gain, Dad?'

Fred sighed. 'I give up. Come on, Daph. I can hear cars arriving. Let's go and greet our guests.'

He offered his arm to his wife and they walked out into the garden.

There was an archway of flowers leading from the house to all the seats laid out in rows on the lawn for the guests, with a small area at the end for the wedding ceremony. Then the marquee was beyond it, with the tables beautifully decorated.

Fred had spared no expense for his daughter's wedding. A group played classical music, ready to burst into the Wedding March when Suzie appeared.

Charles was sitting nervously at the front, with his brother Rodney, who was the Best Man. They were wearing full Morning Dress with Top Hats balanced on their knees.

'Morning, Bert,' said George.

Bert sniffed and raised a hand to balance his hat. 'You're down there on the left,' he instructed, 'Bloody stupid hat!'

Daph smiled and kept stopping to greet the guests as she made her way to the front.

'See you later, luv,' Fred said, kissing her on the cheek and going back into the house to wait for his daughter to come down the stairs.

'Morning Rodney. Got Best Man nerves, have you?' George asked.

'Absolutely! I slept with the ring in its box under my pillow, I was so afraid of losing it. If this is how being a Best Man feels, there's no way I'm ever getting married!'

'Hello Charles,' George said to the groom, 'Alright?'

'Yes,' said Charles.

'Quick, they're coming! Quiet everyone!' shouted Bert.

The band began playing Here Comes the Bride, and Fred proudly escorted his daughter along, followed by Candy gently chaperoning the two little bridesmaids and pageboy.

'George, she's beautiful!' gasped Edward.

'Yeah, it runs in the family,' replied George.

'Actually, I meant Candy,' said Edward.

'Oh,' answered George.

Suzie's designer dress was ivory silk with a short train that didn't need carrying, and she wore a crown on her head made of wild flowers. And the bridesmaids wore matching dresses, but with different coloured sashes.

The ceremony was short and light-hearted. When the registrar asked If any of you has a reason why these two should not be married, speak now or forever hold your peace, there was a lot of predictable coughing, from George, Edward and Stefan, and also from the other side, where some of Charles's university and horsy friends were seated. For a few seconds both sides held a competition as they tried to out-cough each other.

After the registrar held up his hand and the laughter died down, the ceremony continued without any further problems.

Suzie led the way to the marquee on the arm of her new husband, stopping at the entrance, and the guests all lined up to congratulate them.

The band had relocated into the marquee, playing at a low volume so that people could talk, and everyone gasped when they saw the decorations.

'Give us a kiss, Mrs Ponsonby-Ffinch.'

'Oh Georgie, it sounds so FUNNY!'

'Super wedding, Suzie,' Edward said, kissing her on the cheek.

'Thank you, Edward.'

'And didn't Rodney do well, Charles?' Edward added.

'Yes,' said Charles.

Waiters held trays of Champagne, Bucks Fizz and sparkling water just inside the marquee. Other waiting staff walked around carrying bottles, making sure that the glasses were kept topped up while people talked.

'Hello, you must be the famous Candy Fosse. Donald Courtney, old university pal of Charles's.' He held out his hand and Candy shook it. 'Marvellous wedding, wasn't it?'

'Yes, it was,' Candy agreed.

'And an absolutely perfect day for it!'

'Perfect. They call it an Indian Summer, don't they?'

'I believe they do.' Donald took two glasses of Champagne from a passing waiter and handed one to Candy.

'I'm not supposed to,' she giggled.

'Oh come on. You deserve it today. You can't be far off your target by now, and you've got ages to go yet, haven't you?'

'Yes. I'm eight stone twelve now, but it's really hard going. Stefan, who runs the Sweat shop, said I must have nearly reached my normal weight for my size and bone structure. Every time I eat or drink anything extra, I go up a bit again. It's getting a bit depressing at times. I don't want to spend the rest of my life on a diet!'

'Cheer up, you've done really well. And may I say what a beautiful young lady you've turned out to be!'

'Thank you, Donald.' Candy sipped her Champagne.

'We've all been following your progress with great interest, you know, and everyone seems to have had a little flutter one way or the other. Charles told me about it and word spread. It was like the stock market in the pub some evenings, with everyone shouting the odds!' He pulled a face. 'I've lost, I'm afraid. I never thought it was possible to achieve.'

'Oh, I'm sorry!'

'That's alright. Win some, lose some. It's certainly captured the Media's interest. But what are you going to do when it's all over?'

Candy stared into her glass. She looked lost and confused for a minute. 'I don't know,' she sighed, 'I've thought about it a lot. I couldn't face going back to an office job. I've got my Sylphie slimming sales, but that's not what I want either.'

'How about advertising slimming products? I'm sure you'd be in great demand.'

Candy shook her head. 'I don't think I want that sort of work. I don't want to spend my life as Candy Fosse, Reformed Fatty, standing in front of a hideous blown-up picture of my past. I want a completely new way of life, but I don't know what it is I want! Does that sound silly?' She took another sip of her Champagne.

'No, not at all. I understand where you're coming from.' Donald smiled at her with an admiring glance at her figure. 'Why don't you get yourself an agent?'

'What sort of agent?'

'Well, someone who manages famous personalities. They must be able to find some work for you, Candy. Celebs are always in popular demand. You've had some experience in public appearances already, haven't you? I saw you interviewed on the telly.'

'But I'd still be known for being an ex-fatty, wouldn't I?'

'Only for a while, I'm sure. With your looks and personality, no doubt you'd gradually lose your Super Slimmer image and be offered things for being yourself.'

'Do you really think so?'

'It's worth a try, isn't it?'

'I suppose it is. But how would I find an agent?'

'Here, take my card. I'm a stockbroker in the City. We have a lot of important clients, and I meet loads of contacts at social events. I'll have a word with a couple of them that I have in mind and ask around, and if you give me a call on Monday afternoon, I should have some results for you.'

'Ooh, thank you very much!'

'You're very welcome, Candy,' he said, 'Here, have some more Champagne.'

SUNDAY 14th NOVEMBER

111lbs / 7st 13lbs / 50.3kgs

'Four of your refreshing lagers please, Digby, and a White Wine Taste-Alike for the beautiful, and SUCCESSFUL CANDY!'

'That's right, Rodders, rub it in.' Digby glared at Candy. 'You've lost me a lot of money, Miss.' He paused and then grinned. 'But I've enjoyed every minute of it – apart from George's occasional dramas. It's not every day we get to watch a lovely female materialise in front of our eyes. We're going to miss you around here, Candy.'

'Thank you, Digby,' Candy giggled.

Digby poured Candy's Wine Taste-Alike and placed it on the bar in front of her. 'Can I interest you in one of our delicious meat pies to go with that?' he innocently queried.

'Cheating are we, Digby?' George asked him.

'George, the idea never entered my head!' Digby protested, walking away laughing.

'So the Grand Weigh-In's tomorrow, George.'

'Yes Frank.'

'I never thought you'd do it. I changed my mind at the last minute. Lost my money, I have.'

'Sorry to hear that, Frank. You should have had more faith in me.'

'But when we first saw Candy – sorry about this, Candy – it didn't look as though you'd succeed in a month of Sundays! And now look at her. Gorgeous isn't she?'

Everybody nodded their agreement.

'Yeah, she's not bad, is she, Frank?' George agreed.

'It wasn't easy,' said Stefan, 'she worked really hard to achieve what she's achieved. I give you a toast; to Candy.'

'To Candy,' the whole pub said, raising their glasses.

'I'm going to be a very rich man tomorrow, thanks to you,' Old Gubbins said to the inside of his pipe. 'I've struggled on that farm all my life, and now I can afford to retire in comfort.'

'So what's happening to the farm, Gubbins? Edward asked him.

Old Gubbins looked directly at Candy, his blue eyes twinkling in his wrinkled tanned face. 'Grant, your new Dad is selling it for me.'

The door opened and Daph and Fred came in.

'Hello Mum, Dad. What are you doing here?'

'Hello Son. Hello everyone. We've just popped in to have a farewell drink with Candy. Two dry sherries please, Digby, and whatever this gang of layabouts want.'

Digby poured out four lagers. 'No more for me,' Candy said, 'I've still got some more packing to do.'

'Well you've lost me a lot of money, Candy.'

'Sorry, Fred.'

'But luckily Daph had a large bet on you winning too, and she bet more than me, so our loss isn't so bad after all.'

'Serves you right, Dad, for not trusting me.'

'No George,' said Fred, 'It's not that I didn't trust you, it's just that – no, you're right. I didn't trust you.'

'Fred!'

'Sorry Daph. But it was true.'

'I know, Fred, but you didn't need to say it.'

'Mum!'

'Luckily you proved me wrong, Son, and do you know what? I'm really glad you did! Cheers everyone.' Fred drained his glass. 'Come on Daph, I've got a load of paperwork to do.' He reached in his jacket and took out his wallet. He pulled out a handful of notes and put them on the bar. 'Here, Digby,' he said, 'Put this behind the bar for everyone. After all, it's Candy's leaving party.'

Once again glasses were raised, and a queue formed at the bar for free refills. They were all feeling in a party mood.

'Goodbye, Candy. You will keep in touch, won't you?' Daph said, kissing her on both cheeks.

'Course I will,' Candy replied, 'And thank you for putting me up.'

'Goodbye Candy,' Fred said, kissing her. 'We'll miss you. You've been like a daughter to us.' He glared at George as he said it. But George didn't notice. He was talking to Rodney.

As Fred and Daph left, Candy looked at her watch. 'I'd better go,' she said, 'It's nearly 9 o'clock and I've still got things to do.'

Suddenly George grabbed hold of her hand. 'No, come on, let's all go and get something to eat. A farewell meal.'

'Do you think we should?' Edward asked.

George looked at Stefan for his permission. 'What do you think, Stefan? Surely one meal won't do any harm?'

Stefan thought for a few seconds. 'Well she's been a steady 113lbs for nearly two weeks now and she's 111lbs today, so she has a bit of leeway there.'

'Okay, let's go for it then,' said Rodney, 'Let's go somewhere terribly expensive!'

They went to Ricci's Ravioli Restaurant.

Ricci handed out the menus, smiled at Candy and asked them what they'd-a like-a to drink, in an Italian accent.

'Two bottles of your best Champagne, Ricci, while we decide what we want,' Rodney ordered, looking at the others who all nodded their agreement.

Candy chose a fillet steak with an Italian salad, but no potatoes and the men had lobster ravioli with fried potatoes and side salads.

'I haven't had proper bread for a long time,' Candy said, dipping it in garlic flavoured olive oil, 'Mm, it's really tasty!'

'And loaded with calories,' Stefan told her.

'It's lovely to have genuine Italian food,' said Candy. Ricci was one of her best Sylphie customers, but she wasn't going to eat any of that this evening!

Edward leaned forward and whispered. 'We came in here once and caught Ricci talking on the phone. And he had a broad London accent, so don't be fooled by the phoney Italian voice. I'm afraid he's more Clerkenwell than Calabria.'

'Come on, Candy, tell us what you're going to be doing in Hollywood.'

'I tried to tell you several times, George, but you didn't listen, as always. You just took the micky and made fun of it.'

'Well I'm listening now.'

'We're all listening, Candy. We haven't heard it before,' said Edward.

'Yes, come on, tell us all about it,' Rodney urged her.

'Okay. I was really lucky that Charles's friend Donald found me that agent. He earned me a lot of money for those slimming product ads on the TV. And now this.'

'Yes, Hollywood, eh?' Stefan smiled at her encouragingly.

'It's really exciting.' Candy's eyes were shining. 'It's a new series called Villaintry, about a mega-rich American family who are all fighting and feuding all the time. I'm the father's English daughter that he didn't know he had. Snow Laintry.

'Snow?' snorted George.

'George, any more sarky remarks and I won't tell you any more about it!'

'Sorry. My lips are sealed,' George said, hiding his laughter behind his hand.

My mother fell in love with him on one of his business trips to London and they had a short passionate affair. She never told him about me and she always refused to tell me who my father was. Then she confesses everything to me on her death bed. So off I go to claim my rights. My newly-discovered Dad welcomes me. But all his children from his three marriages and his third wife are really jealous, and we all have lots of meaty fights and arguments. It's really good.'

'It does sound like the sort of thing that the public will love,' said Edward tactfully.

'Well they've spent a fortune on it already. They'd chosen all the rest of the cast, but they hadn't found anyone suitable to play Snow. Then my agent happened to read an article about their search, and he recommended me!'

'So you're flying to America tomorrow?'

'Yes, Rodney. George is going to drop me at the coach station after the Weigh-in, and I fly from Heathrow in the afternoon. They've got me first class tickets and I'm being met at the other end and taken to the villa that they've rented for me. It's huge with a pool, a jacuzzi, a gym – really important - a maid and a gardener and beautiful views. Someone's showing me around for the first couple of days, which'll be interesting. I'm expected to start learning my script then as well. And I've got a photo session booked, then it's up at the crack of dawn to have my hair and make-up done, and then off we go – action!'

'And you don't know how long you're going for?' Stefan asked.

Candy shook her head, chewing a piece of her steak. 'The contract's for six months, and possibly renewable if the series is a success, or if one of the family doesn't kill me!'

'Then you can come home,' said George.

'Yes George, I can come home if I don't like it there.' She smiled at him.

She twiddled her glass, watching the liquid reflected through the crystal. Then she looked up. 'And what about you, George? You'll be rich and independent after tomorrow; bets, booze and bed again without your Dad having to pay for it – and without me getting in the way.' She let out a small sigh.

George studied the sweet trolley and decided against it. 'No, I'll pass on that, thanks,' he told the waiter, and the others agreed with him. 'Just five coffees and four brandies, please.'

He leaned his arms flat on the table and regarded Candy. 'I'm actually going into business,' he said.

'Oh George, that's great! Doing what?'

'It was something you said on TV to Sally Rhodes.'

'What did I say?' Candy was curious.

'You said, You see, it wasn't my size that bothered me. I just wanted to be treated like a human being. I hated being ignored.'

'That's right. I hated people talking round me or over me as though I was invisible.'

'There was no chance of that!'

'George!! Well it's true. People would completely ignore me. I hated it. Anyway, what's your new business plan, George?'

'Did you notice all the Before and After people on the Sylphie DVD?'

'Yes, what about them?'

'Well when they were overweight, before their transformation, they took no pride in their appearance. They all had untidy hair, the women didn't bother with makeup except maybe a quick touch of lipstick because they didn't like looking in the mirror, and they didn't wear clothes; they wore camouflage. They all dressed in baggy shapeless things to hide their size.'

Edward nodded. 'You're right, George. They seemed to WANT to be invisible.'

'I'm not sure I quite agree with you both,' Rodney said. 'When you see these documentaries about the Elite in places like Monaco, a lot of the men are pretty big guys, but they all wear expensive, well-cut suits.'

'Yeah, right,' Candy snorted, 'But do you ever see any huge women with them?'

Stefan smiled. 'It's alright to be a big man as long as you have a big wallet.'

'It's definitely a sex thing,' Candy said, 'We used to have a Bank Manager in our town. He'd waddle along the road every day in his shapeless grey suit. He was much bigger than me, and he was a grumpy so-and-so too. There's no way on Earth that they'd have given that job to a woman who was that big, however brilliant she was at her work. Anyway, try finding really pretty clothes when you're fat.'

'Actually, it's more than just appearance. It's ATTITUDE, with a capital A. Just look at your Mother. She's big and bold, and Grant loves her for it. So I'm starting a business called Body Talk. I'll be in partnership with Stefan.'

Stefan nodded. 'We'll be holding a sort of Boot Camp at the Sweat Shop. Our clients will pay a lot for it, and we'll teach them step by step to take a pride in who and what they are, not what the Media tells them they should be!'

'Oh what a good idea!' said Candy, 'But do you think they'll join if they have to pay a lot?'

'It's the only way they'll take it seriously,' Stefan told her. 'If you give away something for free, or very cheap, they won't bother turning up half the time. They'll think it hasn't got any value. If you charge them a large fee, they'll think it's good and they'll make sure they get their money's worth.'

'We'll take it a step at a time,' said George. 'And it will be good for them all to work together as a group and discuss any problems.'

'You're dead right there,' Rodney agreed, 'Do you really think you'd have managed on your own, Candy, without our help or if you'd have lived at home?'

Candy shook her head. 'Not a chance! It's a very lonely thing to do on your own. And you're surrounded by temptation. And of course I was bored with my life as well as being lonely. I think the group thing is a really good idea, and necessary, then if they get disillusioned, they'll always have someone to talk to.'

'It's not just for overweight people,' George continued, 'It's for anyone who's not happy with their appearance. They might have a scar, or a deformity. We're going to get an expert to talk to them about self-confidence, then we'll have something different to interest them every week.'

'Yes,' said Stefan, 'Heads You Win will choose one of them to give a free hairdo to, and do their makeup, then show the others the difference. And they'll take bookings from anyone else who wants to have a different look, with us having a commision, of course. And Marie of Cuddles Boutique will give a talk about what each of them should choose to wear for their figures, also what they should avoid – and of course, it doesn't have to be just women.'

'Lunch will be included,' George added, 'And there will be one of Stefan's team there to explain what they're eating, and how they can plan their food for the week and eat enough and feel full while still enjoying a healthy meal. And what they can snack on in between meals if they feel like they need something more.'

'They'll have half an hour's session in the gym afterwards, or before if they want it. And as their appearance changes, they can buy a Sweat Shop membership at a special rate. But it will be made clear that it's not about losing weight. It's about being content with who you are and learning to be happy with what you see in the mirror.' Said Stefan.

'I think it's wonderful,' Candy gasped, 'And I love the thought that there's always someone who they can talk to. I think the worst thing for me was the loneliness. Anyway, what about you, Edward? It's your turn to tell us what you're planning to do.'

'Well it's funny you should say that.' Edward placed his hands palms down on the table. 'I'm going ahead with my art gallery plan.'

'Wow, you've kept that quiet, old chap!' Rodney exclaimed.

'Yes, I wanted to surprise you all. I'm just finalising details on a place to rent that's ideal. And I've persuaded the lovely Stacy to leave the woodburning business and work for me as the Manageress. She's perfect for the job!'

'So how will you earn a living, Edward?' Candy asked him.

'I'll let artists, sculptors, ceramics and other quality craft workers display their things for a week at a time. And of course, for longer if they want to. I'll charge them, of course, and collect a commission from anything that's sold. There are lots of art galleries in London, but there's nothing around here. We'll advertise their Open Day and provide wine and canapes to try to tempt the guests to buy.'

Everyone made approving noises.

'And what about you, Rodney? Any plans that are going to surprise us?' George asked him.

'Actually I have,' Rodney replied. 'As the son and heir of the Ponsonby-Ffinch Estate, it's time I buckled down and learnt how it runs. Like most of these old stately homes, my parents are always struggling to find ways to raise money to preserve it, and it gobbles it up as fast as they can earn it. So I really need to think up some money-making ideas. But most ideas have already been thought of.'

Candy stood up. 'I've really got to get to bed. I've got a quick session in the gym before the Grand Weigh-in tomorrow, and I'm going to be shattered if I don't get some sleep, especially with the coach journey and the long flight. Thank you for the meal, guys and I'll see you all tomorrow.'

'Yes, see you tomorrow,' George said to his friends, 'Bye Ricci.'

'Bye George. Bye Candy,' they called out.

'Well we've done it,' he said as they walked home.

'Yes,' said Candy, 'And that's the end. You get your home back, and I get a new life.'

'Goodnight Candy.'

'Goodnight George.'

MONDAY 15th NOVEMBER

114lbs / 8st 2lbs / 51.7kgs

'Aagh, George!'

'Ugh!' George nearly leaped out of bed. 'What's up? What's the matter?' He looked at his clock; 6am.

George hadn't realised before that there are two 6 o'clocks in one day.

'I'm 8st 2! I've put on three pounds since yesterday!'

'Yes but you're still below the weight you have to be, aren't you?' George tried to do some calculations in his head, then gave up.

'I know, but I was less than eight stone yesterday morning. Surely that Italian meal and a glass of Champagne couldn't make me put on that much weight!'

'Could it be water retention?'

'Oh I don't know! I'll see you at Stefan's in just over an hour. Don't go back to sleep, will you?'

I will after today, George thought, eyeing up his bed which looked very tempting, and deciding it was safer to stay upright.

He showered and then decided to walk to the Sweat Shop in case there wasn't any room to park.

And he was glad he did. The car park was full, and so was the gym.

There were seats laid out and every one of them was taken. This time entry was by ticket only.

A TV station was setting up its equipment and a woman with a big furry microphone was randomly interviewing members of the audience.

George walked down the side and went through the double doors that led to Stefan's private office.

'Aah, hi George,' Stefan said, looking up from his desk, 'Candy's getting changed.'

'Is her weight OK?' George asked.

Stefan nodded. 'Yes she's fine. And she's had a workout and a swim this morning. I'll go on the stage and introduce you, then Candy. Ready?'

Stefan walked out and everyone went quiet, then applause broke out.

'Ladies and gentlemen,' he said, and then he paused. Everybody waited, trying to read the expression on his face, which was usually impossible with Stefan, possibly due to Botox. Had Candy succeeded, or had she just missed her target?

Stefan continued, 'A year ago we all crowded in here for what we didn't realise was something that was going to go viral on Social Media, and be followed worldwide. It was a challenge that a lot of people thought was impossible; the literal cutting in half of a young lady in twelve months.'

Murmuring broke out as everyone wondered if they were going to win or lose their money.

'I'd like to welcome the man who allowed Candy to live in his house so that we could help her to diet –' Stefan beckoned to George to come forward, '-George Slater.'

George walked onto the stage accompanied by applause. Everyone there knew him.

'Right,' Stefan carried on, 'Here are the scales, which are electronic and accurate to less than a milligram. And here's the man who has been holding our money for us – Booky Bill.' There was more applause as Bill walked onto the stage and stood next to Stefan. 'And now there's only one thing missing, and that's Miss Candy Fosse!'

Candy appeared through the double doors. She was wearing her old Oriental dressing-gown, which reached round her twice now.

Stepping onto the stage, she turned her back on the audience, slowly undid the tie, then turned to face them all and theatrically threw the dressing-gown off, letting it drop on the floor. Then she held her arms up high.

After a couple of shocked seconds, the room erupted, with loud whistles and cheers.

What a difference from the last time, George thought, looking at her. She was wearing a black basque with tiny red bows on it, black stockings and suspenders, a red garter, and black stiletto heels.

'Right, we'll check her weight. Stefan, can you do the honours please? 'said Booky Bill, dramatically producing a hanky and wiping his forehead,

There was some laughter, then everyone settled down and sat quietly, leaning forward so they could clearly hear the results.

Candy kicked off her shoes and stood on the scales. They waited while it wobbled into position, and then stopped.

'Eight stone, that's 112lbs,' said Stefan, 'And if any of you want it in metric, you can work it out for yourselves.'

Everyone laughed again. Some of them took out their phones to convert it into kilos.

'Right, Candy has DONE IT! Shouted Booky Bill, 'So it's a win, and I'll be paying out in half an hour. Give me time to get organised, and form an orderly queue. You don't all need to claim your winnings at once. They'll keep for another day.'

He turned to Candy, bowed and kissed her hand. 'And may I say that this is the most gorgeous filly I've ever had bets on!'

Everyone cheered, whistled and stood up to go while the woman with the furry mike walked on the stage to interview Candy.

***

'Oh, my coach is already here, George.'

'Right, let's get your luggage loaded. Have you got everything?'

'Yes George.'

'Passport? Picnic? Bottle of water? Book?'

'I've got everything, George.'

'It's not like me to check up on you. It's usually the other way round, isn't it?'

Candy nodded, with her head down. She fumbled through her bag, pretending to look through it for something.

'Oh, here's your door key,' she said, handing it to him.

'OK, thanks. Maybe you'll need it again one day.'

'Maybe. Right, I'd better get on board. There aren't many people on it, so I can have two seats. I'd have needed two seats a year ago!'

'Right, goodbye, Candy.'

'Bye, George.'

She turned to go and George called, 'Candy!'

'Yes?'

'Give us a goodbye kiss then!' He put his arms round her and gave her a long, slow kiss on the lips. Then he hugged her tightly.

The driver climbed into his seat and started the engine. He smiled and jerked his head. 'Better get on if you're coming with us,' he said.

'Right, this is it. I really must go now!'

'Okay. And Candy-'

'Yes, George?'

'You will stay in touch, won't you?'

'Yes George.'

'Promise?'

'I promise.'

'The fame won't change you?'

She smiled. 'No George, I'll still be the same old me.'

Candy climbed up the steps and the doors sighed shut behind her.

There was nobody else sitting in the back seats, so she walked there, relieved that she didn't need to make conversation with anyone.

Sitting down, she looked out of the window where George was waving to her, making Phone Me gestures, and she waved back. Then she put her bag next to her and looked out the window again as the coach pulled away. George was walking back to his car and he didn't look round.

It started to drizzle slightly. Candy curled up in the corner, leaned the side of her head against the glass and silently sobbed.

***

'Aah, here's George. Digby-'

'Alright Rodders, I'm doing it.'

Digby poured a pint of lager and slapped it down in front of George, slopping some of it over the bar, which was unusual for Digby.

'Gone, has she?' he asked, knowing the answer and glaring at George.

'Yup. She's safely on the coach on her way to the Wild West.'

'You ought to be ashamed of yourself,' Digby snapped.

'What for?' asked George, picking up his lager.

'Candy is really top quality compared to some of the women who you've picked up in here. And what have you done? You've let her go.'

George put down his lager and held out his arms, genuinely confused. 'Well she couldn't stay with me for ever, could she?'

'She could have stayed with ME for ever,' someone called out.

'Me too!' shouted someone else.

George turned round and picked up his lager again. 'Do you know what they're on about?' he asked his friends.

'No idea,' said Edward.

'Right,' Rodney suggested, 'Where shall we go for lunch today, The Yacht Club, The Golf Club, the Country Club, or here?'

'Excuse me,' a voice behind George said.

He turned his head, and then turned it again, faster.

'I'll excuse you any day,' he told the female behind her. She had very long, straight blonde hair and, even better, she had three equally attractive friends with her.

'I've never seen you lovely ladies in here before,' Rodney told them.

They all giggled and talked at once. 'No. We're fairly local, but we've not been in here before, ever. So we thought we'd give it a try.'

'Yes, we've got the afternoon off and we just couldn't decide where to go,' said one of the blonde's three friends.

'We've been banned from everywhere else,' one of the others added. They all giggled again.

'No we haven't! Take no notice of her,' the blonde hastily said. She took her purse out of her bag and raised it, about to call Digby.

George put his hand over hers. 'No, put it away. This is our treat. To welcome you lovely ladies to our local hangout.'

'Oh, thank you,' they all chorused.

'Digby, two bottles of that stuff that you call Champagne and eight glasses. Oh, you do like Champoo, don't you?' Rodney inquired.

They all enthusiastically agreed that they LOVED Champoo.

'Ok, you girls go and sit over there and we'll bring it over,' Stefan told them, pointing to an empty table in the corner that conveniently had seats for eight people.

George carried his lager and four of the glasses. 'Mind if we join you?' he asked.

The girls all shuffled along to make room and George sat down, followed by Rodney, Edward and Stefan. They had all agreed almost telepathically, as they always did, who was going with who.

'By the way,' said George, 'My name's George.'

ABOUT THE AUTHOR

Lyn Funnell has been passionate about writing for most of her life. At school, she almost always earned a gold or silver star for her weekly compositions.

Her first publications appeared in magazines, followed by twelve collections of short stories and poetry. Many of her short stories feature an unexpected twist, and her work has won several prizes.

Beyond writing, Lyn enjoys entering competitions and has received numerous accolades for her original recipes. Her achievements include winning The Good Housekeeping Millennium Menu competition and being a runner-up in the BBC Chef of the Year competition. She was also one of three runners-up in the Observer Food & Drink Magazine competition and has won prizes in the Fruits of France Recipe, Ocean Spray Cranberry Recipe, Bernard Matthews Rustle Up a Recipe, and Dorling Kindersley Autumn Recipe competitions.

Additionally, she reached the semi-finals of Masterspud and was one of three finalists in The BBC One Show Spag

Bol Competition, earning her the title of UK Spag Bol Queen!

To date, Lyn has published ten books online, with another soon to follow.

She lives in East Sussex and co-runs the online magazine Unknown Kent and Sussex.

www.unknownkentandsussex.co.uk

Available worldwide from Amazon
and all good bookstores

Michael Terence
Publishing

www.mtp.agency

www.facebook.com/mtp.agency

@mtp_agency